Million Dollar Smile

A WWII Novel of Faith and Sacrifice

Paul F. Carlson

Twelve Stones Publishing LLC

Million Dollar Smile
A WWII Novel of Faith and Sacrifice

Published in the United States
by Twelve Stones Publishing LLC
Colorado Springs, Colorado

Library of Congress Control Number: 2025913538
ISBN (Paperback): 979-8-9929459-0-4
ISBN (eBook): 979-8-9929459-1-1

Edited by Courtney Oppel
Cover design by Richard Ljoenes

Printed in the United States of America

Unless otherwise noted, all Scripture quotations are from the King James Version of the Bible (Public Domain).

This novel is inspired by real events and individuals. While efforts have been made to maintain historical accuracy, certain characters, events, and dialogues have been fictionalized or reconstructed for narrative purposes. Any interpretations are the author's own and should not be considered definitive historical accounts.

For more information, visit:
www.milliondollarsmilebook.com

First edition 2025

For Paul and Alta Carlson
and
The men and women who serve our great country.

"For I reckon that the sufferings of this present time are not worthy to be compared with the glory which shall be revealed in us."

Romans 8:18 (KJV)

Air Transport Command Routes

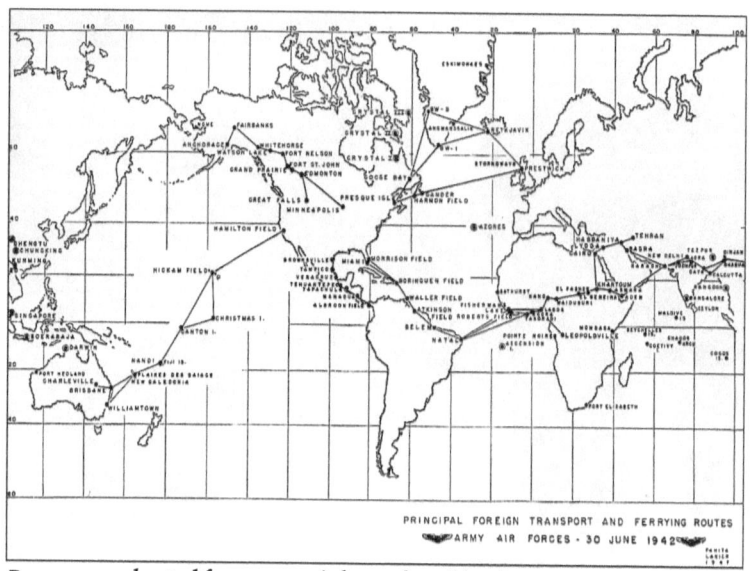

Base map adapted from materials produced by the U.S. Army Air Forces, dated June 30, 1942. Public Domain.

Prologue

February 7, 1943

I t was calm and quiet. Almost too calm and quiet; relaxing, even. The vast stretch of ocean below seemed endless, a slate-gray mirror blending seamlessly with the sky. From his seat behind the co-pilot, Paul looked up from monitoring the radio to glance over his shoulder at the seemingly boundless interior of the C-87 transport aircraft, filled only with the steady hum of the engines. Well, not just the hum; there was also cargo and a handful of military personnel strapped in among the crates and supplies.

He felt the familiar rhythm of flight beneath his feet, a deep drone that usually brought comfort on these long routes across the Pacific. But his training was always there, a steady reminder in the back of his mind. One could easily be lulled into passivity—a dangerous state in a place where constant awareness was vital. In reality, there was always something to do: checking equipment, monitoring radio frequencies, getting updates from the navigator. Flying long-haul missions demanded discipline, even on a calm day like this.

There was something about being in the large aircraft on these long trips that Paul found captivating. To some, the endless hours in the sky might seem monotonous, even dull. But to Paul, even the way the airplane worked—how it cut through the sky, lifted, and carried them across oceans—fascinated him. The thought that he, the crew, and this great aircraft were part of something larger than themselves filled him with a quiet pride. They weren't on the front lines, dodging enemy fire, but their mission was no less critical.

Paul loved flying and loved operating the radio. There was almost nowhere else he'd rather be. Almost. Just another couple of weeks, then he would be back home. Back to his new wife, new family, new life. He couldn't wait; THAT was where he really wanted to be, more than anything else. His mind drifted.

They had been married only a short time, but when they were together, it felt like, well, everything was just ... right. He remembered the moment he said goodbye to leave on this trip. That moment—walking away, turning back, and seeing her wave—was burned into his memory like a photograph.

Once again, he felt the vibration of the engines, the subtle sense of movement.

But then, a faint shift. A slight roll to the left. They were supposed to be starting their final approach on this leg of the trip, though it seemed strange to begin a turn way out here in the middle of nowhere. Still, this crew was top-notch. Relax, he told himself. Whatever it was, everyone here could do their job in their sleep.

Then, a little more of a roll. He again dismissed it—probably just the ocean's wind or an air current. It felt strange, like the moment an elevator starts its downward motion, but also a little bit sideways, tilting. Nothing to worry about, though. But when the angle held, Joe twisted in his seat, just enough for their eyes to meet.

His expression was tense, gaze shifting quickly between Paul and Chuck, lingering there with a flicker of something Paul couldn't quite put his finger on—worry, maybe, or something closer to fear. The unspoken question lingered between them, a moment of hesitation as the roll continued, almost like the aircraft had suddenly lost balance.

Something didn't feel right. The plane's gradual descent should have been controlled and steady. Instead, Paul felt the unmistakable pull of gravity in his gut, like the floor beneath him was tilting slightly forward.

A voice from the cockpit cut through the hum. "Full flaps," the pilot ordered, his tone clipped. Paul froze, his stomach twisting. Flaps this far out didn't make sense—not at this altitude.

Something was dreadfully wrong. They shouldn't be rolling like this.

A quick glance at Joe revealed thinly veiled terror his eyes, while his hands lingered above the controls with a split-second hesitation that shouldn't have been there. As a strong sinking feeling grew in the pit of his stomach and a shot of adrenaline raced through his body, Paul's hands started shaking.

He gripped the arms of his seat tighter as the plane rolled again, steeper this time. His heart thudded against his ribs as a cold sweat broke out along his neck. The altimeter reading, visible for just a second as Joe adjusted the controls, caught Paul's eye—far too low. Was that right? A barely audible mutter from Joe reached his ears. "That can't be right."

Paul turned back to the radio.

"ATC-903, calling Canton tower," he began, his voice steady despite the tremor in his fingers as they hovered over the radio. Silence. Static crackled in his headphones, its sharp hiss overpowering. Paul tightened his grip on the radio console, his knuckles white.

He froze for a moment, his hand pausing over the transmitter. The pitch of the engines had shifted, a faint whine over the steady drone. Now he knew that didn't sound right.

"Joe," he called over the intercom, his voice tight, "are we losing altitude?"

Joe's reply was clipped, tense. "Working on it. Stand by."

Paul's gut twisted. He adjusted the frequency knob on the receiver, his fingers moving on autopilot as he scanned for a clearer line to Canton Tower.

"Canton Tower, this is ATC-903, come in, over!" His voice wavered, but he forced it steady. A hiss of static filled his headphones, grating against his nerves. Paul muttered a curse under his breath—something he rarely did. The weight of the situation pressed down on him.

He flicked a quick glance at the instrument panel, straining to read the altimeter, but Joe's frame blocked his view. Joe was gesturing frantically toward Chuck, his movements sharp and urgent.

Chuck's hands gripped the yoke, knuckles white, his body rigid as he fought against the shifting plane. Joe leaned closer to the controls, his fingers darting over dials and switches in what looked like a desperate effort to stabilize the plane. Paul couldn't make out exactly what Joe was adjusting—the controlled chaos in the cockpit was palpable.

Think, Paul. You can't fix the engines, but you can keep the lines of communication open. Realizing that the rough flight may have loosened the antenna coupler, he began to adjust it with sharp, practiced motions. The static softened and his heart jumped as he heard a faint voice over his headphones.

Before he could respond, the plane rolled sharply to the left. The sudden jolt slammed him against his harness, his head snapping into the bulkhead. He barely registered the pain, his instincts screaming louder than any physical sensation. His first thought was to shout over the intercom for Chuck to stabilize, but he held back. They were doing everything they could. He had to trust them.

Then, without warning, the plane pitched sharply forward, the nose dropping fast. Gravity wrenched Paul forward in his seat, his stomach lurching with the sudden descent. "Chuck, straighten out! Pull up!" he heard Joe shout over the intercom.

The sound around him changed again—the engines strained, their hum turning into a frantic wail as the aircraft plunged into a steep descent. Paul stole a glance back. The officers sat rigid, jaws clenched, hands gripping armrests or resting tensely on their thighs. No one said a word, but their eyes spoke volumes. Paul's fingers shook as he hit the radio again, his voice tight with urgency. "ATC-903, Canton tower ... Mayday, Mayday!"

Paul glanced toward the cockpit again, drawn by an instinct he couldn't name. In a fleeting moment that felt stretched into eternity, Paul saw something that struck him to his core. Joe had leaned toward Chuck, his left hand gripping the pilot's shoulder. For a fraction of a second, Paul thought he saw Joe mouth something—words he couldn't hear but that carried an undeniable weight. Then the moment was gone.

Control was slipping away, and Paul could feel it in every nerve. The last-minute news that he had received before the trip replayed in his mind and he felt a surge of emotion. The ocean rose up to meet them, a slate-gray expanse, vast and unyielding. In that split second, it dawned on him: they were in an unavoidable descent, a final tilt that would lead only into the ocean below. He said a prayer: Lord, if this is my end, hold me fast. Be with Alta. Let her know how much I love her.

The ocean received him. Silence.

Alta.

CHAPTER ONE

Mather Field - August 1942

"**Y**ou lost?"

Runways stretched out in every direction, wide and dusty, lined with rows of military trucks, crates, and soldiers moving with brisk precision. The familiar hum of engines filled the air. Yet it felt different here. More purposeful, even urgent.

He felt slightly out of his element; this was no commercial airport. Here, there were no passengers in neat rows, no bustling civilian crowds. Instead, he saw men in uniform, each with the same hard set to their jaw and determination in their gaze. Some appeared fresh, like him, while others had the seasoned, weary look of men accustomed to the weight of duty.

Paul adjusted his cap and took a deep breath, catching the scent of fuel mixed with dry California dust. This wasn't where he'd imagined himself months ago, but here he was—and he was ready. Or at least he hoped he was. As he scanned the distant runways, a flicker of doubt crept in. Had he made the right decision? His gaze shifted briefly to the sky, and for a moment, his thoughts drifted back to home, to her, waiting for him.

He'd made a promise, after all.

He squinted against the bright sun. He was supposed to report to the operations building for check-in, but the layout of Mather

Field was a maze of identical hangars and runways. His eyes drifted to the horizon, where the faint shimmer of heat waves blurred the edges of the base. He sighed. Maybe he was lost.

"Hey, Mac!"

Paul spun around, startled out of his reverie—he hadn't noticed someone standing behind him. The man trying to get his attention was a young officer in his early twenties, tall and broad-shouldered, with a casual yet confident stance. Sun-bleached hair was tucked neatly under his cap, and a smirk played at the corner of his mouth, lending him an easygoing, slightly mischievous look. His eyes, light green and almost hazel, held a glint of energy that hinted at an unspent drive. Everything about him—from his rolled-up sleeves, revealing tanned forearms, to the way he leaned in with a relaxed air—gave the impression of a man who'd rather be outside and active than confined to a briefing room.

"Are you lost?"

"Uh, I'm not sure," Paul replied.

"Well, do you know where you are?"

"Of course I know where I am."

"That's a good start. Then do you know where you're going?"

"Not particularly," Paul admitted.

"Well then you're lost."

"Thanks a lot, Joe," Paul said, raising an eyebrow and giving his trademark one-sided smile. "But that's not terribly helpful."

"Have we met before?" the officer asked.

"I don't think so. I just got here."

"You called me 'Joe.'"

"Just a figure of speech, I guess. And you are?"

"The name's Joe Mitchell."

"Like the airplane."

Joe let out a hearty "Ha!" and turned to an invisible audience, pointing his thumb back to Paul, "I like this guy." Turning back, he said, "Yes, like the airplane."

Paul held out his hand, "Paul Carlson."

Joe shook it with a firm grip, his grin unwavering.

"Good to meet you, Paul. So, what brings you to sunny California, out here in the dust? You don't look like the type who makes a habit of running around military bases."

Paul chuckled. "You got that right, Joe. Commercial radio operator for United Air Lines, actually."

Joe whistled, impressed. "United, huh? You've got me beat. I was branding horses and fixin' fences before all this."

"So, what brings you to Mather Field?" Paul asked, raising an eyebrow.

Joe shrugged, his casual demeanor intact. "Well, apparently, I'm supposed to be a co-pilot. Not exactly what I had in mind, but I figure if the Army Air Corps thinks I can do it, who am I to argue? Something about aptitude tests, spatial awareness, eye-hand coordination, and all that jazz."

Paul studied him. Despite Joe's laid-back manner and obvious sense of humor, he exuded determination. He had the look of a seasoned officer, like he'd been here for weeks, maybe even months.

"Well, you seem like you know this place. How long have you been around these parts?"

Joe chuckled a little sheepishly. "Got here yesterday. Just enough time to figure out where the mess hall is and take a few wrong turns. I think there was this major I bumped into yesterday. He may still be a little mad at me. Something about a coffee stain on his shirt."

"Yesterday? You could have fooled me," Paul said with a smirk. "Here I was, thinking you were an old hand at this."

"That's the plan, Mac. You know: Act like you know what you're doing," Joe replied with a wink. He leaned in a bit, lowering his voice. "Honestly, we're all in the same boat here. This Air Transport Command is a pretty new thing. Everyone is trying to figure things out. Orientation's tomorrow for all us new fellas. Guess you're stuck with me for now."

Paul felt a mix of relief and amusement. "Good to know. I wouldn't want to be the only one trying to figure things out."

"So, I assume you'll be continuing the radio operator role here?" Joe asked, genuinely curious.

"That's right. I have some experience under my belt, so I thought this was a natural fit. Radios and airplanes, two great things that go great together," Paul replied, feeling a surge of pride. "From what I've heard, there's a ton of supplies to move, and not enough hands to do it. Feels like an important role to fill."

"Oh, I'd say so," Joe replied, nodding. "I guess you'll handle the airwaves, and I'll just try to keep us from falling out of the sky. Between the two of us, I think we'll do alright."

Paul shrugged, his one-sided smile reappearing. "You make it sound too easy. But hey, who am I to argue?"

"Well, whaddya say I show you around a bit? I can show you the mess hall, and maybe even introduce you to that major."

"Joe, I think I'll take you up on that—although I think I'll pass on the major."

"Good thinking. Let's grab some chow," Joe said, clapping Paul on the back.

"Lead the way, partner," Paul replied, following with a grin.

***

"So I guess this is the first, official briefing at Mather Field for us," Paul said, taking a seat near the back of the crowded room.

Rows of folding chairs filled the space, occupied by men murmuring in low tones. Up front stood a podium beside a large chalkboard, scribbled with flight routes and notes. The air was thick with anticipation—and with a few other things. A window or two needed to be opened.

As more people filed in, Joe leaned over casually. "Hey, before things get rolling, take a gander at this!" He pulled a worn photograph from his shirt pocket and handed it to Paul. "Take a look at her!"

Paul examined the picture, admiring the long hair and muscular curves. "She's a beauty!" he exclaimed, perhaps a bit louder than intended.

At that moment, the room fell silent as a stern-looking captain stepped up to the podium. His sharp gaze zeroed in on Paul and Joe at the back.

"What in the Sam Hill is going on back there? Is that a picture of your sweetheart you're sharing with the whole class?"

Joe stood up quickly, unfazed, holding the picture in his hand. "Well, sir, not exactly."

"Care to explain yourself ..." The captain squinted at Joe.

"Mitchell, Lieutenant Joe Mitchell."

"Care to explain yourself, Mitchell?"

Joe lifted his chin. "Sir, it's a photo of my horse, Sage. The best quarter horse in all of Colorado," Joe replied with unabashed pride.

A ripple of laughter spread through the room. The captain raised an eyebrow. "Well, sounds like we've got ourselves a real cowboy. Planning to ride her into the Pacific Theater, are you, lieutenant?"

Joe grinned. "Only if there's room on the plane, sir."

The captain allowed a brief chuckle. "Take your seat, Cowboy. And the rest of you, pay attention."

As the captain prepared to launch into his briefing, Paul glanced at Joe, who seemed pleased despite the reprimand. Paul nudged him with a grin.

"Looks like 'Cowboy' is going to stick," Paul said with a smirk.

Joe shrugged. "Could be worse. At least they know who I am."

Paul chuckled. "Giddy up, Cowboy. Guess we'd better pay attention."

The captain cleared his throat, his eye sweeping across the room as he began. "Gentlemen, welcome to Mather Field and Air Transport Command. If any of you came here looking for the glamor of fighter planes or the glory of bomber squadrons, let me set you straight. The ATC may not make the front page, but our work is no less vital to winning this war."

A murmur of acknowledgment passed through the rows.

"Our mission," he continued, "is logistics. We move troops, equipment, medical supplies, rations, ammunition—everything the front lines need to keep going. The manufacturing machine of the United States is in overdrive. American factories are producing equipment at rates unimaginable before the war. Production alone isn't enough; we have to get everything where it's needed most. This is where we come in."

The captain's demeanor seemed to get even more serious at this point. Paul stole a quick glance at Joe, who seemed immersed in the captain's lecture.

"Let me tell you, fellas," he said, pausing to scan the room, "the Pacific Theater isn't forgiving. It's long stretches of ocean, unpredictable weather, and limited support. Every flight is a test of endurance, skill, and teamwork."

Out of the corner of his eye, Paul saw Joe give a subtle nod, as if steeling himself for the challenge.

The captain continued. "In the coming weeks, you'll be trained in every aspect of Air Transport Command operations. Navigation. Radio protocols. Emergency procedures. For some of you, these skills may be familiar; for others, it'll be a steep learning curve. But by the end," he continued, "you'll know how to handle anything this job throws at you. And make no mistake, it will throw a lot at you."

He paused, letting the gravity of his words settle around the room.

"Many of you will be responsible for long-haul flights, carrying payloads that can't be delayed or diverted. You'll face conditions that demand precision and discipline. A mistake out there isn't just a mistake—it's life or death, for both you and the mission."

The captain's gaze softened just slightly as he continued. "If you have questions, ask them. If you have doubts, work through them. Now is the time. This is where we build the backbone of our forces. You're here because you're needed. And when you're in the air, remember: It's not about medals or recognition, it's about getting the job done."

He scanned the room, giving the men a moment to process. "Are there any questions?"

An officer in the center of the room stood, clearing his throat. "Sir, I noticed we have both Army officers and civilians here. What are the roles of each? How do we work together? And who's in charge during a flight?"

The captain's gaze settled on the officer. "And you are?"

"First Lieutenant Charlie Carter, sir," the man replied, standing at attention.

The captain nodded. "That's a great question, Lieutenant Carter," he replied, nodding. "There will be a mixture of Army Air Corps officers and civilian personnel on each flight. Make no mistake, you'll work together as a team, both in training and on missions."

He paused, letting the men take in the information.

"The Army Air Corps doesn't have enough personnel to cover all the flights needed to move our supplies and troops. United Air Lines has won the contract to operate with us in the Pacific Theater, providing skilled and trained personnel for the effort."

"For most flights, the captain will be a first or second lieutenant from the Army Air Corps. He's in charge, just like on any flight. The co-pilot could be another Army officer, likely a second lieutenant, or a United Air Lines pilot. Navigators may be either Army or civilian." He paused briefly, then continued, "The Army is particularly short on skilled radio operators, so all flight radio operators will be United Air Lines contractors. Any additional crew members, such as mechanics or support, will also come from the commercial carrier's trained personnel."

There were several nods and murmurs of acknowledgment around the room. Satisfied, the captain continued, "Any other questions?"

Silence settled over the rows of men, each man's eyes a little glazed, shoulders sagging under the weight of hours spent in stiff chairs. But the captain wasn't done.

"Good," he said, flipping through a stack of notes on the podium. "Then let's keep moving." Paul stifled a sigh, exchanging a weary glance with Joe. They were in for a long day.

***

Low, weary voices buzzed through the mess hall, broken by the clatter of trays and utensils. After eight straight hours in the briefing room, Paul's head throbbed with the captain's words, still echoing like a distant radio signal. His back ached as he sank onto the bench, every muscle stiff. His mind was packed to the brim.

He slouched over his tray, pushing around lukewarm potatoes while Joe barely lifted his fork across from him. "If every day's like this," Joe mumbled, stifling a yawn, "I might not make it to our first mission." He looked up at Paul, adding, "And didn't your mother ever tell you not to slouch?"

"All the time." Paul chuckled, feeling the exhaustion in his bones. "I think they're testing our limits," he replied, attempting another bite of the overcooked meatloaf. "If we can survive the briefing room, maybe we can survive anything."

The two sat in silence, the fatigue settling around them, until a figure loomed over their table. Paul glanced up, blinking as he recognized the officer from earlier—the one who'd asked the question about Army and civilian roles. Chuck Carter.

"Mind if I join you two?" Chuck asked, holding his tray steady despite his weary eyes.

"Hey! What's up, Chuck?" Cowboy managed to get out.

"Very funny, like I've never heard that one before."

"Oldie but a moldy," Joe shot back with a grin.

"Take the last seat," Paul said, motioning to the empty spot beside him.

Chuck set down his tray and took a seat. Average in height and lean, he had a close-cropped head of brown hair that added to his efficient, no-nonsense look. A precise mustache lined his upper lip, giving his angular face a stern but polished look. His expression was cordial enough, though he held himself with the quiet reserve of someone more comfortable with structure than with small talk.

"You guys holding up after all that?" he asked, giving them a nod.

Joe snorted. "Barely. They should have handed out pillows instead of notes."

Chuck cracked a smile, a flash of white teeth. "Gotta love it!"

"Hey, fellas," Paul said, "how about a quick prayer before we really get started with our meal?"

Joe quickly looked up, pleasantly surprised. "I'd be happy to pray with you. Chuck?"

"You fellas knock yourselves out," Chuck said with a shrug. "I'm gonna dig in."

Paul began to pray. "Heavenly Father, you are Lord of all. We praise you for your name and we praise you for who you are. Lord, we ask for safety and guidance for all here. Please help us to serve to the best of our ability, but only with your help. Lord, we thank you for this food placed before us. We ask you to bless it for our use, and us to your service. And make us ever mindful of the needs of others. In Jesus's name, amen."

"Thanks for that, Paul," said Joe. "I appreciate that."

Chuck smirked, shaking his head as he took a bite of his meal. "Not sure why you guys feel the need to waste your time on things like that. There are more important things to worry about. Things you can actually see."

"You're wrong about that, Chuck." Joe replied, his tone firm and even. "That's the most important thing to worry about. Actually, 'worry about' is not the correct phrase. I'm not worried about it. It's the most important thing to focus on. God, our relationship with Him—it's the foundation of everything."

Chuck squinted his eyes, "Aren't you afraid of what people think, carrying on like that about your invisible friend in front of everyone?"

Paul leaned forward slightly, meeting Chuck's gaze. "I don't fear what people think, Chuck. I fear God, not man."

"Well, that's just peachy. I rely on myself—my abilities and what I can see and touch."

The atmosphere grew tense, and Paul decided to change the subject. "So," he ventured, "what got you into flying?"

Chuck's gaze shifted slightly, his eyes distant for a moment. "Always wanted it," he said, his tone quieter. "I grew up idolizing Lindbergh. Thought maybe I'd be the next one to fly across the ocean someday. Got my engineering degree, joined up with the Army Air Corps, and logged a few months on assignments out east before they transferred me here."

Paul raised an eyebrow. "So you're not fresh out of school then?"

Chuck shook his head. "Not exactly. I started out as a second lieutenant, running training exercises and clocking flight hours in B-25s. Nothing too fancy, but enough to get promoted." He paused, glancing down at his tray with a hint of a wry smile. "Guess the brass figured I'd be useful over here in transport."

Joe looked impressed. "Guess we've got ourselves a real ace over here," he said, nudging Paul.

Chuck's smile was faint, his face betraying just a hint of weariness. "I'll take 'ace' when I've earned it," he replied. "For now, just trying to learn the ropes like everyone else."

"So, what was it like to fly a B-25, Chuck?" Joe asked.

"Those aircraft are more maneuverable than you would think. I enjoyed my time in the B-25 cockpit, it was a pretty fun plane to fly." Chuck responded, with a hint of nostalgia. "Noisy, though. Almost as noisy as another Mitchell I know," he said, turning toward Joe.

"Chuck, I'm touched. I didn't think you'd noticed. I also didn't think you had that in you. My respect for you has just grown—a very little bit."

They fell into a comfortable silence, each focusing on their trays and grateful for the reprieve from lectures, thinking ahead to the long days that lay before them.

***

After dinner, a group of men lingered just outside the mess hall, their voices mixing with the buzz of crickets and the rustle of dry grass swaying in the warm evening breeze. The air smelled faintly of sagebrush from the surrounding fields. For a moment, the weight of the day—briefings, drills, an overwhelming flood of new procedures—seemed to lift, if only slightly.

The conversations drifted, touching on hometowns, homesickness, and the sweethearts they'd left behind. It wasn't late, but the day had been exhausting—physically, mentally, and even emotionally.

Paul stretched, adjusting his cap. "I'll think I'm going to hit the hay. I suspect we've got another long one tomorrow."

As a civilian, he wasn't required to stay on base, but he had decided early on that he would. One reason was camaraderie—these were the men he'd be flying with, after all. The other reason was more practical. He'd heard rumors about quiet resentment from the military personnel toward civilians, especially by officers, who were required to stay on base while civilians could come and go. Paul didn't want to be seen as an outsider.

The Army had also realized this problem of resentment by Army officers, so the decision was made that civilians were to wear

Army uniforms. Paul didn't mind—it helped him to blend in, to feel like part of the team.

"Yeah, me too," Joe agreed, rolling his shoulders. "At least everything's in walking distance here. Heck, we can walk to work or carry our lunch."

Paul blinked, processing the comment. It took a second, but then he got it. Somewhat humorous, he supposed. Joe had a way of saying things that didn't always make perfect sense at first. Maybe that came from spending so much time on the ranch with Sage, where words didn't have to be precise. But even Joe's offhand remarks added to his charm.

Paul chuckled quietly, shaking his head. Before he could respond, he noticed Chuck shifting slightly in his peripheral vision. His hands were stuffed deep in his pockets, his posture unusually stiff.

"I think I might swing by the officers' club," he said, almost as if testing the idea out loud.

Joe raised an eyebrow. "Suit yourself, but don't be late tomorrow. El Capitan might give you an earful."

Chuck's jaw tightened slightly as he glanced toward Joe, his voice carrying a faint edge. "Don't worry about me. I can take care of myself."

Paul caught the tension but said nothing, breaking the moment with a nod. "Alright then. Night, Chuck."

"Good night," Joe added, his tone light.

Chuck gave a small wave as he turned on his heel, heading toward the officers' club. Paul and Joe lingered a moment longer, watching as he walked away. Neither spoke, but Paul caught the brief furrow in Joe's brow, as if some unspoken concern had taken root.

They turned and began walking toward the barracks, the day's exhaustion pressing down on them like a weighted blanket. It was surprising how draining a day filled with briefings and classroom instruction could be. Paul wondered if the other men were feeling as overwhelmed as he was.

In the next few weeks, he knew he'd have to get everything straight in his head. Most of the technical radio knowledge was second nature to him, but the military procedures were another story. And flying long-haul missions across vast stretches of open ocean—that part made his stomach twist a little. The captain running orientation had made it sound daunting.

But he would manage. He had to.

Training here at Mather would be quick and intense. By fall, they'd be flying real missions. Paul was excited, yet also a little nervous. But he figured once they got past the early stages, the nerves would settle.

Pausing outside the barracks, he took a deep breath, letting the night air cool his face, the smell of dust and grass grounding him in the moment. For a second, he thought of Alta—how she was probably already in bed and asleep, as he was hoping to be very soon.

He exhaled slowly, then stepped inside, ready for the few short hours of sleep before it all began again.

***

Paul climbed into his bunk and sat with his pillow propped up behind him, feeling the day's fatigue as he sank into the mattress. The quarters were quiet, save for the murmur of voices drifting from down the hall and the occasional creak of a nearby bed frame. The air carried the faint scent of floor polish and metal, the ever-present tang of the barracks mingling with the lingering sharpness of ink and paper from his notes. He stretched his legs out, letting the stiffness in his back ease, but the tension of the day still clung to him.

Leaning against the wall, he exhaled slowly, his thoughts drifting. He had spent the day immersed in briefings and training sessions, but now, in the quiet solitude of the barracks, he let himself reflect—not just on the day, but on how he had ended up here.

Stromsburg, Nebraska. The family farm. The three eighties of land where he had spent his boyhood exploring, working, and wondering about what lay beyond the fields. He had loved the openness, the space to roam, but as he grew older, he had known he wanted something different. His mild asthma had made the summers on the farm difficult enough, but more than that, he had been drawn to things beyond farming: radios, airplanes, the hum of signals carrying voices across the airwaves.

And then Evelyn. His sister's illness had been a cruel reminder of how quickly life could change. Sixteen years old, full of dreams, and then gone. After that, he had promised himself that he would seize opportunities when they came, that he wouldn't let life slip by without reaching for something more.

That promise led him to radio and aviation classes, and then carried him to Omaha, where he opened up a small radio repair shop. There he could tinker and make a living doing something he loved. And then, United Air Lines. From there, the path to Air Transport Command had fallen into place almost naturally. But as much as he had worked for this, as much as he believed in the importance of what he was doing, it didn't stop the ache of missing home—missing her.

His gaze drifted to his footlocker, where he kept her letters. He didn't need to read them again, he knew them almost by heart, but he reached under his pillow anyway, pulling out the latest one. The paper was soft from the number of times he had unfolded and refolded it, a physical connection to the words inside: "Last night I was talking with the family about us and got so lonesome for you ..."

Paul smiled, running his thumb along the crease of the letter. He could picture her, could hear the way she would have said it—gently, like a confession whispered just to him. She had written about showing off her engagement ring, about her family's approval. He told himself he had nothing to worry about, but still, the thought lingered. These were the people she loved, the ones she trusted the most. Would they see in him what she did? Would he be enough?

He sighed, shaking his head. Of course she thinks so, he reminded himself. She chose you.

The weight of the day settled more comfortably around him, shifting as he let himself sink into the memory of her. He thought of her laugh, of the way her eyes crinkled when she teased him. The way she had looked at him the first time they met, something unspoken passing between them, something that had changed everything.

He exhaled deeply, closing his eyes. The bunkhouse, the regimented life, the training—all of it faded away, leaving only the warmth of her presence in his mind. The whisper of longing remained, but it no longer felt heavy—it was a tether, something steady to hold onto in the midst of the unknown.

Tomorrow, he would wake up before dawn. Another day of lectures, of training, of preparing for whatever lay ahead. But tonight, he had his memories.

Alta.

The thought of her carried him beyond the weariness, past the uncertainty. He let the memory take him back to that moment—the moment the world had shifted. And with that, he drifted into sleep.

CHAPTER TWO

Cleveland Airport - January 1941

E verything happens for a reason. There is no coincidence. There is no luck. Most people who talk about "luck" or "coincidence" misunderstand the bigger picture. Sure, there's probability, but that's not what they mean. Paul would never say, "That is one lucky S.O.B." For one thing, he didn't really like speaking in that manner. For another, the "S.O.B." in question wasn't really "lucky" at all. He was fortunate. Opportunistic. More often than not, he was blessed.

Paul was blessed. He had been in Cleveland at the right time, in the right place. Everything that happened, everything that mattered, had started there.

***

"Glenn Miller? Seriously. Glenn Miller?"

"Sure. What's wrong with Glenn Miller?" Paul couldn't believe what he was hearing. What was wrong with Glenn Miller?

"All I'm tryin' to say is that you need to expand your horizon a bit. Everyone likes Glenn Miller. Don't follow the crowd. Try something different. Like Harry James."

Paul raised an eyebrow. "Harry James? You mean the guy who never met a trumpet solo he didn't like? Sure, he's good, but give me something I can tap my foot to."

His companion leaned back, smirking. "Miller's stuff is fine if you like your jazz watered down and served with a side of tapioca. Harry's got soul. You hear his 'You Made Me Love You'? That's not just music; that's feeling."

"Feeling?" Paul shot back. "I'll tell you what's feeling: the opening of 'Moonlight Serenade.' That's smooth, that's class. Makes you want to grab a girl and dance."

"Yeah, and put her to sleep halfway through," came the quick reply.

Paul laughed, shaking his head. "At least Miller knew how to keep a band in line. With James, it's like everyone's just trying to outplay each other."

"Ever think that's the point? Real musicians letting loose? Besides, not everyone has to play it safe like Miller. Some of us like a little edge."

"Edge is fine," Paul said, a grin forming, "but there's a difference between playing on the edge and falling off the edge. Face it, Harry James is what you listen to when you're trying to impress someone. Glenn Miller is what you play when you're trying to really feel the music and have a good time."

The other man shook his head, chuckling. "You know what? You're impossible."

"And you've got no taste," Paul replied, raising his coffee cup in a mock toast.

As Paul sat in the employee cafeteria of the Cleveland airport, he scanned the room. His gaze passed over a group of young women and settled on her before he realized what he was doing. She was sitting with a few other women, all in conversation, laughter rippling between them. But there was something differ-ent about her—poised yet relaxed, like she belonged there but wasn't trying to draw attention. Her dark hair was styled neatly, the soft curls framing her face, catching the cafeteria's faint light.

She had an easy grace and leaned slightly forward to speak, her lips curving into a smile that seemed genuine, unpracticed. It wasn't the painted-on kind of beauty you might see on magazine covers, it was something softer, warmer—something that made you want to keep looking, as though you'd miss something if you turned away too soon. Smooth, understated, and timeless. Paul thought to himself, if Glenn Miller's music had a face, it might look something like hers.

"Hey, Paul, you with us?" his companion said, interrupting Paul's thoughts.

Paul blinked, realizing he'd been caught staring.

"Who is that?" He nodded toward her, trying to seem casual.

The other man turned, glancing in the direction Paul had indi-cated. "Oh, her? That's Alta Fae," he said with a smirk. "Teletype operator. Sweet, ain't she?"

Alta. He repeated the name silently to himself. It suited her, simple yet elegant. He looked back, trying to commit the moment to memory. She had just tilted her head, laughing at something one of the other women said as her hand brushed a loose strand from her face.

"Sweet, huh?" Paul murmured, more to himself than his com-panion. But it was more than that. He couldn't quite put his finger on it.

"She catch your eye?" his companion asked with a little nudge.

Paul tore his gaze away, suddenly feeling self-conscious. He turned back to his coffee cup, swirling its contents as if it held the answer to that very question. "I was just asking," he muttered, but even as the words left his lips, he knew it wasn't true.

A lot of people would say Paul was shy, though he never liked that description. Shy implied hesitation, an avoidance of people—like an instinctive retreat. That wasn't him. Reserved was better. He liked to think before he acted, weigh his words, be intentional.

But here, now, he knew he wouldn't take too long to act.

He wanted to talk to her, to learn her name from her own lips rather than secondhand. He wanted to know what made her laugh, what kind of music she liked, what she thought about when she was alone. Where she was from, what her dreams were. But mostly, he wanted to ask her out on a date.

And maybe, just maybe, he was shy about that. Because now, at the mere thought of it, a nervous flutter twisted in his gut.

Still, he knew he'd go through with it.

Because in that moment, he knew something else too: Her smile wouldn't just stay with him for the rest of the day. It would linger, like the echo of a melody you couldn't shake, no matter how hard you tried.

***

She needed a break and some coffee with the girls—the perfect little pick-me-up. The cafeteria wasn't as busy as it normally was this time of day, which was just fine with her. The soft buzz of casual conversations blended with the faint clatter of dishes, creating a background noise that wasn't loud enough to grate on her nerves, but soothing in its familiarity.

Alta cradled the warm coffee cup between her hands, letting its heat seep into her fingers. The laughter from the women at her table was like a balm after the chaos of the morning. She couldn't quite pinpoint what about today felt so draining—maybe it was the endless stream of teletype messages, or the monotony of watching words and numbers flicker across the machine. The endless, insistent clack of the keys had followed her into her thoughts, even now. But here, with the aroma of coffee and the company of friends, she felt herself relax, if only for a moment.

One of the girls said something funny, and Alta laughed, a genuine, unguarded sound that came easily with them. She swept a loose curl behind her ear and took a sip of coffee, savoring the brief escape from her responsibilities. Still, there were days when she wished she could close her eyes and let the world carry on without her, just for a while.

She glanced around the room as the laughter at their table settled. Her eyes drifted, half-distracted, until they landed on a man at a nearby table. He was talking animatedly with a friend, his hands gesturing as he made some point she couldn't hear. She noticed his smile at first—broad and genuine, the kind that lit up his entire face.

The other girls caught her looking, and one nudged her gently. "What's got your attention?" she teased, her tone playful.

Alta flushed, turning her gaze quickly back to her coffee. "Nothing," she replied bashfully, but her lips curled into a small, secret smile she couldn't quite hide.

The truth was, something about him had caught her attention. Something in the way he held himself—his broad shoulders, squared but relaxed, as if the weight of the world rested easily there. His dark hair was neatly combed back, just a touch of wave to soften its precision. He had an energy about him, quiet but sure. It wasn't just his looks; something about the way he leaned in when he spoke reminded her of ... she wasn't sure what, exactly. Maybe that kind of steadiness she wished she felt more often herself.

He was talking now, leaning slightly toward his companion, and she could just catch the occasional chuckle in his voice. That smile of his—easy, genuine, and framed by a jawline that looked like it had been carved with care—made her glance again, her curiosity sparked. He didn't look like one of those loud, overconfident types. No, there was warmth to his expression, an openness that made you feel at ease just watching him.

Alta found herself wondering who he was and what he did there. It wasn't like her to linger on a passing face, but something about him felt ... different.

Another girl leaned closer, whispering just loud enough for the table to hear. "That's Paul. He's also with United, works with radios." There was a knowing look exchanged between them. "They call him 'the Swede with the million-dollar smile.'"

"A million dollars, huh?" Alta said, trying to sound unimpressed, but her eyes flickered back to him, just once. Alta raised her coffee to her lips, but the warmth she felt now wasn't just from the cup. Million-dollar smile? Maybe. But there was something else about him, something she couldn't quite put into words, not yet.

***

Gunter Field - January 1941

Chuck was exhausted, but that was fine. This was what was expected of him. He expected it, his family expected it. But that didn't change things right now. The Alabama sun was relentless, even in January, and the damp chill of the early morning had given way to an oppressive, sticky warmth that clung to his uniform. The airstrip shimmered in the distance as waves of heat danced across its surface. His mouth was sand-dry, and he was stiff after hours in the cockpit.

The BT-13 was nicknamed the "Vultee Vibrator" for a reason. It shook and rattled, sometimes fiercely, depending on how much power was pushed through the Pratt & Whitney R-985 engine. The vibrations were unrelenting, a constant hum that turned into a full-body rattle when the throttle opened wide. Combined with the cramped cockpit and the relentless drone of the engine, it was no wonder Chuck felt every ounce of his exhaustion. The vibrations stayed with him even after he climbed out, buzzing faintly in his muscles as if they had seeped into his very being.

This plane was the second phase in a three-stage pilot training program. With flaps, a two-position variable pitch propeller, and a radio for ground communications, it was a step up from the simpler trainers they'd started with. It included two fuel tanks, one in each wing, each holding sixty gallons of fuel. Fully fueled, it could fly for five hours—not that anyone wanted to spend that long in its cramped, unforgiving cockpit. But Chuck had done just that, wrestling the controls through basic maneuvers, steep turns, and touch-and-go landings. His shoulders ached and sweat clung to his back beneath the heavy flight suit.

Training in the BT-13 wasn't just about flying; it was about testing limits. Pushing through the physical strain, the mental fog, and the endless repetition. It was demanding. They wanted to see if he would break under the strain.

Chuck wouldn't. He couldn't

He had too much to prove.

To his instructors. To his classmates. To himself. To his father. Especially to his father.

It seemed like he was never quite able to live up to his father's expectations. Somewhere in the back of his mind, his father's voice echoed: "You're a Carter. We don't fail."

Chuck clenched his jaw. His father had said when he got into MIT, "Great, but how come your grades aren't higher?" Then when he was commissioned, "Good, but why aren't you in combat?" It was never enough.

It seemed like he was always on the precipice of failure.

But failure wasn't an option. Neither was complaining. He tugged his cap lower against the sun and reached for his canteen. The water was lukewarm, but it did the job.

The shrill whistle of an instructor cut through the humid air, snapping him back to the present. "Lieutenant Carter! Quit daydreaming and get your gear squared away! Briefing in ten!"

Chuck stifled a sigh and straightened, his fatigue momentarily forgotten. "Yes, sir!" he barked, his voice steady, even as the edges of his vision blurred with exhaustion. His hands moved automatically, adjusting his gear, checking his logbook. Every movement precise, deliberate, just like everything in his life had to be.

The hangar loomed ahead, its shadow a brief respite from the sun. Inside, the other trainees were already gathering, a mix of faces; some wide-eyed with excitement, others tight with frustration. Chuck slipped into his usual spot near the back, where he could listen without drawing attention.

"Alright, gentlemen," the instructor began, pacing in front of the group. "Tomorrow's evaluation flight will test everything you've learned so far: formation flying, emergency procedures, instrument navigation. If you don't think you will be able to handle it, now's the time to say so."

Chuck didn't even flinch. He knew he could handle it. He had to. He allowed his mind to wander for a moment, back to Boston, to the cold winters, the old stone buildings, the weight of his family's legacy. Back to the letter he hadn't answered yet. The one from his mother, asking if he was eating enough, sleeping enough, being careful enough.

Careful wasn't the point. Getting the job done was. Proving himself was.

But maybe his mother had a point. The sleepless nights, the bad food, the constant exhaustion—it was catching up to him. He had to take better care of himself if he was going to keep this up.

The instructor's voice brought him back. "You'll be paired off for tomorrow's flights. Carter, you're with Donovan. Samuelson, you're with ..."

Great, Donovan.

Chuck nodded, glancing at Donovan, a wiry, sharp-eyed cadet with a perpetual smirk. "Guess we'll see if you're as good as they say," Donovan muttered as they filed out of the hangar, just loud enough for others to hear.

What a louse. Chuck didn't bother with a reply. Let Donovan talk. Tomorrow, he'd let his flying do the talking.

***

Chuck just sat there, kicking himself mentally. He felt sick—not from any physical ailment, but from failure. Today's evaluation flight hadn't gone well. Now, sitting there on his bunk, head in hands, he questioned everything: his ability, his calling, his place here. Around him, the barracks buzzed with muted voices. The slam of a locker door made him flinch, his nerves still raw. His hands trembled as the moment replayed over and over in his mind.

The flight had started off well enough; formation flying was the focus. Donovan was on his left wing. Chuck felt locked in. The Vultee responded as if it were an extension of his own body. It felt good. Then it happened: A sudden downdraft caught his aircraft and forced him down and to the left. The Vultee had shuddered violently as it dropped, the wings fighting to catch lift. Chuck gripped the stick tighter than necessary, his mind blank with fear. He couldn't think, couldn't move. He felt frozen in place, like in a block of ice, body and mind. What was wrong with him?

The instructor's voice barked something sharp through the intercom: "Level out! Overcompensating. Check your ... Don't freeze!" But Chuck couldn't process it. The ground was closing in. When he was finally able to move, his movements were jerky and panicked. He couldn't make his hands do what they needed to do. Then, the instructor's firm hand grabbed the controls from him, and the aircraft leveled out with a bone-rattling jolt.

On the ground, Chuck had sat in silence during the debrief, replaying the moment over and over. He could feel Donovan's smirk burning a hole into the back of his head. He had always believed that training and gut instinct would kick in during a crisis. They hadn't. Instead he froze. If it weren't for the instructor in the back seat taking over, Chuck felt certain he'd be dead—and part of him wondered if that wouldn't have been better.

Now, in the dim light of the barracks, he lifted his head, jaw tightening. This wasn't supposed to happen—not to him. But it had. The doubt gnawed at him, whispering at him with its insidious accusations: You're not good enough. You can't do this. You'll let everyone down. It was like someone was standing right beside him, whispering harshly into his ear, "You're nothing. You should have died out there." The words echoed deep into his soul.

Chuck ran a hand through his dark hair, frustration and self-loathing mounting. MIT had been hard, sure, but this—this was something else entirely. He glanced at the other men in the room, most laughing or relaxed, seemingly unfazed. Was it just him? Or did they feel the weight too, and just hid it better?

Chuck felt like he wanted to talk to someone. But who? He had no friends here. His mother came to mind, but she might tell his father. That was no good. He turned his head up, closed his eyes and opened his mouth as if searching for the right words. None came. He dropped his head, chin on his chest.

There was no one.

But even as the thought passed through his mind, an uneasy sensation lingered. It wasn't just loneliness, it was something deeper, a hollow ache he couldn't name. His chest tightened as if some part of him was straining, reaching, but for what? He exhaled sharply, dismissing the feeling. There was nothing there. And yet ...

He leaned back on his bunk, exhaling slowly. Resolve pushed back against the doubt. This wouldn't define him. Flying was all he had. There was nothing else.

***

Cleveland, Ohio - February, 1941

Paul was nervous. Very nervous, in fact. One would have thought that he had never been on a date before. But was this really a date? After all, it was just lunch, but it seemed like a date. He'd never really gotten a chance to ask her out on a date, but it was kind of funny how it happened. Apparently, both he and Alta had noticed each other at the same time. Their respective friends had noticed that they had noticed, and things just happened. Alta's friends spoke to Paul's friends, and here he was, getting ready to be on a date.

At least he thought it was a date. They hadn't really been introduced or even spoken to each other. Shouldn't they have at least spoken to each other before a "date" had been scheduled? What kind of man was he, letting his friends set him up on a date? At least he thought it was a date. Maybe it wasn't. Maybe it was just two people who didn't actually have the guts to talk to each other showing up at the same time, at the same place, and eating. Maybe they would sit there, not talking to each other. If you really thought about it, they already had a history of not talking to each other. What made him think that this would be any different?

I'm over-thinking this.

Paul took a deep breath and straightened his tie as he glanced at his reflection in the window of the downtown Cleveland soda fountain. It really wasn't much of a tie, just one he wore to work. He was used to wearing it, but now it felt like it was choking him. He dried his palms on his pants. Hands in pockets? Or out?

He'd arrived ten minutes early. After all: If you're not early, you're late—as his father always said. But now he felt ridiculous just standing outside. He decided to step inside and wait.

Inside, the soda fountain was bright and inviting, the air rich with the smell of grilled sandwiches and chocolate malts. The counter was lined with stools, a few of which were already occupied by teenagers sipping on Coca-Colas. Booths along the walls were starting to fill up with lunchtime patrons.

Paul shifted from one foot to the other. Maybe she wouldn't show. Maybe she'd changed her mind. Or maybe she'd realized that agreeing to lunch with some fella she had never even spoken to was a mistake. What was he thinking? He should just leave. Now he felt even more ridiculous standing around just inside the door, looking around at other people enjoying their lunch. He walked over to the counter and leaned on it, trying to look sharp. The door jingled as someone walked in, and Paul instinctively turned to look. His heart stopped for a second.

There she was.

Alta walked toward him, her coat buttoned up against the cold, her cheeks pink from the brisk wind. She paused for just a moment, looking at him with a little sheepish smile. Wow!

"Hi," he managed, his voice cracking, a little higher than he intended. He felt like a teenager.

"Hi," she replied, her smile soft and a little tentative.

Paul gestured awkwardly toward a booth near the window. His elbow slipped off the counter and he struggled to keep his composure—and balance. "I thought we could, uh, sit over there."

She nodded, and they slid into opposite sides of the booth. For a moment, there was silence, the kind that pounded loudly in Paul's ears.

"So ..." he began, trying to sound casual, "I hear they make a pretty good ham sandwich here." And he immediately regretted it. Seriously? Ham sandwich? Their very first conversation. He could have said anything. But he chose to talk about ham sandwiches. Perfect!

Alta's lips bent into a small smile. "That's good to know," she said lightly. "A girl's gotta have standards though. If the coffee's not up to par, we might have a problem. But I do like ham."

The waitress appeared, her notepad at the ready, and Paul breathed a silent sigh of relief. At least ordering food gave him a second to gather his thoughts.

"Coffee, please," Alta said, her voice steady but warm.

"And I'll have the same," Paul added quickly. He glanced at the menu, "And the ham sandwich."

The waitress smirked, her pencil hovering over the page. "You got it." She turned to Alta. "And for you?"

Alta paused, then smiled up at the waitress. "I'll have the turkey club, please."

Paul waited until the waitress walked away before saying, "Good choice."

"Thanks," Alta replied with a small grin as she leaned slightly toward Paul. "And hey, ham sandwiches aren't a bad start."

Paul laughed softly, his nerves loosening just a little. "Well, I'm glad you think so. I was starting to worry I'd ruined my shot at making a good first impression."

She tilted her head slightly, her eyes catching his for just a moment longer than before. "I think you're doing fine."

Paul couldn't help but smile as the tension in his shoulders finally eased. This had been a good idea, better than he'd expected. He would have to thank his friends for the little nudge. Maybe, just maybe, this could turn into something more than just a lunch date.

CHAPTER THREE

Mather Field - September 1, 1942

T he aircraft shuddered as it hit a patch of turbulence, and the constant noise of the four Pratt & Whitney R-1830 Twin Wasp radial engines was momentarily drowned out by the groan of its massive frame. Paul steadied himself against the radio console, his fingers brushing against the radio controls as he kept an ear tuned for any transmissions over the crackle in his headphones.

From the cockpit, Chuck's voice crackled through the intercom, calm but firm. "Hold steady. We're still on course. Paul, confirm our last position with Mather Base."

"Already did. They've got us right where we should be." The headset muffled some of the engine noise, but he could still feel the vibration of the engines through the cabin floor.

Paul adjusted his headset as more chatter came over the intercom. "Alright, listen up," Jimmy's voice came through, slightly distorted but unmistakably cheerful. "We're passing over the grid now, but if my calculations are wrong, we'll end up somewhere in the middle of the Pacific, dodging sharks instead of delivering cargo."

Chuck snorted from the cockpit, "That's comforting, Jimmy."

"It's all about trust," Jimmy replied. "Trust me, you're not gonna be shark bait."

"I trust you about as far as I can throw a pile of manure," Joe chimed in.

"Beautiful. Do you talk that way around your horse, Cowboy?"

Paul couldn't help but grin. Between Jimmy's humor and Joe's quick wit, it was always entertaining. He looked forward to the banter between the crew, and Chuck even got involved every once in a while. But Jimmy took the cake. The man had an uncanny ability to plot a course and make it sound like a stand-up routine.

Jimmy was an interesting character. His humor was in sharp contrast to his obsessive behavior over the smallest of details. His maps were always spread out around him, marked with sharp lines and neat handwriting that showed a meticulousness that Paul could only admire.

The crew had been finalized just about three weeks ago, and Paul had been blessed to have Joe on his flight crew as the co-pilot. The two were quickly becoming close friends, which seemed like an anomaly between civilian and military crew. And wouldn't you know it, Chuck had been assigned as pilot. Jimmy was a late assignment to the crew as the navigator, but he quickly became someone that Paul relied on for his course-plotting skill and steady presence.

This was their final training mission, and the weight of its significance was palpable among the crew. Tensions were high, as success here meant they were ready for the real thing. The plan was ambitious: A 1,200-mile loop starting at Mather Field, heading west toward the coast, then down to Monterey Bay. From there, they would veer offshore for over-water navigation practice, a critical skill for Pacific missions, before turning inland to cross the rugged Sierra Nevada mountains. The route then curved south to March Field near Riverside, where they would simulate a cargo drop. Finally, they would head north, returning to Mather Field.

The entire journey would take approximately twelve hours, testing both the crew's stamina and their ability to work seamlessly as a team.

The training mission was to include navigation over water and a variety of other terrains, along with cargo handling, crew coordination, landing and takeoff practice, weather awareness, emergency procedures, and simulated failures.

It would be a grueling flight session, the most difficult one so far. But this would be nothing compared to a real mission. The distance they would travel for this training would be just one leg of a real trip. The one thought that really kept Paul going was that he was going to be married on September 12. The date had been set, and Alta was ready to move to California. It was less than two weeks away.

But now it was time to focus on the mission, his job, the radio, and the aircraft.

***

The C-87 Liberator Express was a curious beast: a transport plane born from a bomber. With four Pratt & Whitney R-1830 Twin Wasp engines, it was a dependable workhorse, though its thunderous roar made conversation a shouting match, even with earphones. Each engine churned out 1,200 horsepower, propelling the bulky frame through the sky with surprising efficiency.

The airfoil was different than most pilots were used to. The wing was a shoulder-mounted, high-lift, Davis wing. This gave the aircraft high cruise speed and a long range but made for poor low-speed performance and challenging handling.

Inside, the plane was all business—no frills, just rows of exposed ribs and rivets, the bare metal glinting faintly under the overhead lights. It wasn't built for comfort, and the stark interior only seemed to magnify Paul's exhaustion.

There was no temperature control, no pressurized cabin, and no restroom. High altitudes brought bone-chilling cold, while sitting on the tarmac felt like baking in an oven. As for relieving yourself, well, there was a receptacle for that—enough said.

Paul glanced around the interior. For such a big plane, it didn't seem to hold much cargo. The bomb bay doors had been replaced with a solid floor, creating an open expanse for freight or passengers, or both. Cargo doors had been installed where the waist guns of a B-24 would normally be, and the transparent nose had been replaced by another set of cargo doors. The gun turrets were gone, leaving the plane defenseless, stripped down for the sole purpose of hauling men and material across vast distances.

His own workspace, the radio station, was positioned just behind the co-pilot, while the navigator's station, relocated from the nose, sat behind the pilot. The flight engineer's station was next to Paul's.

The C-87's cousin, the B-24, typically flew with a crew of ten. But stripped of its guns and bombs, the C-87 required fewer hands; usually a crew of five, sometimes just four. Even so, the aircraft demanded constant attention in the air. A flight engineer was invaluable, monitoring the engines, fuel and other systems, ensuring the plane remained in working order. The typical crew included a pilot, co-pilot, navigator, radio operator and engineer, each performing critical tasks to keep them airborne.

Paul looked around at his fellow crew members with a sense of gratitude settling over him. In a remarkably short time, they had formed a cohesive team. Each man knew his job, and Paul felt confident in their abilities. The classroom sessions and training flights had played their part, but it was more than that—they shared a common goal, and they were working toward it together.

"Hey Paul, what's the poop on the radio? Are you able to get any Sons of the Pioneers on that thing?" Joe broke in over the intercom.

"Believe me, I've tried, but no luck here. I could sing some 'Cool Water' if that would help," Paul replied.

"I think I'd rather listen to static, but thanks anyway."

"Suit yourself. Alta loves my singing, but then again, she's got some taste. You just hang out around horses all day long."

Paul flashed his trademark smile. The plane's radio wasn't exactly built for entertainment—it was all business. The setup included a BC-348 receiver and a BC-375 transmitter, both dependable and well-suited for the demands of long-haul missions. Paul carefully tuned the frequency, watching the glowing indicator needle slide across the scale. His responsibilities were straightforward on paper but required focus and precision. He was responsible for maintaining clear communication with ground control and other aircraft. He had to monitor frequencies constantly, switching between them as needed, logging every transmission in meticulous detail. Emergencies could arise at any moment, and it was his job to ensure the radio was ready to relay distress calls or vital instruction.

The equipment itself could develop problems, not because of the quality, but because of the operating environment. Vacuum tubes could fail, connections could loosen, and interference could garble signals. Paul always carried a toolkit and spare parts and was prepared to fix whatever went wrong mid-flight. He couldn't count the number of times he'd had to swap out a tube or re-solder a wire in turbulent conditions.

Today was a good day for radio work. The skies were clear and the interference was minimal. Paul settled into his seat, fine-tuning the radio's antenna coupling to improve reception. As he made the adjustments, the faint static faded. He logged the current frequency in his logbook and jotted down the time and coordinates.

He usually found the work engrossing. Having frequencies to monitor and reports to write made the hours pass quickly. But today, his thoughts were not completely on his work. As much as he loved the rhythm of the job, his heart was somewhere else—with someone.

Back in August, Paul had walked into a jewelry store in Cleveland with a purposeful stride. Purposeful, albeit with a hint of nervous tension. He'd picked out a ring—a simple gold band with a modest diamond flanked by two smaller stones, simple yet elegant, just like her—and tucked it safely in his pocket. With his leave approved, he had traveled to Cleveland, determined to ask the question that had been running through his mind for weeks.

It wasn't a surprise, not really. Their letters had become more frequent, their words warmer over the past few months. He'd even noticed a touch of impatience in her tone, as though she were waiting for him to catch up to what they both already knew. It felt natural, inevitable.

At dinner, in a quiet little place she liked, Paul reached for her hand across the table. His fingers brushed hers, steady despite the thundering in his chest. The warm glow of candlelight flickered in her eyes, and for a moment, he almost lost himself in them.

Paul took a breath and spoke softly. "Alta Fae, you know I'm not the kind of guy for big speeches." He paused, gathering his thoughts. "But I also know that I don't want to go another day without knowing you'll be my wife."

Her lips parted slightly, her breath catching, but she didn't speak.

His thumb brushed over her knuckles, grounding him. "I love you. I love everything about you. And if you'll have me, I promise I'll do my best to make you happy for the rest of my life."

A slow smile spread across her face, the smile that always made his heart flip in his chest.

He swallowed hard. "Alta, will you marry me?"

Her smile had lit up the room, and she hadn't hesitated. "Yes," she'd said, her voice soft but full of certainty. Just like that, his world shifted, clearer and brighter than ever before.

Now, here he was, finishing his final training at Mather Field. Soon, they'd embark on extended missions across the Pacific. He and Alta had decided they didn't want to wait. They'd be married before his first mission.

He turned his attention back to the radio, performing his duties with renewed focus, but thoughts of Alta gave him a quiet sense of purpose that made the hours feel shorter.

***

The flight to the coast and the over-water navigation practice had been fairly uneventful, aside from a few patches of turbulence. Jimmy had done a solid job plotting course changes as they flew west of the California coastline, the vast expanse of the Pacific stretching beneath them. Now, as they crossed the Sierra Nevada, the terrain presented new challenges.

The mountains were unpredictable; air currents could shift suddenly, and pockets of turbulence kept them on their toes. Paul kept his focus sharp, his hands resting near the radio controls as he monitored the 14.025 MHz frequency. Just as outlined in the pre-flight briefing, he was listening for instructions from Mather base.

The steady drone of the engines filled the cockpit, but then a burst of static crackled in Paul's headphones, snapping him to attention.

"Transport 102, this is Mather Base," came the transmission. "Simulate engine failure on engine three. Do you copy?"

Paul adjusted the radio frequency slightly, ensuring the signal came through clearly, and keyed the transmitter on 14.225 MHz. "Mather Base, this is Transport 102," he replied. "Copy that, simulating engine failure on engine three. Transport 102, over."

The high frequency (HF) bands were well-suited for long-distance communications between aircraft and ground control. These frequencies bounced off the ionosphere and made communications over vast distances possible.

Paul swiveled in his seat, switching to the intercom. "Chuck, Joe, they want us to simulate an engine failure. Engine three."

"Roger that," Chuck responded. His tone was calm, but Paul could detect an edge—Chuck was focused. A slight change in pitch vibrated through the plane as Chuck throttled back engine three. The C-87 responded immediately, yawing to the right.

"Engine three failing," Joe announced, reaching for the controls. "Feathering now."

Paul quickly logged the event in his notebook. Behind him the flight engineer made some adjustments on the engine control panel and monitored the oil pressure and RPM readings. His role was to ensure that the simulated failure didn't escalate into a real emergency. He gave a thumbs up to Joe—everything looked normal.

"Feathered," Joe confirmed a moment later. Outside, the propeller blades on engine three slowed and aligned with the airflow, reducing drag. The plane steadied, but the strain on the remaining engines was evident in the slightly deeper growl.

"Let's see how she handles," Chuck muttered, his hands firm on the yoke. He made careful adjustments, compensating for the asymmetric thrust. The C-87 responded sluggishly, its weight and the high-altitude air density combining to test Chuck's skill. Below, the Sierra Nevada's jagged peaks loomed, their rugged faces bathed in the late morning sun.

Paul looked around at his fellow crew members. Joe was scanning the instruments with an intense focus, his mouth in a tight line. Jimmy, ever calm, was already recalculating their flight path, his pencil scratching against the chart in quick strokes. The flight engineer stayed quietly focused, monitoring the gauges and ready to jump in if needed. They were working as a seamless team.

In that moment, Paul felt a surge of certainty—this was what he wanted for his profession. Of course, he wouldn't stay on Air Transport Command missions forever, but he wanted to continue solving problems, working through procedures, and collaborating with a tight-knit crew like this one. And he wanted to fly.

Still, the toll this life took on Alta weighed heavily on his mind. He had received a letter from her last month, the strain evident in her words: "What I wish is that this war was over, and you were working here in Cleveland instead of me not knowing where you are or are going to be."

Her words echoed in his thoughts, a reminder of the sacrifices they were both making. After they were married, he knew he would have to find a way to balance these long trips with family life. He owed that to her. But he also knew Alta understood the demands of the war. She was working grueling hours herself, supporting the effort stateside. It wasn't easy for either of them, but they shared a quiet resolve to endure it together.

When the war was over, he would find a job closer to home, maybe at the Cleveland airport. Until then, they would both have to make sacrifices.

The intercom buzzed again and Chuck's voice cut through the background noise. "Paul, let Mather know we're simulating engine three failure. Everything's under control."

Paul keyed the transmitter again. "Mather Base, this is Transport 102. Engine three failure simulated; all systems stable."

"Transport 102, Mather Base. Copy that. Engine three failure simulation successful," came the reply. "Throttle up engine three and continue the mission profile. Mather Base out."

Paul switched back to the intercom. "Mather Base confirms successful engine three failure simulation. Throttle up engine three and continue with mission."

"Roger that. Starting engine three."

Paul settled back in his seat, the weight of the simulation easing slightly as they pressed forward to the next waypoint.

***

Joe sat in the co-pilot's seat, scanning the horizon for the runway at March Field. The terrain below shifted into neat patterns of farmland and roads, a stark contrast to the rugged Sierra Nevada they'd just crossed. He adjusted his headset, the steady drone of the engines filling the cabin, and his gaze flicked to the instrument panel out of habit. Everything looked good—textbook, really. But his mind wasn't entirely on the cockpit.

He liked flying, sure. But it wasn't where his heart was. Not really. He missed Sage. He missed the ranch.

Sage wasn't just a horse; she was his partner, his friend. On more than one occasion, she had saved his life, literally, pulling him out of danger when instinct alone wouldn't have been enough. Figuratively, she had steadied him, kept him grounded during moments when life's weight threatened to crush him. God had put her in his life for a reason, and for that, Joe was eternally grateful.

Then there was the sheer joy of riding. It was something that a person who had never been in the saddle before could ever truly understand. On horseback, there was power, freedom—a partnership between man and animal that transcended words. The way a horse could read your movements, anticipate your intention—it was like flying, but without the noise. Joe cracked a faint smile, thinking: A good horse is better than just about anything else. Even a bad horse is better than most things.

His thoughts drifted further back, to the rolling pastures of his family ranch, Mitchell Quarter Horse Ranch near Hayden, Colorado. He had grown up there, surrounded by the rhythms of ranch life. The furthest he'd ever gone from home was when he left for college at Colorado A&M in Fort Collins. At the time, he'd thought that was the adventure of a lifetime.

Joe had earned his degree in mechanical engineering, which, he figured, had caught the Army's attention and landed him in aviation. He had a knack for understanding machinery, and the engineering program had sharpened that skill. But while he'd excelled with equipment, his true gift was with the livestock. That was why he'd added a minor in animal husbandry—it just felt right. Still, the Army hadn't sent him to the cavalry; they'd handed him aptitude tests that steered him into the cockpit instead of the corral.

Now, here he was, thousands of feet above California, watching for runways instead of fence lines. The radio crackled, pulling him back to the present. Paul's voice filtered through the intercom, calm but terse, relaying instructions from March Base. Joe focused on the distant horizon again, his trained eyes picking out the faint lines of March Field's runways against the California landscape.

Right now, duty came first. He'd made that choice when he signed up, and he didn't regret it. He wanted to serve, to do his part, and he was learning to appreciate the precision and teamwork of flying. Still, there was part of him that longed for the simplicity of a saddle beneath him and the wide-open sky above.

As the C-87 began its descent, Joe took a deep breath, his hands steady on the controls. There would be time to think about Sage later. For now, it was time to focus on the approach.

"Joe, you've got the yoke. Take us in," Chuck's voice came over the intercom, calm yet firm.

"Roger, I have the ship," Joe replied, glancing over at Chuck briefly before setting into his role.

Paul's voice came over the intercom. "March Tower says to enter the pattern from the north and line up for runway two-four. Winds are calm."

Joe nodded, keeping his eyes on the instruments and the horizon. "Copy that. Runway two-four. Let them know we're entering the downwind leg."

Paul keyed the transmitter. "March Tower, this is Transport 102. Entering downwind for runway two-four."

Joe guided the C-87 into the traffic pattern, bringing it down to pattern altitude, about 2,500 feet above sea level. His right hand lay steady on the yoke, while his left adjusted the throttles to maintain their descent rate. The plane felt heavy, especially after the engine failure simulation. Even so, the C-87 was responding well, and Joe focused on keeping the turns smooth and controlled.

"Transport 102, cleared to land runway two-four. Winds now five knots, variable," Paul relayed from the tower.

"Cleared to land, runway two-four," Joe repeated. He adjusted their heading, turning onto the base leg and then final approach. Ahead, the wide expanse of the runway stretched out, its edges shimmering slightly in the midday sun.

As they descended, the air grew choppier. A slight crosswind had developed, rolling off the hills nearby and pushing the plane gently to the right. Joe compensated, angling the nose slightly into the wind and keeping a firm hand on the yoke.

"Bit of a crosswind," Chuck said over the intercom. "Watch your alignment."

Joe nodded, his focus narrowing. He nudged the rudder pedals, bringing the nose back in line with the runway centerline. The controls felt sluggish now, a common trait of the C-87 at lower speeds, but he kept his corrections small and deliberate.

Then, at about 300 feet, the plane suddenly dropped. A downdraft, likely caused by uneven heating on the surrounding terrain, pushed them abruptly downward. Joe's heart leapt as the altimeter needle fell faster than he expected.

"Power up!" Chuck's voice snapped through the intercom, and Joe reacted immediately, easing the throttles forward and raising the nose slightly to arrest the descent. The engines roared in response, and the C-87 stabilized, though the ground felt uncomfortably close.

"I got it," Joe muttered, steadying his breathing. He rechecked their alignment and airspeed, compensating for the crosswind again. This was no time to overcorrect; small, measured inputs were key here.

The runway rushed up to meet them, and Joe transitioned into the flare, pulling back on the yoke gently to soften their landing. The main wheels touched down with a firm thud, followed by the nose gear. The plane rumbled down the runway, its weight settling onto the tires.

"Transport 102, welcome to March Field," Paul relayed from the tower as Joe slowed the aircraft, easing it off the runway onto the taxiway.

Joe exhaled deeply, his grip on the yoke relaxing as Chuck gave him a quick nod of approval. "Nice recovery," Chuck said. "That downdraft could've been bad."

Joe cracked a smile, the adrenaline still coursing through him. "Thanks. I'll take that as a win. I really had to work hard at keeping calm and not overcompensating."

Chuck's jaw tightened, and his expression suddenly shifted, like a door that had been wide open was suddenly slammed shut. He looked distant and morose, with a tinge of fear. What's that all about? Joe wondered.

"Chuck, you seem off. Everything alright?"

Chuck's head snapped toward him, "Yes, I'm fine!" he shot back. "Let's get through the post-landing checklist."

"Fine," Joe said, backing off, caught a little off guard. "Let's do it."

"Engines set to idle," Chuck started, his voice clipped.

"Check."

"Propellers adjusted to full forward position."

"Check."

"Retract flaps to fully up position."

"Check."

Chuck's tone stayed brisk and professional as they worked through the rest of the checklist and Joe followed his lead, but the tension hung in the air. Something was clearly bothering Chuck, but whatever it was, he wasn't going to talk about it.

As they taxied to the parking area, Joe glanced quickly at Chuck, who stared straight ahead, fierce determination set in his face. He'll talk when he's ready, thought Joe. But now they had to finish up and get through the simulated cargo drop.

***

Paul stood by the C-87 in the early afternoon California sun, watching the ground crew perform the simulated cargo unload. As they worked through their procedures and checklists with practiced efficiency, Paul scanned the area. It was a near-perfect day in Riverside, California: clear skies, a slight breeze, and temperatures in the mid-seventies. After hours cooped up in the aircraft with the constant drone of the engines, the open air and nice weather felt like a gift.

His gaze wandered across the tarmac, taking in the orderly bustle of the base. Then he spotted Chuck standing in the shade of one of the hangars, his face tilted toward the sun as he stared into the distance. There was something about his posture—rigid, yet unguarded—that caught Paul's attention.

Joe had mentioned Chuck's sudden shift in demeanor after landing, and Paul couldn't shake the feeling that something was weighing heavily on him. He hesitated, unsure if now was the right time, but then that familiar nudge came: a quiet yet insistent urging, like a hand on his back, guiding him forward. It wasn't something Paul could fully explain, but he'd learned to trust it. More often than not, that subtle prompting led him to do the right thing.

Taking a deep breath, Paul started toward Chuck, the sound of his boots on the pavement blending with the faint buzz of activity around them. Give me the right words, he prayed silently.

"Hello, Chuck. Nice day, isn't it?" Paul said as he approached the hangar.

Chuck didn't seem to notice Paul approaching, and he suddenly snapped back from wherever his thoughts had taken him at the sound of Paul's voice.

"Yes, very nice. It's good to be on the ground for a little bit."

"Yeah, I agree. So, how are things going for you? This is a lot to take in, especially with the thought that our next flight will probably be a real mission. Are you holding up alright?"

Chuck opened his mouth to respond, then stopped, his brow furrowing. He started again, but paused once more, finally blowing out a slow breath. When he spoke, his voice was flat.

"I don't think I can do this," he said suddenly. "This is all I've ever wanted, and now I don't think I can do it."

Paul blinked, caught off guard. He hadn't expected that—Chuck wasn't the type to open up. He especially wasn't the type to open up and admit doubt.

"What makes you say that? From my seat, it seemed like everything went very smooth. You did a great job. The entire crew did, and that's a reflection on you."

"I could have frozen again."

Paul frowned. "What are you talking about? I've never noticed you to freeze."

"During my flight training, my plane caught a downdraft, and I froze. Joe experienced something similar, and he worked through it with no problem."

"Chuck, those were two very different circumstances. And you've got a lot more experience now. You are a great pilot, and I have complete confidence in your abilities."

"Thanks," Chuck muttered. "I used to have complete confidence in my own abilities too. Now I'm not so sure. I'm not sure if I should even be here."

"Listen to me, Chuck. Everyone has doubts. Even the person who seems to have the most self-confidence struggles with them. Probably more than most. But here's the thing: when we rely completely on our own abilities—our own understanding—we will always feel like we're falling short. No one can live up to every expectation, whether it's from others or from ourselves."

Chuck turned to face Paul, his expression tight with frustration. "Who else's understanding would I possibly rely on?"

Paul hesitated, praying for wisdom. "Chuck, God has you here for a reason. Maybe even a reason you don't or can't fully understand. That's who you need to rely on: God."

Chuck's face darkened, and he turned away abruptly. "Geez, I thought that this was the direction the conversation was heading. Don't talk to me about God. He either doesn't exist, or He isn't interested in me. Either way, we're done here."

Paul watched as Chuck stalked off, his shoulders tense, his steps quick and deliberate. For a moment, Paul dropped his head, letting out a slow breath. He could have felt like a failure. But he reminded himself of what he'd just said: Relying on his own understanding wasn't the answer.

He prayed silently, hoping that, even if Chuck hadn't been ready to hear it, the seed of truth had been planted. Sometimes, that's all you can do.

***

Mather Field - September 3, 1942

"So you're not going to invite me to the wedding?" Joe said, feigning indignation. "After all we've been through, and I'm not even important enough to get an invite?"

"Honestly, I don't even know when it's going to be at this point," Paul replied with a sigh. "I need to get a telegram out to Alta lickety-split."

The final training mission had been a success. The simulated cargo drop went off without a hitch, and the flight back from March Field to Mather Field had been smooth. Several simulations had come through the radio during the long flight, but nothing the crew couldn't handle with ease. They were ready for the real thing now.

Things were moving quickly. The successful training flight had been on September 1, and the next day they'd been notified of their final crew assignments. Their base of operations would be Hamilton Field, the West Coast headquarters for the Air Transport Command. Men training at Mather were now preparing to move to Hamilton, and everything would be in place by the start of the following week.

Their first real mission was already on the books: September 12, a long-haul flight to Brisbane, Australia. That date posed a significant problem for Paul. Alta was coming to California September 12, and they were supposed to get married.

He'd tried to schedule everything through the mail, but coordinating it was no easy task. Over the past several months, Alta's letters had become more frequent. Sometimes one arrived every day. Paul wished he could write her more often, but it was hard to find the time, or the words.

Now, he and Joe sat in folding chairs just outside the barracks, faces tilted up as they watched the California sunset. The late-afternoon heat had faded to a pleasant warmth, softened by a breeze drifting in from the west. Most of the men nearby had stripped down to white t-shirts and uniform trousers, taking advantage of the cooler air.

Out of the blue, Paul spoke up, his gaze still fixed on the horizon.

"When I was in high school, I had this Model T Ford. Drove it to school just about every day. Couple times a week, I'd stop at the neighbor's place down the road a piece, pick up their girls, and give them a ride to school. I spent a lot of time with that car—driving it, tinkering with it. That car was important to me back then. You grow up on a farm, you learn to drive young. Same as I suspect you did on a ranch. By the time I got that car, I was an expert driver—or at least I *thought* I was."

Joe gave a short chuckle, and Paul smiled faintly.

"One day," Paul went on, "I was driving those neighbor girls to school. We were talking, laughing, having a good time—until I hit some washboard on the road. Lost control, and the next thing I knew, we were in a ditch. The girls were shook up pretty bad; one was crying. I dinged that car up pretty good. Took weeks to get it fixed."

Paul paused, his voice softening. "In that moment, I realized two things. First, those passengers, those girls, were *my* responsibility. Their safety and well-being were in my hands. And second, that car? As much as I loved it, it wasn't what really mattered. People are what matter. Relationships. The folks we care about."

Paul turned to look at Joe, his expression earnest. "You're important to me, Joe. I just wanted you to know that."

Joe, caught off guard, shifted in his chair but offered a small, genuine smile.

Paul stood and stretched, taking a deep breath. "Alright, let's go get some chow."

As they started toward the mess hall, Paul added with a small grin. "But, once we're settled in a new place, I want to have you over for supper. You can meet my new wife, and we'll figure out how a cowboy like you's gonna get along out here in California. Something tells me you'll have to bathe a bit more often than you're used to."

"Hey!" Joe shot back with mock offense. "I've gotten along just fine so far. Well, except for that incident when I first got here. Oh, and maybe that mix-up down at the docks ..." He trailed off, shaking his head. "On second thought, maybe I do need some help."

Paul laughed and clapped him on the back.

Joe grinned. "So, where do you two plan on living once you're hitched? I assume you've got something lined up by now."

"I asked her in a recent letter," Paul replied. "We're thinking San Mateo. It's a bit of a drive to Hamilton, but we figure it's worth it."

Joe gave a low whistle. "San Mateo, huh? Sounds pretty sharp. I'm looking forward to meeting her, and I think you're gonna do alright out here, Paul. You and Alta both. And by the way—happy birthday."

He gave Paul a friendly punch in the shoulder as they stepped into the mess hall. They each grabbed a tray, loaded up on food, and found a couple of seats toward the back. The meal was nothing special—standard mess hall fare—but tonight, it didn't matter. The weight of training was behind them, and for the first time in weeks, Paul let himself relax. They'd done it. Training was finished. Soon, they'd be on a real mission.

For now, though, he just enjoyed the moment—the food, the company, and the quiet satisfaction of knowing they were ready.

CHAPTER FOUR

Cleveland Airport - June 1942

Alta felt the familiar sting behind her eyes, threatening tears she didn't have time for. Tensions at work had been mounting since Pearl Harbor, and today was no better. The war had changed everything and some of her coworkers weren't handling it well. Snapping at each other had become the norm, and there was little patience to go around.

Everyone felt the weight of the war, but some took it out on others. Earlier that morning, a sharp exchange between two operators over a malfunction had left the room tense and quiet. Alta had tried to mediate, but her calm suggestions were met with muttered frustration. She couldn't stand how the stress turned people against each other.

The teletype room was a relentless clamor of typebars and machinery, its air heavy with the smell of oil and ink. Alta's head throbbed in rhythm with the noise, a constant reminder of the tension that had been growing in the office since Pearl Harbor.

Paul's latest letter was tucked safely in her bag, its creases soft from being unfolded and refolded so many times. He was in Chicago now, training for the Air Transport Command. The thought of him in another unfamiliar city, surrounded by strangers, made her ache for him all the more.

When the ATC had called for civilian volunteers to fill critical roles, Paul had signed up immediately. That was who he was: always ready to help, to do his part. She was proud of him for that, but it didn't make it any easier to be apart.

Her fingers hovered over the keys for a moment, the rhythmic clatter of other machines filling the room. Once she began typing, the machine would instantly transmit each character over the line. A record of the message would also be printed locally on the sending teletype machine itself. There was no margin for error—every keystroke mattered, and mistakes were immediately visible to anyone who read the printout. It wasn't just a physical effort; it was a mental one, requiring focus and precision.

She missed Paul terribly and looked forward to his letters. They were a lifeline, but they weren't enough. He was in Chicago now, but where would he go next? He didn't even know. That uncertainty pulled at her, a constant undercurrent to her days.

Alta blinked back the sting in her eyes and resumed typing, forcing herself to focus. She was doing her part too. Even here in Ohio, commercial airlines were deeply involved in the war effort. Cargo runs, troop transports, maintenance—all of it fell to civilian hands as military resources were stretched thin. Alta's job in the teletype room was more important than ever. Every message she sent or received—flight schedules, cargo manifests, military orders—carried weight. The room hummed with purpose, but it was exhausting.

Her shifts were longer now, draining her physically, mentally, and emotionally. To make matters worse, she was being trained in radio operations in case they needed to reassign her. It wasn't that she couldn't learn it, but the idea of taking on something new, something so critical, felt overwhelming. The thought of being responsible for managing vital communications filled her with a gnawing anxiety she couldn't quite shake.

Up in the radio room, she'd often struggle to pick out signals from the crackling static, her ears straining to make sense of the disjointed bursts of sound. The hum of the equipment and the occasional squeal of feedback didn't help, layering chaos over her concentration. She found herself holding her breath as she worked, hoping that she would be able to pick out the next signal.

Though there were moments when she enjoyed the challenge—when the codes came through cleanly, and the message clicked into place—she was always relieved when her time in the radio room was over. She couldn't help but wonder if she'd ever truly be at ease with it.

Still, she pressed on. Everyone was making sacrifices these days. That's what you did when the world was at war.

As she finished typing the message, she leaned back in her chair, taking a rare moment to just breathe. Her hand slipped into her pocket, brushing against Paul's letter. She pulled it out and unfolded it carefully, her eyes scanning the familiar handwriting.

The tension in her chest eased slightly as his words transported her out of the stifling room, reminding her of brighter days and quieter moments.

His words gave her strength, but they also reminded her of the ache in her heart. She traced a line with her finger, one she had read a hundred times: "I'm counting the days until I can see you again. I know it's hard, but Alta, you're the strongest person I know."

The line made her heart ache with equal parts gratitude and guilt. She knew he meant it, but she couldn't help feeling selfish for asking him to visit her in Cleveland so often. Did he see it that way? He never said so in his letters, but Alta couldn't shake the thought that she was pulling him in too many directions, adding one more burden when he already carried so much.

Taking a deep breath, she folded the letter carefully and tucked it back into her pocket. The machines clattered on, but this time, the noise felt a little easier to bear. Alta resolved to write him tonight—not about her headaches or the tension at work, but about how proud she was of him. He believed in her. Maybe she could start believing in herself too.

Paul was always on her mind, but now, as she sat there, her thoughts stretched beyond him. She wondered how the war was affecting people in other parts of the country—young men leaving home, families waiting anxiously for letters, factories running at full tilt to supply the troops. Even beyond America's borders, the war had changed the world. Cities she had only read about in papers—London, Paris, Manila—were caught in the tide of history, their people enduring hardships she could scarcely imagine.

***

Kelly Field, San Antonio, Texas - July 1942

The Texas sun beat down like a hammer, relentless and unyielding. Even in the shade of the hangar, Joe could feel the heat radiating from the tarmac, the soles of his boots sticking faintly to the ground with every step. A bead of sweat slid down his temple, soaking into the collar of his khaki shirt. He swiped at it absently, his gaze fixed on the multi-engine trainer parked nearby, its metallic surface glinting under the midday glare.

Kelly Field was alive with activity. Planes roared overhead, their engines a constant drone against the shouting of instructors and the clamor of mechanics. The base was bursting at the seams with trainees, so much so that tents had been pitched to serve as makeshift hangars and barracks. It felt overcrowded, chaotic. Nothing like home. The dusty air carried the tang of aviation fuel, sharp and acrid in the heat.

In Colorado's Yampa Valley, June was a time for green pastures, wildflowers, and cool breezes that carried the scent of pine and sagebrush. Most days, he'd be out on Sage, riding the fence line or working three-year-olds in the round pen. He could almost feel the reins in his hands, the rhythmic sway of Sage's gait, and the quiet satisfaction of a day's work done well. If he closed his eyes, he could feel the saddle beneath him. The thought brought a faint smile to his lips, though it faded as quickly as it came.

Joe leaned against the side of the hangar, the hot metal biting into his back, and let his mind drift further. Luke would have loved watching the planes roar across the sky, seeing his kid brother getting ready to fly bombers. Luke had always been the steady one, the one who kept Joe in line when he got into trouble. And Joe had gotten into his fair share of it.

He laughed softly to himself, shaking his head. Actually, Luke had probably saved him from worse trouble than he'd ever admit. But when Luke passed away, it felt like the whole world had caved in. Joe had been barely fifteen, and suddenly, the ranch felt too big and the work too heavy. Still, there was no time to dwell on it. On a ranch, you cowboyed up and kept going, no matter what. Even if your heart was broken.

Maybe that's why he clung so fiercely to Sage. She'd brought him through that time—the worst time of his life. People talked about being grateful, but to Joe, gratitude always had a direction. He was grateful to God—for Sage, for the ranch, for salvation, and now for this chance to serve in an important way.

His attention returned to the AT-10 sitting in the blistering sun, its twin engines ticking faintly as they cooled. He had just wrapped up another training flight in basic navigation and formation flying. It wasn't the first time he'd flown with another pilot in the right seat, and it wouldn't be the last. Still, each flight brought new lessons, new challenges.

The AT-10 Wichita was a twin-engine trainer, designed to bridge the gap between single-engine trainers like the BT-13 and the multi-engine bombers he'd soon be flying. Its lightweight plywood airframe—used to conserve metal for combat aircraft—gave it a distinctive feel, responsive but less forgiving. The cockpit, a snug side-by-side setup, required teamwork and precision, especially in tight formations or emergency drills.

He stepped away from the hangar wall, stretching his shoulders as he replayed the morning's sortie in his mind. The takeoff had been smooth, but the crosswinds during the landing approach had kept him on his toes. That was the thing about flying: There was no time to let your guard down. Every move mattered and every adjustment was a test of his instincts and training.

"Mitchell!" The sharp bark of an instructor's voice jolted Joe from his thoughts. He turned to see Captain Rawlings striding toward him, clipboard in hand, his sun-weathered face set in its usual scowl.

"Yes, sir!" Joe straightened, wiping his hands on his trousers.

"You've got another flight this afternoon," Rawlings said without breaking stride. "Simulated engine failure. You'll be flying with Lieutenant Edwards. He needs refining."

"Yes, sir," Joe replied, masking the flicker of irritation that sparked at the mention of Edwards. The younger officer had a reputation for being overeager, the kind of guy who thought confidence could make up for a lack of skill. He wasn't a bad guy, but he needed to pay a bit more attention to important details.

As Rawlings walked away, Joe exhaled and turned back to the AT-10. A simulated engine failure wasn't his favorite exercise. It was one of the more nerve-wracking drills they did. But it was necessary. Out there, in a real bomber with a real crew, you couldn't afford to panic when things went wrong.

Joe ran a hand over the smooth metal of the plane's fuselage, feeling its heat under his palm. He thought of Sage again. Flying wasn't so different from riding her. It wasn't about brute force; it was about balance, trust, and knowing when to guide gently or rein in hard.

Joe squared his shoulders and headed for the briefing room. A cowboy always saddled up—even when the ride was rough. Luke had taught him that. Sage had proven it. And now, it was time to live it.

***

Edwards was a pain in the horse's you-know-what. The training flight had been beyond frustrating. Edwards wasn't ready for this—not by a long shot—but he thought he was. That was the problem. As soon as they wrapped up the post-flight checklist, Joe scrambled out of the plane and strode briskly across the tarmac toward the hangar. He needed to put some distance between himself and Edwards before he said something he'd regret.

Unfortunately, Edwards was close on his heels.

"Hey, Mitchell!" Edwards called after him, his voice carrying over the hum of activity on the field. "What are you going to tell Rawlings about me?"

Joe kept walking, jaw tightening as he ignored the question.

"Hey! I asked you a question," Edwards insisted, quickening his pace. "What are you going to tell the captain about me?"

Joe glanced over his shoulder without breaking his stride. "I'm going to tell him you need a bath."

Edwards stopped for half a beat, then sped up again, his voice tinged with indignation. "No, seriously. What are you going to tell him about my flying?"

Joe came to an abrupt halt, spinning on his heel to face Edwards. The younger pilot nearly stumbled to avoid colliding with him.

"Oh, seriously?" Joe repeated, his voice dripping with sarcasm. "You really want to know what I'm going to tell him—seriously?"

"Yes," Edwards shot back, crossing his arms. "That's what I asked."

Joe took a deliberate step closer, lowering his voice to a barely contained low growl. "Fine. I'll tell him you should go back to single-engine planes. That you have no business being in advanced flight training. That maybe—just maybe—you don't have any business being in the cockpit at all. And, for good measure, that you still need a bath. Does that cover it?"

Edwards' face reddened, but he didn't respond right away. Joe could feel the tension rising, but he didn't care. His patience, never his strong suit, had run out the moment Edwards ignored his instructions during the simulated engine failure.

Joe turned sharply and resumed his march toward the hangar, leaving Edwards sputtering behind him. He knew he shouldn't have lost his temper. Patience—"forbearance," as his Bible called it—was something he prayed for regularly, but it wasn't his natural inclination. And today, it was nowhere to be found.

"Why would you say that?" Edwards called after him, his voice louder now, in obvious disbelief. "I'm a great pilot!"

Joe stopped again, this time only long enough to shoot a look over his shoulder. He clenched his fists and his jaw tightened further as he fought the urge to snap. "That's the problem, Edwards. You're overconfident. You don't listen. You don't take criticism. And today, you almost got us killed. That's why."

Without waiting for a response, Joe turned and stalked off toward the hangar. He needed some space, and maybe a moment to pray for the patience he so obviously lacked. Edwards would have to figure the rest out on his own.

As he entered the hangar, the air inside felt even heavier than outside, pressing against him like a hot, sticky blanket. Sweat rolled down his sides and he realized, in all fairness to Edwards, that he probably needed a bath too.

He dropped into a seat near the front, grateful for the brief solitude before the briefing began. The quiet gave him a moment to collect his thoughts and say a silent prayer. He prayed that he could handle situations like this better, with less anger, more patience. But incompetence rubbed him the wrong way. Mistakes were one thing; everyone made them. But refusing to learn, to improve—that was different. That wasn't just a mistake. That was a liability.

Other pilots began filtering into the hangar, their boots echoing faintly against the concrete floor. Joe watched as Edwards trudged in, his shoulders stiff, his gaze flitting briefly to Joe before he veered toward a seat on the far side of the room. Joe let out a slow breath. Distance was probably best for now.

He straightened in his chair, his focus shifting as the captain strode into the hangar. Joe tucked his frustration away. There was no time for grudges when there was so much to be learned, and so little time left in which to learn it.

***

Chicago Municipal Airport - July 1942

Chicago wasn't Paul's kind of place. It was too fast paced, too crowded. He preferred quieter, more familiar surroundings. Yet, here he was, immersed in the city's ceaseless energy, training as a flight radio operator at Chicago Municipal Airport.

The Chicago airport buzzed with constant activity. One of the busiest airfields in the world, it had become a critical hub for both civilian and military aviation, its runways alive with the roar of engines and the hum of wartime urgency. United Air Lines had set up a dedicated training program here to support the war effort, and Paul had jumped at the chance to be part of it. When the announcement went out, he didn't hesitate; he expressed his interest immediately.

Now, he was one of thirty United Air Lines employees selected for this specialized training. It was intense and fast-paced, much like the city itself, but Paul didn't mind. This opportunity felt tailor-made for him. Airplanes and radios—two things he had loved for as long as he could remember—came together in a way that allowed him to serve his country.

Paul had taken many radio courses and had extensive experience in radio work, including the time running his own small radio repair shop in Omaha. But this was different. The stakes were higher, the scope broader. These weren't just radios for entertainment or local communications, they were the lifelines that could mean the difference between survival and disaster for pilots braving the vast, perilous stretches of the Pacific.

The training days were grueling but satisfying. Mornings often began in a classroom, where an instructor drilled them on Morse code, their hands hovering over the telegraph keys as the rapid-fire dots and dashed filled the room. As Paul tapped out a sequence, he imagined Alta in Ohio, her fingers hesitating over the same dots and dashes. The thought made him smile. He couldn't wait to tease her in their letters about who would decode faster. He already knew her answer would be playful and competitive.

Afternoons were spent on the tarmac or in a grounded aircraft, where they learned to dismantle and reassemble radio sets, troubleshooting common issues under the supervision of seasoned engineers.

Today's training focused on emergency procedures for what to do if a signal was lost over the Pacific. With a headset clamped over his ears, Paul adjusted dials on a simulated SCR-287 radio, straining to catch faint signals through the static.

The instructor's voice cracked in his ear: "Signal's weak—tune it in." Paul's fingers moved quickly, spinning the frequency knob until the static cleared, a faint transmission breaking through. He jotted down the message. By the end of the session his neck ached and his temples throbbed, but he felt a growing confidence in his skills.

Outside, the buzz of activity at the airport was constant, with planes landing, engines roaring, and ground crews bustling. Paul paused to watch as a DC-3 took off, its silver body gleaming in the sun.

At lunchtime, he walked to the cafeteria with one of his classmates.

"Catch *Mrs. Miniver* yet?" his classmate asked as they passed a movie poster.

Paul nodded. The story of ordinary families facing extraordinary challenges was still fresh in his mind.

"Yeah," he said, his voice quieter. "Reminded me of Alta—people like her are fighting this war in their own way."

The themes of duty and resilience felt personal, even comforting, in a way that he hadn't expected. He was sure that Alta would have loved it. Maybe they would have a chance to watch it together someday.

At lunch, he glanced at a newspaper left on a nearby bench. The bold headline declared, "Victory at Midway!" Reports of the June 4–7 battle were everywhere, detailing how American forces had delivered a decisive blow to the Japanese Navy. The mood around the training program had shifted after that news, becoming hopeful, even determined.

For all the challenges, Paul felt a deep sense of purpose here. This was where he was meant to be, and he would give it everything he had. Still, his thoughts drifted to Alta. He could picture her sitting down to write another letter—the familiar curve of her handwriting filling the pages. He missed her terribly and thought about her a lot. He was hoping that she thought of him just as much.

He had sent Alta a simple, thin bracelet—nothing fancy, just something small to remind her of him. He hoped she wore it often, that each glance at it brought her a bit of comfort, just as sending it had steadied him. It wasn't just a gift, it was a promise, a small token of their connection, something to remind her that wherever he was, his heart was with her. He thought of their future together, the life they would build after this war, and the hope of it filled him with quiet determination.

After lunch, as he sat at a radio console, his thoughts turned back to the training. Each day brought its challenges, but it also brought him closer to Alta—closer to the life they were building, one day, one letter, one small step at a time.

CHAPTER FIVE

Hamilton Field California - September 19, 1942

The steady drone of the engines filled the cabin as the C-87 leveled off at 10,000 feet. Outside, the endless blue of the Pacific stretched toward the horizon, a vast, empty expanse that felt both thrilling and daunting. Paul leaned back in his seat, taking a moment to savor the stillness. They were finally in the air, heading toward Hickam Field in Hawaii. It felt good. In fact, it felt really good.

It had been a long, hard road getting here, full of months of training, setbacks, and uncertainties. But here they were, the crew of ATC-903, on their first real Pacific Theater mission. At this altitude, the air was cool but comfortable, with just enough of a chill to keep them alert. The crew settled into their routines, their movements fluid and practiced, as Paul tuned to the radio frequencies outlined in the mission profile.

As he adjusted the dials, his thoughts wandered. So much had fallen into place to get him here. He still couldn't believe how perfectly everything had worked out. The mission had been delayed a week due to logistical issues, shifting the departure date to September 19. That delay was a blessing—one he couldn't attribute to anything but God's perfect timing. It meant the wedding could go ahead as planned on September 12.

Well, almost as planned. Getting married in California had turned out to be harder than he'd expected. Timing was tight, and the local options didn't seem to fit. Paul had hoped for a ceremony in a Swedish Lutheran church, but none were nearby. Alta had arrived in California expecting to be married that day so they could move into their new place. If the wedding didn't happen, she'd have to find somewhere else to stay—a situation neither of them wanted.

Paul shook his head with a faint smile, remembering the scramble to figure it out. As it turned out, military men had a knack for knowing where to go and how to get things done. When someone suggested Reno, everything clicked.

"Reno?" Alta had asked, raising an eyebrow. "Isn't that the place where people go to gamble?"

Paul had laughed, taking her hands in his. "Maybe. But it's also the place where we can get married quickly. And they've got a Swedish Lutheran church. So this is no gamble—it's perfect."

The trip to Reno had been a whirlwind, but standing in front of the reverend, looking into Alta's eyes, had made it all worth it. The world beyond those church doors faded away, and for those brief, shining moments, it was just the two of them, promising forever.

Paul smiled to himself as the memory faded, replaced by the reality of the mission at hand. He glanced at the other crew members, each focused on their tasks. It wasn't just the mission that mattered to him now; it was the life waiting for him after this war. Alta was his future, and every mile they flew brought him closer to it.

The cargo hold was packed with vital supplies for the war effort: crates of engine parts, boxes of medical supplies and equipment, and even a few bundles of parachutes destined for a unit in Brisbane. Everything had been meticulously loaded and secured before takeoff, but the weight of it was always on everyone's mind—literally and figuratively. The cargo was their lifeline to the front, and it had to arrive intact.

Paul had just finished logging the latest radio check when Chuck's voice crackled over the intercom, tight and clipped. "Paul, can you check the cargo? Make sure nothing shifted during takeoff."

"On it," Paul replied, setting aside his headset and unbuckling his harness. From his radio station, he could see part of the cargo hold through the narrow space behind the cockpit, where rows of crates were strapped down and secured. Still, Chuck was right to be cautious; the rough takeoff might have jostled something in the deeper section of the hold.

He moved toward the narrow ladder leading down into the main cargo area. The air grew cooler as he descended, the muffled hum of the engines replaced by the creak of the airframe and the faint vibration under his boots. Once at the bottom, he ran a practiced eye over the crates and supplies, noting that everything seemed secure. Still, he tugged at a few straps and double-checked the heavier loads, just to be sure.

Satisfied, Paul climbed back up to the radio station, strapped in, and keyed the intercom. "Cargo's secure, Chuck. No surprises back there."

"Good," Chuck said after a moment. His voice softened slightly, though there was still a thread of tension. "Thanks."

Paul settled back into his seat and slipped on his headset. His eyes flicked toward the cockpit. He couldn't see Chuck from here, but he could imagine him gripping the yoke a little too tightly, his mind racing through every possible worst-case scenario. It wasn't just Chuck—everyone was feeling the weight of this first mission. The stakes were real now, and there was no room for error.

Still, Paul felt a sense of calm. The routines they'd drilled into themselves during training were paying off, each task flowing into the next. They had prepared for this moment, and now it was time to trust that preparation—and each other.

The first leg of their mission, from Hamilton Field to Hickam Field, spanned approximately 2,400 miles. Cruising at a speed of 200 miles per hour, the journey would take an exhausting eleven to twelve hours. It was a grueling flight, but the crew found solace in knowing they'd have a three-day layover in Hawaii before continuing their journey. From Hickam Field, they would proceed to Canton Island, then on to Fiji, New Caledonia, and finally Brisbane. The entire mission would take Paul away for two weeks—a significant stretch, but one he had prepared for with quiet determination.

He glanced out the window at the vast, unbroken expanse of ocean below. Each mile brought them closer to their destination—and closer to the life he was building with Alta.

***

Hickam Field, Hawaii

The barracks weren't much to look at—plain wooden walls, the faint scent of mildew, and mattresses that looked like they'd seen better decades. Joe tossed his duffel on one of the bunks, testing the springs with a cautious push. Yep, this wasn't the Grand Hotel, but it'd do for a couple of days. Besides, he didn't plan to spend much time here anyway. Hawaii was calling, and Joe Mitchell wasn't about to let this rare opportunity slip by.

"You're really gonna drag me around, aren't you?" Paul asked with a grin, flopping onto the bunk opposite Joe's.

"Drag you?" Joe shot back, raising an eyebrow. "Paul, you're gonna be thanking me when you're sipping coconut water on the beach and swimming in the ocean."

Jimmy chimed in from the doorway, arms full of gear. "Don't forget the hula girls, Joe."

Paul rolled his eyes. "You two are hopeless."

Joe laughed, turning to Stan, who was meticulously unpacking his bag. "How about you, Stan? You in?"

Stan glanced up, hesitating. "Maybe. Depends how things shake out."

Joe nodded, not pressing further. Stan wasn't the type to be rushed. Chuck, on the other hand—well, getting him out of the barracks would be the real challenge.

It was too late to go anywhere now anyway, and they were all tired. But tomorrow ... tomorrow would be top-notch! For now, it was just time to get settled in.

As Joe sat down on the thin mattress, his mind wandered to last week when he finally had the chance to meet Alta. The newlyweds had just settled into their little place in San Mateo and invited Joe over for dinner.

Paul had greeted him at the door, practically beaming. "Joe, meet Alta. Alta, this is Joe Mitchell."

"Mitchell, like the airplane. It's nice to finally meet you, Joe," she'd said, warmly shaking his hand.

Joe grinned, turning to Paul. "Paul, you've outdone yourself; she's way out of your league. Marry this girl again, just to be sure." Turning back to Alta, he added, "It's a pleasure, Mrs. Carlson."

Alta laughed, her wit as sharp as her handshake. "Still getting used to 'Mrs. Carlson,' but I think I like it."

She was exactly what Joe had expected from Paul's stories: confident, quick-witted, and full of warmth. Over dinner, the three of them fell into easy conversation, trading stories and laughter. For the first time in a while, Joe felt completely at home.

The tapping started halfway through dessert. Soft, rhythmic. Joe paused mid-bite, his brow furrowing.

"Do you two hear that? It's like a faint thumping."

Paul and Alta exchanged a glance. "I don't hear anything, do you, Alta?" Paul said, barely suppressing a grin.

"There it is again!" Joe leaned down slightly, glancing under the table. Paul's hand was tapping lightly against the underside.

"What are you two up to?" Joe demanded, pointing a mock-accusatory finger. "That's Morse code, isn't it? You're talking about me!"

Alta giggled, "We're just tapping 'I love you.'"

"Yeah, Joe," Paul continued, "we wouldn't dream of gossiping—well, not unless it's about your hygiene."

Joe threw up his hands. "Romantic Morse code? That's so sweet, I think I'm gonna be sick."

"You just wait, Cowboy," Alta replied. "We're gonna find you a girl that'll make you want to tap out sweet nothings in code."

"Yeah, that'll be the day." Joe chuckled, shaking his head. "I don't think you'll ever catch me doing that—maybe just a few grunts here and there, though," he added.

With that, he puffed out his chest and gave a few exaggerated, caveman-like grunts, slapping the table for emphasis. The table erupted with laughter.

That night, they stayed up late, talking about everything from faith to flying. Joe left with a full belly and a full heart, knowing that his best friend had found someone truly special.

Now, as Joe unpacked in the dim barracks, he smiled at the memory. Tomorrow promised adventure, but tonight, he'd drift off remembering the warmth of that little San Mateo home and the laughter around the dinner table.

Joe hadn't had any serious relationships of his own. There'd been a few girls he dated briefly in high school, but nothing lasting. Ranch life had kept him busy, and by the time college rolled around, his focus shifted to studies and preparing for the future. Besides, his upbringing had instilled in him a belief that relationships shouldn't get serious unless marriage was a real possibility. If it wasn't headed in that direction, it wasn't worth the heartache.

That was fine with him. He trusted God to guide his steps, knowing that if marriage was part of the plan, the right person would come along at the right time. Until then, there was plenty to keep him busy. And now, he had an example to look to. Paul and Alta's marriage wasn't just a love story, it was a compass. Their faith, their partnership, and the way they supported each other was everything Joe hoped to find someday.

He ran a hand through his hair and stretched out on the bunk, staring at the ceiling. Maybe tomorrow would be the day he'd finally convince Chuck to relax. Or maybe he'd just find a beach, soak up some sun, and let the Hawaiian breeze carry his thoughts back to the possibilities waiting for him down the road.

***

The morning hadn't started smoothly. As the commanding officer, Chuck had the final say on where they would go for R&R—or whether they'd even leave the base at all. And Chuck hadn't made it easy. His reluctance to let the crew venture out wasn't exactly a surprise. He had a knack for focusing on duty above all else, even when the opportunity for a break presented itself.

It was Paul who finally swayed him. Calm and methodical, Paul had pointed out the benefits of a short trip: A visit to Pearl Harbor to pay their respects, followed by an afternoon at Waikiki Beach for a bit of much-needed downtime. Even Chuck couldn't argue with the reasoning. The military itself encouraged rest and relaxation, recognizing it as vital for morale.

"Fine," Chuck had said, crossing his arms. "But we stick to the schedule. No wandering off."

Joe grinned at Paul once Chuck's back was turned. "You're a miracle worker, Carlson. I thought we'd be stuck in the barracks all day."

The visit to Pearl Harbor was somber, as expected. Almost a year had passed since the surprise attack, but the devastation still hung heavily in the air. Standing near the harbor, the crew gazed silently at the waters where the USS *Arizona* lay submerged, a stark reminder of lives lost in the blink of an eye. They reflected in their own ways: Stan crossed his arms tightly, his expression unreadable. Jimmy removed his hat, holding it against his chest. Paul stood quietly, the weight of it sinking in. Even Joe, usually quick with a joke, remained uncharacteristically subdued.

Paul couldn't help but think how quick and fleeting this life was. You had to make every moment count. Make every minute mean something. Above all, every word and action should glorify God.

Chuck lingered at the back of the group, his posture rigid. If he felt the same determination and resolve as the others, he kept it to himself. But something in his gaze—a hard, distant look—suggested he wasn't immune to the moment's gravity.

As they drove away from Pearl Harbor, the mood inside the vehicle was heavy. The juxtaposition between the somber visit and the stunning beauty of Hawaii was impossible to ignore. Towering palm trees swayed against a backdrop of turquoise waters, a stark contrast to the images of smoke and fire that still haunted the harbor.

By the time they neared Waikiki Beach, the tension began to ease, thanks largely to Joe. He'd decided to start teasing Chuck, a risky move, but one that seemed to lighten the atmosphere.

"I really can't wait to see you trying to balance on a surfboard," Joe said with a mischievous grin, elbowing Paul for emphasis. "What I don't want to see, though, is the sun reflecting off your bare chest. I may need to avert my eyes, or at the very least need some dark sunglasses."

Chuck shot him a sidelong glance. "Yeah? Well, at least I won't be showing off a farmer's tan."

Paul wasn't sure if Chuck was actually playing along or slightly offended, but either way, the jab earned a chuckle from the others.

Jimmy, sitting in the back, leaned forward. "Let's face it, fellas—none of us are winning any beauty contests. But we're about to find out if Joe's as good in the water as he claims."

Joe leaned back with mock indignation. "I'm a natural-born athlete, Jimmy. Just you wait."

"Shoveling horse manure doesn't count as a sport, Cowboy," Jimmy replied.

As the Dodge WC Command Car crested the final hill, Waikiki Beach stretched out before them like a postcard come to life. The sparkling turquoise water seemed endless, framed by swaying palm trees and soft, white sand. The rhythmic crash of the waves reached their ears, mingling with the distant chatter of beachgoers.

For the first time in weeks, the weight of the war seemed to lift, if only slightly.

Laughter filled the vehicle, lighter and more frequent now. The crew, cramped but in good spirits, leaned forward to get a better look at the stunning view. Even Chuck, ever the stoic, allowed himself a rare smile as he guided the car down the winding road toward the beach parking area.

Paul shifted in his seat, feeling the rough canvas beneath him and the lingering warmth of the midday sun radiating from the metal of the vehicle. Though the Dodge was sturdy and had plenty of room for all five of them, the stiff suspension and jostling over the uneven roads had left them all eager to stretch their legs.

As they pulled into the lot, Chuck parked the vehicle under the shade of a towering coconut tree, the engine rumbling to a stop. Paul swung his legs over the side and hopped down, brushing off the dust that had settled on his trousers during the ride. The smell of salt and seaweed filled the air, a refreshing change from the motor pool's fumes and the dry heat of the barracks.

Paul took a deep breath, letting the fresh sea air fill his lungs. The tension from the morning seemed to evaporate, replaced by a sudden burst of energy. He turned to Joe, who was already grinning ear to ear, a mischievous glint in his eye.

"Well," Paul said, gesturing dramatically toward the inviting waves, "are you ready to embarrass yourself on a surfboard?"

Joe clapped him on the back. "Oh, you'll see, Carlson. By the end of the day, I'll be surfing circles around you."

Chuck rolled his eyes as he grabbed his gear from the back of the Dodge. "Let's just hope no one ends up in the hospital," he muttered, though there was a trace of amusement in his voice.

The crew began unloading their things, the camaraderie easing into something lighter, more natural. For now, they were just a group of guys at the beach, having some fun and sharing some laughs.

***

Waikiki Beach

The evening air, which carried the mingling scents of salt water, roasted pork, and tropical flowers, wrapped around Jimmy as he stepped onto the warm sand. Tiki torches flickered in the breeze, their flames casting playful shadows across the crowd. The rhythmic sound of ukuleles filled the air, accompanied by the soft hum of voices and an occasional burst of laughter.

Jimmy had seen plenty of gatherings back home in Iowa, but nothing like this. The energy was different—unhurried, welcoming, almost reverent. The locals moved with a natural grace, their smiles genuine as they placed leis around the necks of the crew. He couldn't help but grin as the soft petals of the lei brushed against his sun-warmed skin, releasing a faint, heady perfume.

A year ago, the idea of standing barefoot on a Hawaiian beach, sharing laughs with a crew bound for the far reaches of the Pacific, would have seemed like something out of a storybook. Then the United States had entered the war and everything changed. He had always loved maps and land navigation. This coupled with a suppressed desire for adventure prompted him to sign up for a navigator position with Air Transport Command. Now, here he was, on R&R in Hawaii.

"Didn't know I'd be getting dressed up for this," he joked, adjusting the lei as Joe clapped him on the shoulder.

"This ain't dressed up, Jimmy," Joe replied with a chuckle, his eyes twinkling in the torchlight. "Now, if you were wearing one of those grass skirts ..."

"Please don't even finish that sentence," Jimmy shot back, though the corner of his mouth twitched in amusement. Jimmy shook his head, grinning. Joe always knew how to lighten the mood, no matter where they were.

The crew moved toward the long tables set up near the edge of the beach. Piles of food were arranged in a colorful spread: Roasted pig with crispy skin, platters of tropical fruit, steaming bowls of rice, and something wrapped in leaves that Paul was eying cautiously.

"Try it, Paul," Jimmy teased, grabbing a plate. "It won't bite you."

"I've never been that adventurous when it comes to food," Paul replied, "but I'll take your word for it. But remember, I know where to find you." Paul smiled his trademark smile as he followed suit and filled his plate.

As they settled in, Jimmy glanced around the circle of faces—his crew, the locals, other soldiers, and civilians—all gathered together for this brief escape from the war. It struck him then how different they all were yet how easily they shared this moment. It was too bad that this one little slice of fellowship couldn't be shared with everyone. Maybe then there wouldn't be a war.

As the music swelled and a group of dancers stepped forward, their movement fluid and hypnotic against the backdrop of the setting sun, Jimmy's thoughts wandered back to the afternoon. Then, the laughter and camaraderie had been just as plentiful.

The surfing had been a mix of triumphs and wipeouts, with Joe taking center stage, as usual. "I'm a natural!" Joe had proclaimed after managing to stay up for all of five seconds. Then there was his second attempt, which was much more spectacular.

He was actually doing pretty well. Then, seemingly out of nowhere came an unexpected wave, towering behind him. For a short moment, it looked like he might conquer it. But then, in an instant, it crashed over him with a force that sent his board flying. For a few heart-stopping seconds, there was no sign of Joe.

Paul had already taken a step toward the water, his heart pounding. Just as he was about to jump into the water, Joe emerged, sputtering and grinning, no worse for the wear, other than a mouthful of seawater.

Chuck, surprisingly, had joined in for a while, though his serious demeanor hadn't fully left him. Still, Jimmy had caught a rare smile as Chuck paddled back to shore, dripping and triumphant after a particularly good ride.

Paul was obviously having a blast, a smile never leaving his face as he himself had a few good, albeit short rides on the surf.

Jimmy chuckled at the memory, knowing that this would be a day he would remember as long as he lived. His attention snapped back to the present as a platter of roasted pork was passed his way. He filled his plate again and took another bite, leaning back to savor the smoky flavors.

Jimmy leaned over toward Joe, "I was just thinking about this afternoon. You call that surfing? You spent more time underwater than on the board."

"You just don't know real talent when you see it, Jimmy," Joe shot back, his grin widening. "Only surfers who really know what they're doing can pull off a demonstration like that."

Jimmy rolled his eyes, giving Joe a good-natured punch on the shoulder. "What were you demonstrating? How to drown?"

Laughter rippled between them as the ukulele music swelled again. Jimmy leaned back, letting the sounds of the night wash over him—the crackle of the fire, the soft murmurs of waves, the hum of conversation. As Jimmy watched the firelight flickering against the star-speckled sky, it struck him that moments like this—laughter shared with friends over a meal—were the true victories in a world at war. Here, on this beach, in the shadow of war, laughter and friendship felt like a defiance of the darkness threatening to swallow the world.

***

San Mateo, California

Alta lay awake, staring at the ceiling as the soft glow of moonlight cast shifting patterns across the room. The house was silent, save the occasional creak of settling wood and the distant, lonely wail of a train whistle. Back in Ohio, she had always found the sound comforting—a familiar presence in the night. But here, in this unfamiliar town, it only emphasized how alone she felt.

A new house. A strange city. No friends yet.

She exhaled softly, turning onto her side. That had to change. Tomorrow, she would get out of the house, go shopping, find a church. That would help.

This wasn't the first time she had been away from home, but it was by far the hardest. After high school, she had worked as a nanny, saving every penny she could for school. Then came Kansas City, where she had moved with her sister Mildred to attend the Midland Radio and Television School. It had been an exciting time in her life—her first taste of true independence. The city was bustling and alive, and though it had been unfamiliar, at least she had Mildred. Together, they had explored, laughed, and adjusted to a new world.

Then Cleveland. Her first real job. The rhythm of the airport, the sounds of distant engines, the clatter of the teletype machines—it had been overwhelming at first. But she had grown into it, learned to love the energy of the place. And even then, her hometown of Bainbridge had only been thirty miles away. Home was still close enough to touch.

Here, though, home felt impossibly far. And Paul was even further.

She sighed, drawing the blanket up around her shoulders. She had known what this life would be, what it meant to marry a man who flew. She had told herself she was ready. But knowing it and experiencing it were two different things.

She tried not to dwell on that. She would take things one day at a time. Get involved in a church. Make friends. She could do this.

Her mind drifted to Paul, wondering where he was at that very moment. Thousands of miles away, flying through the night. Was he awake? Was he thinking of her too? The ache of his absence pressed against her chest, heavy and sharp. But then, as if carried by a whisper, a familiar verse came to mind: "He that dwelleth in the secret place of the Most High shall abide under the shadow of the Almighty. I will say of the Lord, He is my refuge and my fortress: My God; in him will I trust."

Paul had pointed out that verse to her during one of their late-night talks about faith, his voice steady and certain as he shared the words. Now, they wrapped around her like a protective shield, a lifeline between them, stretching across the distance.

She let herself sink deeper into the bed, her heartbeat steadying, the loneliness easing just enough. The moonlight seemed softer now, gentler. And with God's promise holding her fast, she closed her eyes and finally drifted into a peaceful sleep.

CHAPTER SIX

Canton Island Approach - September 21, 1942

The engines droned steadily as the sun began to dip below the horizon, casting a warm, golden glow over the endless Pacific. Canton Island was close but invisible, swallowed by the vast expanse of the ocean. The crew had been in the air for hours, and fatigue was starting to creep in.

The evening luau at Waikiki Beach had been the highlight of the trip. The next day had been all business as the crew reviewed the mission profile and the plan for the next leg of the journey. They hadn't left the base all day, and it was a bit of a relief to get back in the air and continue the journey across the Pacific.

Paul adjusted the dials on his radio, listening for the faint signal of the Canton Island radio beacon that would guide them in. Static crackled in his headset as he fine-tuned the frequency. The signal seemed distant, weaker than Paul had anticipated. He frowned, his finger working instinctively over the controls.

"Paul, verify our position with the beacon," Chuck's voice came over the intercom, clipped and tense.

Paul exhaled. "Roger that, but I'm having trouble locking onto the signal. I'm unable to get a fix from Canton. Triangulating instead."

"We can't afford any mistakes here. Get that position verified as soon as possible," Chuck snapped, tension threading through his voice.

Jimmy chimed in from his navigation station, pencil scratching over the map. "We're looking good based on the charts, Chuck. Heading's steady. But yeah, a beacon fix would be comforting."

"And I'm just up here filling in as the mission ornament. How am I doing?" Joe cracked over the intercom, his voice light, but clearly aimed at breaking the tension.

Jimmy didn't miss a beat. "You're doing just fine, Joe. You look great."

"Glad to know my charm isn't wasted," Joe quipped, then shifted to a more business-like tone. "In all seriousness—Chuck, did that altimeter get calibrated back at Hickam? Are we really that low?"

Chuck's voice came back clipped. "It was tight, but I verified the calibration myself. That reading should be correct, although it would be nice if we could get a reading from the Canton tower."

Paul leaned closer to his equipment, adjusting the gain and tweaking the frequency knob. "I'm tuning in on two additional signals now. Should have a triangulated position in a minute."

Paul didn't need to glance at his watch to know time was running short. They'd need to make visual contact with the island soon, and the last thing they wanted was a missed approach over open ocean at night.

Static hissed in his ear as he switched channels, his fingers deftly aligning the direction finder. He jotted down two bearings on his notepad, then cross-checked them with Jimmy's chart. "Alright, triangulated position confirms we're tracking right."

"Still no signal from Canton?" Chuck asked, his tone sharpening.

Paul shook his head, though Chuck couldn't see it. "Nope. It's weak—interference, maybe atmospheric conditions. Let me give it another shot." He switched back to the Canton frequency, twisting the dial with precision.

Stan's calm voice broke through the tension. "Engines are steady, fuel's on track. Let's keep her smooth, Chuck. We'll get there."

The intercom crackled to life again, this time with Joe's voice. "Hey, Paul, if you don't find that beacon soon, we'll end up making new friends with the fish down there. No pressure."

Paul smirked despite himself. "Just keep working on your tan, Joe."

As the static cleared for a brief moment, Paul caught a faint, rhythmic tone—the beacon's identifier. His pulse quickened, and he fine-tuned the dial until the signal stabilized. "Got it! Weak, but usable. Signal confirms we're right where we should be."

"Good," Chuck replied, his tone softening just a fraction. "Let's bring her in."

The crew collectively exhaled as Paul locked the position into the log. Canton Island was still just a shadow on the horizon, but they were getting closer. The engines hummed steadily as the C-87 pushed forward through the dusk. Outside, the Pacific's endless expanse shifted from golden hues to deep, shadowy blues as night crept in. The tension in the cabin was easing, but the crew remained focused.

Paul leaned back slightly, his shoulders relaxing now that the beacon signal was locked in. He adjusted his headset and glanced over at Jimmy, who was still bent over his map, tracing their route with a pencil.

"Anything on the horizon yet?" Paul asked.

"Not yet," Jimmy replied, squinting through the navigator's window. "But we should be close. Keep your eyes peeled."

Chuck's voice broke through on the intercom. "Alright, gentlemen, we're coming up on visual range. Everyone stay sharp—this isn't a runway at Hickam. Canton's strip is short and surrounded by ... well, nothing."

Joe leaned forward in his seat, peering out the side window. "Short and surrounded by nothing. Sounds like my love life."

Stan chuckled softly from his station, his voice carrying just enough humor to keep the mood a little lighter. "Engines look good. Oil pressure is stable. All systems are good."

As they descended closer, the faint outline of Canton Island emerged from the shadows—a dark smudge against the shimmering ocean. The atoll's distinctive flattened-horseshoe shape became clearer, its lagoon gleaming faintly in the waning dusk. From this distance, the island looked almost tranquil, a small patch of serenity in the middle of the vast Pacific.

"There it is," Jimmy said, pointing to the island as it became clearer. "Canton Island, dead ahead."

"Good eyes, Jimmy," Chuck replied, his tone steady but still holding a slight edge of tension. "Paul, how's that signal?"

Paul double-checked the beacon, ensuring their position remained accurate. "Holding steady. We're on course."

As they approached, the airstrip came into view—a narrow strip of land barely distinguishable from the surrounding terrain. Small lights marked the runway, flickering like fireflies in the dark.

Chuck visibly tightened his grip on the yoke. "Alright, fellas, this is where we earn our paychecks. Let's make it smooth."

"You're getting paid? I thought we were just doing this for fun," Joe replied.

Paul sat a little more relaxed in his seat, his eyes glued to the faint lights of the runway.

"Flaps set," Stan reported, his voice calm but deliberate. "Throttle steady. Descent looks clean."

The C-87 shuddered slightly as the landing gear extended, the vibrations coursing through the cabin. Outside, the lagoon glittered like a bed of stars—but Paul kept his focus locked on the task at hand.

The final moments were tense but controlled as the aircraft aligned with the runway. The wheels touched down with a jolt, followed by the screech of rubber on asphalt. The engines roared as Chuck brought them to a slow, rolling stop near the edge of the strip.

"Welcome to Canton Island," Chuck announced, exhaling audibly over the intercom.

The crew exchanged relieved glances as the engines powered down. Outside, the faint glow of lanterns and the movement of a few figures signaled their arrival.

Paul unbuckled his harness and stretched. "Well, that was a ride."

"Yeah," Joe added with a grin. "And the best part? Chuck might get to take a shower."

Stan stood and stretched, his calm demeanor intact. "Let's get the cargo squared away and find out where we're bunking tonight."

Jimmy glanced out the window again, taking in the quiet beauty of the island. For now, they had made it. Tomorrow would bring another leg of their journey—and with it, new challenges. But tonight, they would get a well-earned rest.

***

Canton Island

After a long and exhausting flight, Stan was relieved to finally be on solid ground, even if it was on a remote atoll in the middle of the Pacific. The island was a narrow strip of land encircling a vast lagoon, its flat terrain barely rising above sea level. As he stepped off the plane, the first thing that struck him was the airfield: a single, packed coral runway stretching out before him, its surface gleaming faintly under the evening twilight. The layout was straightforward. The airstrip ran from the northwest tip of the island, with the deep blue expanse of the Pacific Ocean on one side and the tranquil turquoise lagoon on the other. The contrast between the churning ocean waves and the serene lagoon waters was striking.

Stretching from the northwest tip to the south was a cluster of Quonset huts and canvas tents that served as living quarters and operational centers. The Quonset huts, with their semi-circular corrugated steel structures, looked hastily assembled, yet sturdy enough to withstand the island's unpredictable weather. Nearby, supply depots were neatly organized, with stacks of wooden crates labeled with stenciled markings and rows of fuel drums lined up precisely. A makeshift control tower stood near the end of the airfield. Its raised wooden platform offered a panoramic view of the entire runway, and a tattered windsock fluttered atop a pole.

The air was thick with a blend of scents: the sharp tang of salt from the ocean, the pungent odor of aviation fuel, and the earthy aroma emanating from the crushed coral underfoot. The only sounds were the distant hum of generators, the occasional clatter of tools from maintenance crews, and the murmur of voices exchanging terse instructions. The isolation of the island was palpable. With the nearest inhabited land hundreds of miles away, it felt like a solitary outpost on the edge of the world.

As the crew made their way toward their assigned quarters, Stan's eyes continued to wander. On one side, the vastness of the Pacific stretched endlessly, the horizon melding seamlessly with the sky. On the other, the lagoon lay calm and reflective, its surface mirroring the scattered clouds above. Coconut palms dotted the shoreline, their fronds swaying gently in the breeze, casting dappled shadows on the ground from the moonlight.

"Not exactly the Ritz," Joe muttered, breaking the silence.

Stan gave a small nod, his gaze still fixed on the horizon. Exhaustion weighed heavily on him. At this point, it didn't matter whether they were staying at a luxury hotel or in a makeshift hut, all he craved was sleep.

"Yeah, well, I guess it'll do for what we need," he replied, his voice tinged with resignation.

As they settled into their quarters—a dimly lit Quonset hut with cots lined against the walls—Stan couldn't help but reflect on the island's strategic importance. Despite its desolate appearance, Canton Island played a crucial role during the war as a trans-Pacific refueling stop and strategic military outpost. This was a place of transit, a brief respite in their journey, a spot to refuel both planes and weary bodies before pressing on with their mission.

Before the war, Pan American World Airways had used the island as a stopover for its flying boat service, a lonely outpost along their Pacific route. But despite its admittedly brief history in aviation, it still felt underdeveloped—almost makeshift, as if the whole base could be packed up and abandoned at a moment's notice.

Stan exhaled, fatigue settling into his bones. "Time for some sleep," he muttered to Joe. "Tomorrow's another long one."

"You got that right." Joe stifled a yawn. "Have a good night, Stan."

"Same to you, Joe."

Stan lay back on his cot without bothering to undress. The cot's stiff canvas stretched under his weight, the scent of salt and oil lingering in the still air. His eyelids grew heavy, and before his head fully hit the pillow, he was out.

***

Paul didn't think he'd sleep well. The thin mattress and the humid air didn't make for ideal conditions, but the exhaustion won out. One minute he was laying his weary head down, and the next, sunlight was streaming into the barracks, signaling a new day.

The rest of the crew had already made their way to the makeshift mess hall, but Paul and Joe were running late.

"I told you to get up sooner," Paul grumbled as they hurried down the sandy path. "Now we're rushing around like the Keystone Kops trying to catch a runaway trolley."

"What can I say? Beauty sleep doesn't just happen," Joe quipped, brushing off Paul's admonishment.

Paul shot him a sideways glance. "Ain't that the truth. But it never seems to help you much."

"Hey!" Joe retorted. "I'll have you know that ..."

Joe's witty comeback was cut short as he barreled into what felt like a brick wall. Hot liquid splashed between them, and Joe stumbled back, spinning to face what—or rather, who—he had collided with.

In front of him stood a man of average height but commanding presence. His steely blue eyes locked onto Joe's with calm intensity, and his posture was as straight as an iron rod. His salt-and-pepper hair was cropped short, and his crisp khaki uniform, now bearing a sizable coffee stain, hung neatly despite the recent collision. There were no insignias on his collar, but the authority he radiated was unmistakable.

"Hey, buddy, watch where you're going!" Joe blurted out before fully registering the situation.

Paul's stomach dropped as he nudged Joe hard in the ribs. During wartime, it was never a good sign when you came across someone who was obviously an authority figure, but didn't have any rank insignia. "Joe, I think you'd better—"

"I think you'd better listen to your friend," the man continued, his voice steady, calm and unshakably firm. His words carried a weight that silenced Joe mid-protest.

Paul jumped in, hoping to salvage the moment. "Sir, please excuse my friend here. He hasn't had breakfast yet, and he gets a little grumpy."

The older man's piercing gaze shifted to Paul, softening slightly. "You don't have to call me 'sir,' son," he said evenly. "But your companion here does."

Joe, oblivious to the storm clouds gathering over him, waved dismissively. "Why should I call you 'sir'? I don't even see any rank on your collar."

A flicker of amusement crossed the man's face, though his tone remained steady. "Well, do you see the large coffee stain on my shirt now? Son, I have two shirts with me on this trip. This one and another with bloodstains. So I'd prefer to keep this one coffee-only." He gestured to the spreading stain with a calm, almost bemused air, but his steely eyes held Joe in place.

Paul's face paled as realization hit. "Joe! I believe we have Admiral Chester Nimitz standing in front of us."

Joe's mouth opened, then shut quickly as he took a half-step back, his eyes widening. "Admiral ...?"

"Yes, lieutenant," Nimitz said, his lips bending into a faint smile. "Admiral Chester Nimitz. And you just welcomed me with a nice coffee stain."

Nimitz stood there, unshaken, his calm demeanor as solid as the Pacific fleet he commanded. Even the coffee stain on his shirt seemed insignificant in the face of the quiet authority he exuded.

Joe's ears burned red as if he'd stepped too close to one of the hot airplane engines. He shuffled his feet, his usual bravado crumbling under the admiral's piercing gaze. Joe fumbled for words, his usual confidence gone. "I, uh, Admiral, sir ... I didn't mean to, uh ..."

Nimitz raised a hand, cutting him off. "No harm done—well, except to my shirt. But let me give you a bit of advice, son." His voice remained measured, but it carried an undeniable authority. "When you're moving through life—or down a path to breakfast—you should always keep an eye on where you're going. Be on the lookout for who might be in your path. You never know what's coming your way. But if you keep your eye out, you can usually avoid a bigger mess than some coffee on your shirt."

Paul exhaled the breath he didn't realize he was holding. "Sir, thank you for your understanding. The lieutenant here, and I, will make sure to be more careful."

Nimitz gave a small nod, his tone shifting to something almost fatherly. "Good. Now I'd suggest you two get to breakfast before it's all gone. And it looks like I need some more coffee."

Joe's face burned with embarrassment as he stammered, "Yes, sir! Right away, sir!" As he ran off toward the mess hall.

Paul lingered for a moment, catching Nimitz's eye. "Sir, I just wanted to say it's an honor to meet you. Thank you for everything that you're doing."

Nimitz's expression softened further. "Thank you, son. And thank you for what you're doing. Without men like you moving supplies and cargo, the front lines wouldn't have what they need. Your work may feel small at times, but it's vital. Never forget that."

Paul nodded, feeling both humbled and proud at the same time. "I appreciate that, sir."

"And I told you," Nimitz added with a slight smile, "you don't have to call me 'sir.'"

"With all due respect, sir, I think I do."

At that moment, Joe returned, a steaming cup of coffee in hand, looking like a chastised schoolboy. "Here you go, sir. I, uh, hope this makes up for earlier."

Nimitz took the cup with a gracious nod. "Thank you, lieutenant. And don't sweat it. Just remember—watch your step."

The admiral looked at each man in turn, then said, "Fellas, let me tell you something: Everyone stumbles. Early in my career, I ran a ship aground—a failure I'll never forget. But what matters isn't the mistake. It's whether you rise from it stronger, or let it sink you. Tell me—what is your mission?"

"Well, sir, we're moving cargo on a C-87 to Brisbane," Joe replied.

Nimitz's demeanor suddenly became more focused, more serious and firm. "No! That's not how you tell me. You tell me that you are moving supplies on a critical mission across the vast expanse of the Pacific Ocean. That your cargo cannot be lost or even delayed. You tell me that your efforts are critical to the war effort. That you are brave men, doing your duty. That's how you answer my question, because that's the truth, and it's no small thing! It's vital!" Nimitz's blue eyes burned like a hot flame, passion exuding from his very person.

Nimitz then turned with the precision of a ship's rudder, striding away with a measured confidence that left a tangible weight in the air. The breeze picked up, rustling the palm fronds as if the island itself acknowledged the man's authority.

Paul stood rooted in place, his mouth gaped open in awe, the admiral's words reverberating through him. He felt as though Nimitz had reached inside him and flipped a switch, illuminating the purpose behind their mission with blinding clarity. This wasn't just cargo—they were carrying lifelines, hope, and victory itself.

Paul looked at Joe. Joe looked at Paul. Both men were caught up in a moment that seemed to stretch on forever. Joe finally broke the silence, his voice softer than Paul was used to.

"You think he really meant that? About our work being vital?"

Paul nodded slowly, the admiral's words still echoing in his mind. "Yeah, Joe. I think he did. And I think he is right. Let's go get some breakfast—I can't wait to tell the other fellas."

Paul and Joe continued down the sandy path toward the mess hall, their boots kicking up small puffs of dust with each step. The sun had climbed higher in the sky, its warmth intensifying with every passing minute. Soon, they'd be back in the air, pressing on in the next leg of their mission. But for now, there was a brief moment to pause, to refuel—not just the plane, but themselves. First, breakfast.

***

As far as mess halls went, there wasn't much to Canton's. The low buzz of conversation had dwindled to almost nothing as most of the men had already finished breakfast. Only Chuck's crew and a few stragglers remained, scattered at other tables. The faint smell of powdered eggs and burnt coffee lingered, clinging to the air like an unwelcome guest. Chuck sat at the far end of the table, arms crossed, the corners of his mouth pulled into a scowl.

For some reason, this island really rubbed him the wrong way. Maybe it was the nothingness of it all—just a God-forsaken patch of coral and sand in the middle of nowhere. Or maybe it was that the war felt distant here, like an afterthought. He hated that. He wanted to be doing something, moving forward. Not just sitting here, waiting.

It didn't help when Paul and Joe burst in twenty minutes late, practically glowing with excitement. Paul was carrying a tray piled high with breakfast, while Joe trailed behind, a cocky grin plastered on his face. Chuck glared at them as they slid into their seats, interrupting the relative calm.

"Guess who we just talked to?" Joe started, barely able to contain himself.

"Betty Grable!" Jimmy shouted from across the table, not missing a beat.

"Glenn Miller?" Stan guessed, looking up from his plate with a smirk.

Paul raised his hands for silence, exasperation laced with amusement. "No—only the most important person in this part of the world, other than Roosevelt himself."

"You talked to Bing Crosby?" Jimmy said incredulously, earning a round of laughter from the table.

"No, no, no," Paul said, waving off the suggestion. "Admiral Nimitz. Joe and I just had a conversation with Admiral Chester Nimitz! Well, first Joe spilled coffee all over him, then we had a conversation."

The table went quiet for a moment, everyone staring at Paul as if he'd just announced they'd met Santa Claus.

Jimmy leaned forward, his voice low and skeptical. "You're telling me that *you two* talked to *the* Chester Nimitz? The man running the entire Pacific Fleet?"

Paul nodded emphatically. "That's exactly what I'm saying."

"I had heard he was on the island," Chuck muttered, his voice flat. "But why would he waste his time talking to you two jokers?"

Chuck was slightly annoyed and a bit jealous. Here was a civilian and a guy who didn't really even want a career in the military, and they'd had a brush with greatness.

Joe puffed out his chest, clearly reveling in the attention. "We just kind of bumped into him. I spilled coffee on him—accidentally, of course—then I went to get him more coffee. And then he told us how much he admired us."

"Well, that's not exactly what he said," Paul corrected, rolling his eyes.

"Details, details," Joe said, brushing him off.

Chuck sat back in his chair, arms still crossed, his expression unreadable. "Alright, Paul, enlighten us. What did *the* Admiral Nimitz have to say to a couple cargo-haulers?"

Paul leaned forward, elbows resting on the table, and launched into a recounting of the chance meeting. His words were deliberate and his face lit up as he spoke, his admiration for the admiral shining through. He described the calm authority in Nimitz's voice, the way he had spoken with conviction about the importance of their mission, and the parting words that had left both Paul and Joe standing there like awestruck schoolboys.

The table was silent as Paul finished. Even Chuck's scowl seemed to soften—just a little.

Jimmy broke the silence with a low whistle. "Well, I'll be. You really did meet him."

"Not just met him," Joe chimed in. "He gave us a pep talk. Said we were doing vital work. Pretty much called us heroes."

Stan chuckled. "Sounds like you were lucky he didn't throw you in the brig for spilling his coffee."

Paul smirked. "Yeah, well, let's just say Joe was on thin ice there for a minute."

Chuck finally spoke, his tone more contemplative than usual. "Nimitz doesn't waste words. If he told you something, he meant it." He tapped his fingers on the table, his gaze distant. "Might do us all some good to remember that."

For a moment, the table fell into a companionable silence, each man lost in his own thoughts. It wasn't every day you had a brush with greatness—especially in the middle of the Pacific.

Paul suddenly broke the silent reverie. "So, Joe, it seems like you're moving up in the world."

"How do you mean?" Joe asked, raising an eyebrow.

"Well, first there was that major at Mather. Now it's Nimitz on Canton. I guess next it's what—Roosevelt in D.C.?"

Joe grinned, leaning back in his chair. "I think you're right about that, Paul. Anyone know Roosevelt's schedule? I've got a coffee cup with his name on it."

Laughter erupted around the table, except for Chuck, who stood abruptly, his chair scraping against the floor. "We need to get ready to leave. Everyone finish up, stow your gear, and be ready to depart at 0800. I'm going to get some air."

He returned his tray and stepped outside, the sunlight glaring against the sand. As he walked along the edge of the airstrip, Chuck's thoughts churned. He respected Nimitz deeply, and the admiral's words carried great weight, convicting him about the importance of their mission. But even as he felt inspired by the encounter, a hollow ache settled in his chest.

Something was still missing—something he felt all too keenly but maybe was beginning to understand.

***

The early morning sun painted the horizon with shades of gold and pink as Chuck walked along the edge of the airstrip. The scent of salt and the faint sound of surf in the distance were constant reminders of their isolation on this patch of coral in the vast Pacific. Chuck's boots crunched softly against the sand, but his mind wasn't on the mission or the logistics of their departure, it was on the conversation he'd had with Paul just a few nights ago in Hawaii.

It had been their second night at Hickam, before they were to depart for Canton the next day. Chuck was sitting at a table in the officer's club, nursing a whiskey and soda, when Paul appeared seemingly out of nowhere.

"May I join you, Chuck?" Paul asked, his tone friendly but measured.

Chuck glanced up, a little surprised. "Uh, sure, Paul. Didn't expect to see you in here."

"Just looking for a change in scenery, I guess," Paul said, setting a glass of club soda with a lime on the table as he took a seat across from Chuck. "I was just wondering how you're doing. You've seemed a little distant today."

"I'm doing fine," Chuck replied, swirling the ice in his glass. "Just ready to get on with the mission. I get tired of just sitting around."

"Yeah, I get that," Paul agreed. "Though yesterday was fun. Some well-deserved rest for all of us."

"I suppose." Chuck seemed about to say more but hesitated. He exhaled slowly and took another sip of his drink.

Paul studied him for a moment. "Tomorrow will be a long day. Any concerns about the flight?"

Chuck shook his head. "No, not really. Seems like it'll be pretty standard. But it'll be nice to have some work to do." He paused, staring at the melting ice in his glass. "Although, lately work doesn't seem to be enough either."

Paul tilted his head slightly, his curiosity evident. "What do you mean?"

Chuck glanced up, his brow furrowed. "Can I tell you something in confidence, Paul?"

"Of course."

Chuck leaned back, his chair creaking. "I don't know how to put it, really. I always thought flying was my thing. That once I was a pilot and in command, I'd feel ... fulfilled, I guess. But it's not happening. No matter how much I focus on work, it never seems to be enough. I don't know what's wrong with me."

Paul didn't respond immediately, his expression thoughtful. After a moment, he said quietly, almost to himself, "A God-shaped hole."

"What does that mean?" Chuck asked, his tone carrying a hint of defensiveness.

"You've probably heard of Blaise Pascal," Paul began.

"The seventeenth-century mathematician?" Chuck said, raising an eyebrow.

Paul nodded. "He was that, among other things. But later in his life he wrote about philosophy and theology. He described what people now call the 'God-shaped hole.' Basically, he said people try in vain to find meaning in their lives, to fill a void with everything around them, but nothing works. He wrote, 'This infinite abyss can be filled only with an infinite and immutable object; in other words, by God Himself.'"

Chuck remained silent, his expression unreadable. Paul pressed on. "You see, Chuck, you'll never find ultimate meaning in things, work, or even relationships. There's only one thing that can give your life true meaning. Only one thing that can fill the void."

Chuck leaned forward slightly, his voice laced with sarcasm. "Let me guess—you're going to say 'Jesus.'"

"That's exactly right," Paul replied evenly.

Chuck snorted. "Why do you people always have to bring God and Jesus into everything? Why are you always trying to convince other people? What's in it for you?"

Paul sat back, considering his words. "Chuck, let me ask you something. Will you listen and take this seriously?"

Chuck hesitated, then nodded reluctantly. "If it were anyone else, I'd say no. But I respect you, so go ahead."

Paul leaned in, his voice steady and deliberate. "Imagine someone running as fast as he can. You know something he doesn't: there's a sheer cliff ahead, hidden until it's too late. You know that if he keeps going, he'll run right off the edge and lose everything on the jagged rocks below."

Paul paused, letting the image sink in. "Now, imagine you recognize that person. Maybe he's someone you barely know, maybe he's someone you care about. Either way, you'd do everything in your power to stop him, wouldn't you? Shout, wave your arms, block his path, do whatever it takes to get his attention."

Chuck nodded slowly. "Yeah, I'd stop him."

Paul's voice softened. "That's why Christians talk about Jesus. We believe that void you feel—the one you're trying to fill with work and other things—it's leading you toward that cliff. And we want to help you stop before it's too late."

Chuck stared down at his drink, his jaw tight. "What are you telling me, Paul?"

"I'm telling you that you're running toward that cliff. You're trying to fill an infinite void with finite things. But there's only one way to fill it. And that one way will be your salvation."

That conversation was clear in Chuck's head, and as he felt the morning breeze on his face, Paul's words echoed in his mind. A cliff. A void. A life spent chasing things that never quite satisfied. He couldn't deny that the emptiness Paul had described was real. But what if Paul was right? What if he really was running toward that cliff—and just didn't want to see it?

CHAPTER SEVEN

Canton Island Departure - September 22, 1942

They were getting a late start; it was already pushing 0830, and the crew had just finished reviewing the flight plan to Fiji. The Pacific sun climbed higher, casting long shadows over the sparse Canton airstrip. There was a hint of salt in the air, mixed with the acrid smell of fuel and grease. A rhythmic clatter of tools echoed from the nearby hangars.

Stan Kowalski leaned against the edge of the fuselage, clipboard in hand, his eyes scanning the rows of maintenance notes from the Canton ground crew. Most of the entries were routine—fuel topped off, a minor adjustment to the trim tab. But one note stopped him cold: "Flap actuator stiffness noted during taxi testing. Requires further inspection at the next major maintenance interval."

Stan frowned as he tapped his pencil against the clipboard. "Next major maintenance interval" wasn't exactly comforting when you were about to embark on a ten-hour flight over the open Pacific. The words stuck in his mind, like an itch he couldn't scratch. He could almost hear his old instructor's voice: "If something doesn't feel right, it probably isn't. Go with your gut." Small issues had a nasty habit of turning into big problems when you were cruising at 10,000 feet with no place to land. The note wasn't flagged as critical, and the plane hadn't been grounded, but that didn't make him feel any better.

He worked his way up to his station and glanced around the cockpit. Chuck was running through his own pre-flight check with practiced efficiency, but his jaw was tight, his movements quick and slightly jerky. The man was on edge again—Canton Island seemed to have that effect on him. Or maybe there was just something else on his mind. Joe was in his seat, assisting Chuck with the checklist. Paul and Jimmy were busy checking their respective stations, their voices faint through the intercom.

Stan took a breath, weighing his options. He didn't want to be the one to cause a further delay; but then again, flaps weren't something you wanted to gamble on, especially over the Pacific. He decided he should mention it to Chuck.

Stan keyed the intercom. "Hey, Chuck. Quick heads-up—there's a maintenance note here about the flap actuators stiffening during taxi testing. It's not marked as critical, but it says to address it at the next major maintenance interval."

There was a pause before Chuck's terse reply. "Thanks, Stan. Log it, and we'll make sure Brisbane looks at it. We're already thirty minutes behind, and we can't delay any more."

"Copy that," Stan muttered, jotting the issue into the logbook with a pencil pressed hard enough to leave indentations. One more thing to keep an eye on.

He closed the clipboard and stowed it, taking a moment to glance out the cockpit window. The Pacific stretched ahead—vast, blue and unforgivng. He shook off his unease and started the pre-flight engine checks. This wasn't the first time he'd flown with a less-than-perfect maintenance report. Still, something about this one gnawed at him.

Stan was from Fall River, Massachusetts, a place as gritty and hardworking as the people who lived there. His family had worked in the local textile mills for generations, but Stan had always wanted something different. Motors fascinated him—how they worked, how they fit together, and how even the smallest part could cause a failure if overlooked. That fascination led him to engineering school and eventually to working as a civilian flight engineer for the Air Transport Command.

He liked to think he brought a bit of Fall River with him wherever he went. The lessons he'd learned back home—about hard work, precision, and humility—were tools he used every day. But more than that, Stan carried the quiet resilience of someone who had seen tough times and pushed through them.

Outside, the ground crew began hand-turning the propellers, each engine cranked several times to clear oil pooled in the cylinders. The rising sun glinted off the fuselage as mechanics signaled the cockpit, their gestures deliberate and crisp.

"Check engine three," Chuck's voice crackled over the intercom, his tone crisp.

Stan responded, flipping switches with practiced ease. "Fuel valves open. Ignition switches set. Engine three ready."

"Start engine three."

"Starting engine three." A heartbeat later, the engine sputtered to life, its roar filling the cabin. Stan's eyes darted across the gauges, scanning for anomalies. Satisfied, he gave the next report. "Hydraulics on-line. Engine three stable."

Each engine came alive in sequence, the vibrations shuddering through the aircraft like rolling thunder. The ground crew stood vigilant with fire extinguishers, their practiced movements almost ritualistic. Inside, the cabin hummed with the rhythm of systems coming on-line and the low murmur of the crew settling into their roles.

Stan took a moment to glance out the window. The endless expanse of the Pacific stretched out before them, its beauty stark and unforgiving. He adjusted his headset and muttered to himself, "I'll keep an eye on those flaps."

The aircraft lumbered down the runway, engines roaring as it taxied. The next leg of their journey was starting. They were ready—or so they hoped.

***

The roar of the engines was a constant, steady presence, the only assurance of normalcy as the crew pressed deeper into the vastness of the Pacific. The ocean stretched below in a restless, heaving expanse, its surface darkened by the gathering storm.

Stan glanced out the small window at his station. The sun had been their companion for the first five hours of the flight, but now, gray tendrils of storm clouds reached across the sky. He keyed the intercom.

"Chuck, looks like we're heading into some nasty weather. You want to adjust altitude?"

Chuck's voice came back tense and sharp. "Negative. Stick to the flight plan."

Stan frowned but didn't press the issue. He knew Chuck wasn't the type to take serious suggestions lightly. Something about Canton had gotten under his skin. Something happened there.

Paul's voice cut through the intercom, calm and reassuring. "Visibility's dropping fast up here. We might want to get those turbulence checklists ready."

Jimmy leaned back in his navigator's seat, swiveling slightly to look at the rest of the crew. "Nothing like a little excitement to keep us on our toes, huh?" His grin faded fast when he caught Chuck's glare. He cleared his throat and turned back to his charts, muttering, "Just saying."

The turbulence began with a light jolt, the kind that might have gone unnoticed if not for the growing tension among the crew. But within minutes, the jolts turned into violent shudders and the aircraft groaned in protest of the storm's battering winds.

Stan's hands moved instinctively, his eyes darting around the console. He keyed the intercom again. "Hydraulics are holding steady, engines look good. Whatever was affecting the flaps at Canton doesn't seem to be affecting any other systems."

Chuck shot back quickly, annoyance evident in his voice, "I don't need a play-by-play, Stan. Just monitor the systems and let me know if anything is abnormal."

Joe shot Chuck a sideways glance from the co-pilot's seat, his voice carefully neutral. "Easy, Chuck. We've been through worse."

"Have we?" Chuck snapped, fighting the plane as it bucked. His knuckles were white on the yoke, his jaw clenched. "Because this feels like plenty to me."

Paul glanced back at Stan, his expression calm but questioning. Stan gave a slight nod, signaling that he was unfazed by Chuck's response.

The storm closed in and rain hammered the widows with such force it sounded like gravel. The horizon vanished entirely, replaced by a swirling gray void. The instruments became their only connection to reality, each dial and needle a lifeline in the darkness.

Jimmy's voice broke the silence. "Hey, anyone want to hear about the time I plotted a course right to the middle of a jungle, instead of an airstrip? Might take the edge off."

Paul chuckled softly, but no one else joined in. Even Jimmy lost heart as the plane jolted again, rattling loose a clipboard that clattered to the floor.

Stan steadied himself against the wall, muttering under his breath. "Come on, old girl, hold together."

He chanced another glance at Chuck, who was focused, but his expression betrayed something else. Some inner turmoil that mirrored the storm. Joe's glance toward him suggested he noticed it too.

"You OK, Chuck?" Joe's voice was steady, but the weight behind the question was unmistakable.

Chuck didn't look up, his focus fixed on the instruments. "I'm fine," he muttered, but the edge in his voice suggested otherwise. Joe hesitated, then nodded, turning his attention back to the controls.

Stan's voice came through again, more urgent now. "We've got lower oil pressure readings on engine four. Nothing critical yet, but I'm watching it close."

Chuck exhaled sharply. "Do more than watch it, Stan. Fix it."

Stan bristled but held his tongue. "Doing my best."

They were now in the worst of the storm. The C-87 was being thrown around like a toy plane, with rain pelting the fuselage like machine gun fire. The plane jolted violently, pitching them downward as if struck by a giant hand. Stan's stomach lurched; he gripped the console instinctively.

He scanned the console as the storm battered the plane. The C-87 groaned and shuddered, its engines roaring in defiance.

"Oil pressure non-existent in engine four," Stan said urgently into the intercom, his voice sharp but steady. "Engine four out. Joe, feather that engine."

"Feathering engine four," Joe replied as the plane lurched again, jostling Stan around in his harness.

"Confirmed. Engine four feathered. Throttle up engine three to compensate."

"Throttling up engine three," Joe said. "Chuck, we're off course—compass reading shows we're off five degrees."

"Correcting," Chuck snapped, fighting the yoke with clenched fists. "Paul, get me a beacon fix."

Paul shook his head grimly. "Negative. I'm not picking up a signal on any of the mission profile frequencies. We may have lost the HF antenna."

Stan's stomach sank. "We could try the trailing wire antenna. Might be able to pick something up."

"Do it," Chuck ordered decisively.

Stan unbuckled his harness and motioned to Paul to follow him down to the cargo area. The turbulence was relentless, tossing them against bulkheads as they wrestled with the trailing wire assembly. Rain hammered the fuselage as the storm raged on, making every movement a fight against the bucking plane.

Finally, after what seemed like a lengthy struggle, the wire antenna was deployed and Paul connected it to the radio feed. They stumbled back to their stations, strapping in as Stan keyed the intercom.

"Trailing wire connected. Paul adjusting antenna coupler."

Paul deftly worked the dials, his face a mask of focus. "Stand by. Adjusting for beacon frequency from Fiji." The cockpit fell silent, every eye on Paul as he adjusted the gain. Then, his expression shifted, a spark of relief breaking through.

"Got it! Beacon signal locked. Plotting now." Paul relayed the coordinates, his voice calm but resolute. "We're on course for Fiji."

Chuck exhaled sharply. "Nice work with the radio."

"Great flying, Chuck," Stan replied.

Chuck was a great pilot—there was no doubt about that. Stan could see the potential for him to be a great leader, too. But there was something in him, something that seemed to crack under pressure. Stan couldn't quite put his finger on it, but at times, it felt like Chuck was wrestling with himself as much as the controls.

The cabin shook as the plane lurched again, loose equipment rattling with each jolt. Stan glanced at the rest of the crew, strapped in and focused, then back at Chuck. His grip on the yoke had loosened, but the tension in his eyes hadn't faded. With one engine out and the storm still raging, the fight was far from over.

For now, though, they'd weathered the worst. The Pacific stretched ahead, dark and dangerous, but Fiji was somewhere beyond it.

***

Fiji, South Pacific

The post-flight checklist was complete, but the flight hadn't been easy. It felt like a dark shadow, clinging to Chuck, no matter how he tried to shake it. He remained in the pilot's seat long after the others had disembarked, staring at the empty cockpit and replaying every decision he'd made during the last leg.

Outside, the scene was almost surreal in its tranquility. The turquoise water beyond the airstrip shimmered under the late-afternoon sun, a hue so vibrant Chuck doubted it could be real. Coconut palms swayed gently in the warm breeze, their fronds rustling like whispers against the distant buzz of the airfield. The raging storm felt like a distant memory, yet its weight lingered on Chuck's chest.

He unbuckled his harness slowly, his hands trembling just enough to frustrate him. Rising from the seat, he adjusted his flight jacket, as if the motion alone might help him pull himself together. But his legs felt heavy as he made his way to the exit.

Disembarking into the humid air, Chuck blinked against the sudden brightness. The smells of the island hit him first—salt carried on the breeze, the earthy aroma of damp grass, and faint traces of engine oil from the airfield. Nadi Airfield was alive with activity. Ground crews refueled planes, checked engines, and rolled carts laden with supplies across the tarmac. These same ground crews would have some significant work to do on their C-87 before departure tomorrow morning. The murmur of voices, the occasional shout, and the distant rumble of another aircraft created a backdrop of subdued activity.

Chuck walked around to the front of the plane, his boots crunching against the gravelly surface of the tarmac. He saw a spot near the front landing gear and lowered himself onto the metal step of the forward gear door. Sitting there, he rested his forearms on his knees, his head bowed slightly.

The plane loomed behind him. The stress it had endured was visible, a testament to the storm they'd barely escaped. One of the ground crew gave him a polite nod as he passed, but Chuck didn't respond. He couldn't. His thoughts were too tangled, fragments of fear, self-doubt, and exhaustion warring in his mind.

The storm hadn't just tested the aircraft, it had tested him. And while the plane had made it through with one engine feathered and a few more maintenance notes to address, Chuck wasn't so sure about himself. He didn't have any maintenance notes for himself. The weight of the decisions he'd made—or almost failed to make—pressed down on him like the humidity in the air.

From his vantage point, he could see the line of parked aircraft further down the tarmac, their silhouettes stark against the backdrop of the lush green mountains that rose beyond the airfield. Fiji was beautiful, almost otherworldly, but its serenity only deepened the dissonance inside him. The calm felt like a cruel joke.

Somewhere behind him, he heard Stan's voice, steady and calm as always, probably coordinating with the ground crew. Paul's laugh carried faintly on the breeze—an easy, unguarded sound that made Chuck's chest tighten. How could they shake it off so quickly? How could they move forward so easily when he was still roiling in the storm's aftermath?

Chuck sighed and ran a hand over his face, staring out at the turquoise blue sea. He envied its stillness. He closed his eyes and felt the warm, tropical breeze blow through his hair. He thought about what it would be like to drop all his cares and just stay here—to cast everything away and feel some peace.

Chuck opened his eyes and looked behind him as he felt a presence approach. Paul was walking up from the back of the plane toward him.

"That was some great flying today, Chuck," Paul said as he crossed his arms and leaned against the fuselage. "I don't think I've seen a better display of skill in a pilot."

"Well, thanks, Paul, but that's not exactly what I'm feeling. I could have done a better job. Handled things better. Made quicker decisions."

"It was a tough situation, Chuck. It wasn't just the storm; we also had several systems failures. It was stressful."

Chuck stood up and faced Paul. "I'm not sure why I'm telling you this. I probably shouldn't be since I'm the commanding officer."

"It's OK, Chuck. You have my respect regardless. And hey, I'm just the civilian radio operator," Paul responded with a smile. "Would you like me to pray with you?"

Chuck dropped his head with a slight chuckle, "You never give up, do you?"

"Well, there was this time I was trying to teach Alta how to serve in tennis, without hitting the net. I felt like quitting then."

The tension seemed to lift as Chuck had a real, genuine laugh and clapped Paul on the back. "Thanks Paul, I needed that. I need to go see a man about a horse. I'll see you in a bit."

As Chuck walked away, Paul shouted after him, "I don't think Joe has any horses on board the plane, but you can certainly ask him."

Chuck turned back and looked at Paul with a hearty "Ha!" and continued toward the hangars.

It amazed him how just a few words from Paul could lighten the weight he carried. Chuck wasn't used to confiding in people—it wasn't his nature—but with Paul, it felt different. There was something steady about him, something that put people at ease. He never spoke down to others, never made them feel small. Instead, his advice came without judgment, his reassurance without pretense. Chuck carried that thought with him as he approached the hangar, feeling lighter than he had moments before.

***

No response—figures. These pilots were something else. Hot shots who thought they were better than everyone else. Sam shook his head, irritation bubbling under the surface. All he'd done was give the guy a polite nod, just to acknowledge him. The pilot had barely looked his way. Staring off toward the ocean like he was the only man on the airfield. They're all the same, Sam thought. Fly in, expect their planes to be taken care of, then off to the next destination without so much as a thank-you.

He glanced back at the pilot as another crew member—a slim guy with an easygoing posture—walked up to him. Their voices were low, the words lost under the background noise of engines and an occasional shout from a ground crew member. Sam turned his attention back to the aircraft.

The C-87 loomed in front of him. He walked around to the back of the plane and ran a hand over the slick metal of the tail section, muttering to himself, "Another one just holding together, huh?"

"Hugh!" he called out, spotting his colleague near the tool cart. "Grab the maintenance report for this C-87, will ya? Serial 41-23903."

"Sure thing," Hugh called back, wiping his hands on a rag before jogging toward the cockpit.

Sam walked along the plane's flank, his boots crunching against the gravel tarmac. The heat pressed down on him, the sticky humidity clinging to his skin. He wasn't complaining though. If he had to be stuck somewhere, Fiji wasn't the worst place. The island had a beauty to it, with its green mountains and turquoise waters. Not that he got to enjoy it much. The shifts were long, the traffic constant, and the time off too rare to make it to the beach. Still better than some dusty airfield in the middle of nowhere, he thought, then chuckled. Technically, this is the middle of nowhere.

Hugh returned, handing over the maintenance log. "Looks like she had a rough one," he said, nodding toward the plane. "Guessing that storm chewed them up pretty good."

"Yeah," Sam replied, flipping through the log. "HF antenna's gone." He pointed up at the gap where the wire should've been strung along the fuselage. "That'll need replacing."

He walked around to the nose of the aircraft, stopping as he noticed the number four engine. The propeller was feathered, a clear sign it had been shut down in mid-flight. "Engine trouble too," he muttered, kneeling to inspect the housing. He made a quick note in the log and moved on.

"Everything else looks standard," Hugh said, peering over Sam's shoulder.

Sam nodded, flipping to the last page of the log. His eyes stopped at a note written in small, neat script: Flap actuator stiffness noted during taxi testing. Requires further inspection at the next major maintenance interval.

"'Next major maintenance interval,'" Sam read aloud, his voice tinged with skepticism. He tapped the entry with his pen. "Figures."

"Think it's a problem?" Hugh asked.

Sam shrugged. "Not now, maybe. But flaps aren't something you want to gamble on." He closed the log with a sigh and looked back at the pilot, who had just stood up from his seat and started walking toward one of the hangars. As he walked, the man paused, turned back slightly, and let out a laugh—sharp and genuine—before continuing on. Sam followed the pilot with his gaze, noticing the man's shoulders seemed a little less tense now.

"They were lucky this time," Sam muttered. "We should probably take a quick look at it before they head to Brisbane."

Hugh followed his gaze. "You think he's one of the good ones?"

"Don't know," Sam said, turning away. "Guess we'll see."

Sam walked back to the hangar to grab more tools, trailing behind the pilot. His boots scuffed against the tarmac; the sound must have caught the man's attention because he stopped and turned. Sam braced himself for a curt question or a dismissive comment, but instead, something unexpected happened.

"Hey, Mac," the pilot said, his voice carrying over the din of the airfield. "Thanks for working on our plane. It means a lot. We had a rough time out there, and I appreciate your expertise in getting her in the air again."

Sam blinked, caught off guard. "Uh, sure, Lieutenant. Yeah, she looks pretty banged up, but we'll get her purring again."

"Thanks, uh …" The man hesitated, raising an eyebrow.

"Flemming. Corporal Sam Flemming."

"Thank you, Corporal Flemming," the officer said, offering a slight nod before turning on his heel and continuing toward the hangar.

Sam stood there for a moment, watching him go. Well, I'll be, he thought, a faint smile tugging at his lips. I guess he is one of the good ones.

***

The early evening air outside the base was warm and carried the mingling scents of tropical flowers, briny sea breeze, and the faint smell of wood smoke. Paul, Joe, and Jimmy strolled along a narrow dirt road, their boots kicking up puffs of dust. The buzz of the market ahead grew louder with every step—vendors calling out in cheerful voices, laughter, and the faint jangle of island music drifting through the air. Chuck and Stan decided to stay behind on the base, each doing his own thing to catch up on some much-needed rest.

"This is what I call a proper break," Jimmy said, tipping his hat back to take in the scene. "Beats staring at maps and storm clouds any day."

Joe chuckled, his hands resting loosely in his pockets. "Don't get too comfortable, Jimmy. Chuck might have us patching up the plane ourselves if he thinks we're having too much fun."

Paul grinned, shaking his head. "Chuck is under a lot of stress and going through some things of his own. Let's just enjoy this while we can, who knows when we'll get another chance?"

They meandered past rows of stall and tables, each one a colorful snapshot of Fijian life. Piles of ripe bananas and pineapples glistened under the flickering light of kerosene lamps. Wooden carvings of turtles and warriors lay beside woven mats and jewelry made of seashells. Brightly dyed fabrics shimmered like molten color in the fading sunlight.

Paul slowed as they reached a table covered in small pennants, each one embroidered with the name of a different place. His hand hovered over one in particular.

"Fiji," he murmured, picking up a pennant with a palm tree stitched in vibrant green. The word stood boldly across the top in white letters. "What do you think, Joe? A good keepsake or too touristy?"

Joe shrugged, a small smile playing at his lips. "You? Tourist? Never."

Jimmy snorted. "Yeah, Paul, go ahead. Something to show Alta when you're back stateside."

Paul smiled as he handed a few coins to the vendor. "Something to remind me of this place, too," he said, almost to himself.

As Paul tucked the pennant under his arm, Joe stopped in front of another table, pointing to a small mound of knotted brown roots. "What I'd really like to know is, what are *these* things?"

"That's ginger, Joe," Paul replied.

"You mean like for ginger ale? That's what I'm ingesting when I drink ginger ale?" Joe's voice was incredulous.

Jimmy clapped him on the shoulder. "You're expanding your horizons, Cowboy. There's more to life than eggs and bacon."

"Yeah, sure. There's steak too."

Paul laughed as they continued down the row. A woman behind a table caught their attention, calling out, "You want to drink coconut juice?"

Joe stepped closer, curious. "Coconut juice? Now this I've got to try. How much?"

"Fifty cents," the woman replied, motioning to a young man standing nearby.

"OK," Joe said with a grin. "I'll try it for fifty cents."

The young man picked up a coconut and an enormous knife, and with practiced precision, began chopping away the husk.

"Now that's what I call a knife!" Jimmy exclaimed, as his eyes widened.

The blade whistled through the air as it struck, each cut clean and deliberate. Paul, Jimmy, and Joe stood mesmerized as the young man worked. When the coconut was stripped bare, he deftly drilled a hole with the knife, inserted a straw, and handed it to Joe.

"That was amazing," Joe said, accepting the drink. He took a sip and his eyes widened. "Oh, geez, sweet. This tastes great!"

Jimmy reached for his own wallet. "Well, don't hog all the culture, Cowboy. I'm next."

Paul chuckled, watching the growing friendships unfold. The simple pleasure of the moment—the laughter, the warm air, the vibrant market—was a welcome reprieve from the relentless pressure of the war. For now, they were just three friends sharing a rare moment of relaxation. He only wished Alta could be there to share it with them.

As they strolled out of the market and back down the dusty road, a comfortable silence fell over them. The rhythmic crunch of their boots in the dirt was broken only by the occasional rustle of palm fronds in the breeze.

Joe spoke up, his voice thoughtful. "So, what did you mean when you said Chuck is going through some things of his own? Is he OK? Anything we can do?"

Paul glanced at Joe, then at Jimmy, measuring his words carefully. "All I'll say is that he's at somewhat of a crossroads. For him, figuring out the right path is … a struggle. He has a lot on his mind, and sometimes self-doubt gets the better of him."

Jimmy frowned, his voice softening. "Didn't realize it was that bad. Chuck's always seemed so … in control."

Paul nodded. "He's good at keeping up appearances, but that doesn't mean he's not wrestling with something inside. The best thing we can do is be supportive. Stay strong in your faith, and help guide him, gently. Chuck's got a lot of weight on his shoulders. Support from friends might make the difference."

Joe exhaled, nodding slowly. "Yeah, I can do that. I just hope he knows he's not in it alone."

"He'll figure it out," Paul said, his voice steady. "In the meantime, we'll walk with him, and not push him."

The three men continued their slow shuffle past the scattered stalls, the glow of the market fading behind them as the horizon turned a deep shade of amber. Though the road ahead was uncertain for all of them, Paul felt a quiet conviction settle over him, perhaps another push from that unseen presence, that still small voice gently guiding him.

"Well, fellas, I suppose we had better head back and hit the sack. We have another long day tomorrow," Joe's voice came, calm and relaxed. "I'm glad we did this. I think we all needed it."

They slowly walked back to the base, the soft breeze at their backs like a comforting embrace at the end of a long day.

CHAPTER EIGHT

Brisbane, Australia - September 23, 1942

T he short layover in Fiji had been a welcome reprieve from the stresses of flying, especially after the storm they had battled on their way in. But Paul noticed the tense atmosphere return to the crew before their departure from Nadi Airfield. The storm's aftermath had shaken even the most seasoned among them. Fiji had offered a brief chance to breathe, but it hadn't erased the weight of the mission. Still, Paul thought, the relative calm of the last two legs was something to be grateful for.

One moment during the flight from New Caledonia to Brisbane stuck with Paul. It wasn't much—probably something the other crew members hadn't even noticed. They were on a quiet stretch of the flight, the engines droning steadily and the air smooth for once, when Joe's voice crackled over the intercom.

"How did we end up here, fellas?"

"What do you mean, Joe? Other than through hard work?" Jimmy replied, his tone light but curious.

"How is it," Joe continued, his voice thoughtful, "that we end up here, looking out over God's beautiful creation, doing His work, while others never really got the chance?"

There was a long pause before Jimmy responded, a hint of uncertainty in his voice. "I ... I don't know, Joe. I guess we're just lucky."

The exchange had been brief, and the rest of the crew probably dismissed it as another of Joe's musings. But Paul sensed there was something deeper behind those words. He made a mental note to follow up with his friend when the time was right.

From Fiji to New Caledonia, the flight had taken around six hours. New Caledonia to Brisbane was another five, with a stop in Nouméa for refueling. Thirteen hours in total wasn't a grueling stretch by wartime standards, thanks to the stopover in Nouméa, but it was long enough to remind everyone that this wasn't a vacation.

Paul glanced out the small windows as the C-87 began its descent. The sprawling city of Brisbane came into view, its skyline a mix of industrial smokestacks, warehouses, and a scattering of taller buildings. It was a far cry from the remote outposts they'd visited, and its bustling airfield hinted at the scale of the war effort.

As the plane touched down, a jolt ran through the fuselage. Paul felt the familiar vibrations of the landing gear engaging the runway, followed by the rumbling deceleration as Chuck brought the aircraft to a steady roll. The crew exchanged tired but relieved glances, each of them visibly glad to have reached their destination. Really, it was a significant milestone.

The engines wound down to a low hum as the plane taxied to its assigned spot on the crowded airstrip. Through the window, Paul saw rows of other planes—transport aircraft like theirs, as well as bombers and smaller fighter planes. Ground crew swarmed like ants, directing traffic, refueling aircraft, and hauling cargo.

"Welcome to Brisbane," Jimmy said over the intercom, his tone carrying a hint of sarcasm. "Home of tight schedules and question-able coffee."

Paul chuckled and unbuckled his harness as the plane came to a stop. The cargo doors creaked open, and a wave of warm, humid air rushed in. It carried the scent of fuel and distant eucalyptus, a mix that somehow managed to smell both foreign and familiar.

He grabbed his flight bag and stepped onto the metal stair-case leading down to the tarmac. Around him, the bustling airfield buzzed with energy. Mechanics barked orders, engines roared to life, and forklifts rumbled past, hauling crates marked with mili-tary stencils.

Stan stayed behind near the cockpit, talking with the Brisbane ground crew about the maintenance log. Paul decided to linger, curiosity drawing him closer to the conversation.

"Flap actuator stiffness," Stan said, handing over the log. "It held up fine on this leg, but I'd still take a close look."

One of the mechanics, a wiry man in grease-stained overalls, frowned as he skimmed the entry. "We'll clean and lube it, see if that sorts it out."

Paul glanced at Stan, noting the engineer's furrowed brow. It was the same look Stan always had when something didn't sit right.

"I dunno, fellas," Stan said, crossing his arms. "What if that actuator's more worn than it looks? If the flaps deploy uneven-ly—even by a few degrees—it could throw the whole bird into a roll we can't stop." He shook his head. "Control's already sluggish on approach. At low speed? We might not have enough aileron to correct it. Lubing it might smooth things over for now, but that wear's still there. It'll just get worse."

The mechanic straightened, irritation edging into his voice. "Listen, fella, we've got dozens of planes coming in here almost every hour. We just don't have the time to do a deep dive into every minor issue. We'll lube it, and that should be good for now."

Stan held the mechanic's gaze for a moment, then exhaled sharply, his shoulders dropping slightly. "Uh, sure. I understand. It'll probably be fine until we get back to Hickam. Maybe they'll have the proper resources to deal with it there."

Paul winced at Stan's comment, though he silently agreed. It wasn't the kind of remark that endeared you to a ground crew, but sometimes a little pushback was necessary. He caught Stan's glance as they turned to leave and offered a small nod of encouragement.

As they walked toward the barracks, they caught up with the rest of the crew, who were waiting in a shaded area near the edge of the airfield.

"What'd you find out, Stan?" Chuck asked, his arms crossed as he leaned against a crate.

"That we're going to have to live with the flap issue, at least until we get back to Hawaii," Stan replied. "But it should hold up. The ground crew will lube it, and that ought to keep it working for now."

Chuck nodded, his expression neutral. "Let's hope they're right."

"Well, I just hope we can get some good chow here," Joe chimed in, the tension breaking slightly with his grin. "I need some real food."

"Anything that doesn't come from a can is just fine with me," Jimmy added, rolling his shoulders as if to shake off the weight of the day.

Paul chuckled as they started walking toward the barracks together. The conversation shifted to lighter topics, but Stan's lingering unease about the flap actuator stuck with Paul. He glanced back at the plane one last time, its silver fuselage catching the early evening sun, and felt a nagging in the back of his mind.

***

The night air carried the mingling scents of grilled meat, smoky coals, and sea breeze, the combination somehow comforting after the long flight. Near one of the larger hangars, a makeshift barbecue had been set up, complete with long tables and benches cobbled together from crates and planks. A smoky haze drifted lazily under the glow of hanging lights, casting warm yellow patches on the dusty ground.

The gathering was casual, open to anyone on base who wanted a hot meal and a moment to unwind. The faint buzz of conversation and occasional bursts of laughter created a lively, almost festive atmosphere.

Paul stood near the edge of the gathering, sipping from a tin cup of lemonade. He glanced toward the food line, where mechanics and air crews filed past grills loaded with sizzling sausages and thick cuts of steak. A few tables featured bowls of coleslaw, baked beans, and roasted sweet potatoes, their golden-orange edges caramelized to perfection. At the far end of the spread, a large platter of lamingtons—sponge cake squares coated in chocolate and shredded coconut—caught his eye, a hint of local flavor among the otherwise standard fare.

Joe and Jimmy were near the food line, chatting with a couple of mechanics. Their laughter carried easily over the din, a sharp contrast to Chuck, who leaned against a crate a few paces away. With his arms crossed and his gaze fixed somewhere beyond the airstrip, Chuck's expression hovered between boredom and discomfort.

"Not your scene?" Paul asked, stepping closer to Chuck.

Chuck shrugged without looking at him. "I'm just not much for crowds."

Paul nodded, understanding. Chuck had been quieter than usual since they'd landed, though that wasn't entirely unexpected. The mission, the storm, and the constant demands of leadership—it all seemed to weigh on him.

"Let's walk," Paul suggested. "Get some air."

Chuck hesitated for a moment, then nodded. "Yeah, good idea."

Paul waved to Joe and Jimmy, gesturing for them to join.

"Where's Stan?" Paul asked, as Joe and Jimmy walked up.

"Uh, he's over there by the meat," Jimmy replied, nodding toward the grill. "Finally taking a break from his flap detective work."

Joe stuck two fingers in his mouth and let out a shrill whistle that turned several heads. "Hey, Stan! Mosey on over here!"

Paul chuckled as Stan looked up, rolling his eyes but starting their way, a plate of food in his hand.

"Nice one, Joe," Chuck muttered under his breath, just loud enough for the group to hear. There was a touch of annoyance in his voice.

Stan joined the group, his plate piled high with sausages and sweet potatoes. "You know, I was just about to enjoy my dinnah in peace," he muttered, though the corners of his mouth twitched with a hint of amusement.

Paul grinned. "Don't worry, Stan. I bet you can walk and eat at the same time."

"What was that you said you were going to enjoy—dinnah? What's that?" Jimmy teased, grinning as he leaned toward Stan.

The group laughed. By now, they were getting used to Stan and Chuck's Eastern accents, but it was still fun to needle them now and then.

"Oh, at least I can say 'mountain' properly," Stan shot back with mock indignation. "Hey, Joe, say 'mountain.'"

"Moun'in," Joe replied with a broad grin. "See? Us folk from Colorado can speak correctly. We're the ones who don't have an accent."

The laughter lingered as the five men began moving away from the hangar, their pace unhurried and conversation light. The sounds of the barbecue faded behind them, replaced by the quieter hum of the airfield. Overhead, the stars began to peek out, dotting the deepening night sky.

"So, Joe," Chuck started, his tone sharp, "were you always a loudmouth, or is that a skill you've been perfecting lately?"

Joe snorted, not missing a beat. "Well, Chuck, at least I'm not moping around all the time like some teenage girl who just got dumped."

Paul frowned slightly, his glance at Joe asking, What's going on here?

Chuck's posture stiffened and his voice developed a harder edge. "Some of us, Joe, can't just bounce around through life cracking jokes and trying to be the center of attention. Some of us have real things to deal with."

"Oh, yeah?" Joe shot back, stepping closer. "And I suppose those real things mean you can treat everyone else like garbage? News flash, pal—you're not the only one with problems."

Chuck's jaw tightened, and he took a step toward Joe. "You'd better watch yourself. In case you've forgotten, I'm your commanding officer."

Joe squared up, his fists clenching. "Good for you, sir," he said with biting sarcasm. "But rank doesn't give you the right to act like you're the only one who's got it rough."

Jimmy raised his hands, stepping between them. "Hey, come on, fellas. "Let's cool it, huh?"

"Cool it?" Chuck snapped, brushing past Jimmy. "How am I supposed to cool it when this loudmouth is always in my face?"

Joe's voice rose, cutting through the tension. "And how am I supposed to deal with this guy acting like his problems are the only ones that matter? You want to pull rank on me? Fine! But that doesn't make you better than the rest of us!"

Paul had heard enough. He stepped between them, his voice calm but firm. "That's enough. Both of you. Chuck, being the commanding officer means more than pulling rank—it means setting a tone for the rest of us. And Joe, you know better than to throw punches at someone you're supposed to respect and trust. And I know you do. So whatever's eating at the two of you, sort it out without tearing each other, and the rest of us, apart."

The tension held for a long moment as both men glared at each other. Finally, Chuck exhaled sharply and took a step back, his shoulders stiff. Joe held his ground for a beat longer, then unclenched his fists, muttering something under his breath that Paul couldn't quite make out.

Paul let the silence hang for a moment, then spoke evenly, his voice cutting through the charged air. "I think it's time we call it a night," he said, his voice even and measured. "We've got a debrief on the trip tomorrow, and we'll need clear heads for that. Can you two shake hands and move on?"

Chuck shook his head slightly, his lips pressed into a thin line. "I agree that we should call it a night," he said, his voice low, "but I think that's all I can handle for now."

Joe snorted softly, the sound laced with frustration. "Fine by me," he said, his gaze still fixed on Chuck. "I'll see you at the debrief."

Paul sighed inwardly at the rift that had opened between them. He glanced at Jimmy and Stan, who both looked uncomfortable but said nothing. Turning back to Chuck and Joe, he softened his tone, but kept it pointed. "Listen, you two don't need to be friends. But we're a team, and we've got a job to do. That means working together with respect, even when it's hard."

Joe nodded, the stiffness in his posture easing slightly. Chuck didn't respond immediately, but he gave a brief nod before turning and walking a few steps away, his back to the group.

"Guess that's as close to a handshake as we're getting tonight," Jimmy quipped, his voice light. "So, uh, who's up for one more lamington before bed?"

Paul gave a small smile, grateful for Jimmy's attempt to lighten the mood. "Not a bad idea. I think we could all use something sweet to end the night."

Joe shook his head. "I'll pass. I'm heading to the barracks."

"Actually, I'll walk with you," Paul said, falling into step beside him. The air had cooled, and the quiet of the night felt like it pressed down on them like a weight.

"You all right?" Paul asked after a moment, his voice calm.

Joe shrugged, stuffing his hands into his pockets. "I'm fine," he said, but the edge in his voice told a different story. "Chuck just gets under my skin sometimes. Acts like he's the only one carrying a load. I guess my frustration just boiled over tonight."

Paul nodded, letting the silence stretch between them before replying, "Maybe part of it is because he doesn't know how to share the load. He keeps things to himself and lets the pressure build up. And," Paul hesitated, choosing his words carefully, "he doesn't have the faith that we do. That makes it harder."

Joe didn't reply, his gaze fixed on the path ahead. Paul decided not to press further, knowing the conversation would happen when Joe was ready. For now, the most important thing was keeping the crew together, even if the cracks weren't fully mended.

As they reached the barracks, Paul's thoughts drifted to Alta. He missed her fiercely.

***

Alta sat at the small desk in their apartment, the soft glow of the lamp casting a warm circle of light over the paper in front of her. The pen felt heavy in her hand as she paused, staring at the blank page. She knew Paul might never see this letter, with him somewhere over the Pacific and the unpredictable nature of wartime mail. But writing to him felt like the only way to bridge the miles between them.

She took a deep breath and began, "My Dearest Paul".

The words came haltingly at first, but as the thoughts flowed, the pen moved steadily across the page. She wrote about her day—how she had finally found a Lutheran church nearby that felt welcoming, and how she had spent the afternoon chatting with their new neighbors, who seemed nice enough. She continued: "Once you get back from your trip, we can start going to church together. I know you wouldn't want to have a wife that's a heathen."

She paused and chuckled at the little inside joke they shared.

"Life here feels so quiet compared to what you must be experiencing," she wrote, pausing again to gather her thoughts. "The most exciting thing I did this week was bake a cake for Mrs. Evans down the hall. She's expecting a baby soon, and I thought she could use a little treat. But it's nothing compared to the work you're doing. I hope you know how proud I am of you."

Her gaze drifted to the small bouquet of flowers on the table. Every time she saw a gardenia, she thought of Paul, standing at the flower stand in San Francisco, handing her one with a smile that could light up even the foggiest day. The memory brought a bittersweet smile to her lips.

"Do you remember our trip to Golden Gate Park?" she wrote, her hand moving a little faster now. "The seals playing in the waves, the cool breeze from the ocean, and all those beautiful gardens? I can still smell the salty air and feel the slight weight of the gardenia in my hair. That day feels so far away now, but it's one of my most cherished memories."

She paused again, glancing toward a photograph of them together at Big Basin, the towering redwoods behind them. The picture didn't do the trees justice, nor did it capture the wonder she'd felt standing beneath them. The memory of the deer they'd encountered—the one that came so close, only for the picture to turn out too dark—brought a soft chuckle.

"We were here together in California for such a short time before you left for the trip, but even in that short time, we experienced some wonderful things. One day, when all this is over, we'll go back to Big Basin. We'll stand beneath those redwoods again and marvel at how small we are in comparison. There's so much I still want to see with you, so many adventures waiting for us."

Her pen hesitated as her thoughts turned more somber.

"I pray for you every night, Paul. For your safety, for your strength, and for your return. I know you're doing God's work out there, and I have faith He will bring you home to me. Until then, I'll keep writing, even if you never get these letters. It helps me feel close to you."

She signed the letter with a flourish and set the pen down, staring at the words as if willing them to reach across the miles to him. Folding the paper carefully, she slid it into an envelope, though she knew it would likely never leave the apartment.

For a moment, she sat in silence, the weight of the empty apartment pressing down on her. Then she stood, crossing the room to the small vase on the table. She touched one of the petals of the gardenia, her thoughts drifting to Paul's smile and the warmth of his hand in hers. She wondered what he was doing right now, what he was thinking about and what he was feeling.

The vast distance and the big difference in time made her feel completely disconnected from him. She supposed he was on the other side of the world right now, in Australia, a place she had only read about. She hoped that he was taking care of himself. She hoped that he was safe. Mostly, she hoped that he was thinking of her and their life together.

"I'll keep waiting," she whispered, her voice barely audible in the quiet room, "no matter how long it takes."

***

Stan was the first to arrive in the mess hall for breakfast. Normally, he wasn't much of a breakfast person—just a cup of coffee and maybe a slice of toast. But this morning, his stomach reminded him that skipping meals probably wasn't a good idea. Maybe it was the tension from the night before, or maybe he was just overdue for a decent meal. Either way, he decided to give the powered eggs a shot this morning.

He found an empty table, set down his tray, and took a sip of coffee. It was bitter and overly strong, but it was hot, and that was what mattered. There was something about coffee first thing in the morning—the warmth of the cup in his hands, the ritual of the first sip—that made even the worst brew bearable.

A couple of minutes later, Jimmy sauntered in, his tray piled high. He slid into the seat across from Stan, grinning. "How are the powdered eggs this morning? Nothing like a plate of reconstituted greatness to start the day."

Stan smirked, pushing his plate slightly forward. "They're fine, but they burnt my toast."

Jimmy raised an eyebrow, then leaned back with exaggerated disbelief. "Burnt toast? Now hold on a second—there's no such thing as burnt toast."

Stan tilted his head, puzzled. "What are you talking about?"

"Think about it," Jimmy said, gesturing with his fork. "Toast is made from bread, which is already baked. Toast is really just burnt bread, right? So saying toast is burnt is like saying water is wet. It's a tautology."

Joe appeared with his own tray, sliding into the seat next to Stan just as Jimmy finished his proclamation. "I think he's got a point," Joe said, grinning as he took a bite of his eggs. "Toast is toast, no matter how light or dark it is."

Stan shook his head, rolling his eyes. "You would agree, Joe. You two are ridiculous."

"You are absolutely correct. It's ridiculous how observant and wise we are," Jimmy said, raising his coffee cup in a mock toast.

Jimmy grinned as he took a bite of his toast—extra dark, of course. "You know, Stan, you engineers are too practical. You're missing the philosophical side of breakfast."

Stan smirked, shaking his head. "I'll leave the philosophy of toast to you two poets. I've got enough to worry about without debating rhetoric."

As the men laughed, Chuck entered the mess hall, looking slightly better rested but still carrying an air of tension. He grabbed a tray and joined the group, followed closely by Paul. As Chuck sat down, Stan noticed that Joe appeared to avoid eye contact. Obviously the previous night's disagreement still weighed on each of them.

"Morning, fellas," Paul greeted, sliding into a chair beside Stan. "What's the topic today?"

"Burnt toast," Jimmy answered. "Turns out it doesn't exist, according to Socrates and Aristotle here."

Chuck gave a faint chuckle as he scooped some eggs with a fork. "If this is the best conversation of the morning, I think I'll stick to my eggs."

Stan smiled, but his thoughts began to drift. As the others ate, joked, and talked about the day ahead, he found himself staring at his cup, the flap actuator nagging at the back of his mind.

Finally, he spoke up, his tone a little subdued now. "Listen, I've been thinking about the flap actuator."

Jimmy paused mid-bite, his expression puzzled. "Flap actuator? That's a bit of a leap from breakfast philosophy."

Stan ignored the comment, his eyes on Chuck. "The ground crew says it's fixed, but they only cleaned and lubed it. If there's real wear on the actuator, it might hold up for a while, but not forever."

Chuck set his coffee down, frowning. "You think it's still a problem?"

Stan hesitated, glancing around the table. "I can't say for sure. But it's one of those things that can bite you when you least expect it."

Paul leaned forward, his expression serious. "Is there anything else we can do before we start back?"

Stan shrugged. "Not here. Brisbane doesn't have the resources for a full replacement. I'll keep an eye on it, but when we get back to either Hickam or Hamilton, we'll want to insist on a closer look before we take on another mission."

The table fell silent for a moment, the weight of Stan's words settling over the group. Chuck broke the silence, bringing everyone back to the present. "Let's finish up here. We've got a briefing to get to, and the rest of the day is ours. Tomorrow, we start the trip home."

Despite the earlier banter about toast, no one seemed inclined to linger over their breakfast. One by one, the men quickly finished eating, pushed back from the table, gathered their trays, and headed out. The long trip out had worn on them, and last night's argument only confirmed that tensions were running high.

It would be good to get back. The next mission would feel different—more familiar, less uncertain. The excitement of the first trip had already faded, replaced by fatigue and short tempers. Yeah, Stan thought, I'm ready to go home.

He was the last to step out of the mess hall. The morning sun was high in the sky, bright and relentless. He took a deep breath, rolled his shoulders, and followed the rest of the crew toward the briefing room.

***

The briefing held no surprises. Their next mission would mirror this one—long flights, multiple stops, and bad coffee. Only this time, they'd be transporting personnel and equipment. They'd bring back army men finishing their tours, along with some worn-out airplane and Jeep parts headed stateside for repairs.

It had been a long trip, and Paul had conflicting feelings about it. In some ways, it felt like it had sped by. But when he thought about each individual leg—all the course corrections, the endless engine checks, the fatigue settling in his bones—it seemed like they had left Hamilton a lifetime ago. What was the saying? The days are long, but the years are short. In this case, it was: The flights are long, but the mission is short.

For some reason, the briefing had driven that home for him.

"So, what do you think, Chuck?" Paul asked as they walked out of the briefing room, the late morning heat already thick in the air. "Can we handle another mission?"

Chuck nodded, his stride unhurried. "We gained some good experience on this one. I'm sure we can handle just about anything."

There was something in his voice, though—something hesitant and measured. Paul had spent enough time with him to notice when Chuck was holding something back.

As they neared the airfield, Chuck slowed, watching the others drift toward the barracks. "Hey, Paul, can we talk for a minute? Before we get to the barracks?"

Paul adjusted his step to match Chuck's. "Sure. What's on your mind?"

Chuck hesitated, shoving his hands into his pockets. "I don't know exactly how to start this, but ... I guess it's about last night. The argument with Joe."

Paul stayed quiet, letting him work through it.

"I know I shouldn't have lost my temper like that," Chuck admitted, his gaze fixed on the horizon. "Joe rubs me the wrong way sometimes, but it's not just him. It's everything. The mission, the pressure, being responsible for you guys. Sometimes it feels like too much, and I don't always know how to handle it."

Paul nodded. "It's not easy, Chuck. You're in a tough spot, but you're doing the best you can. That's all anyone can ask."

Chuck stopped walking and turned toward him. "Do you really think that? Because sometimes, it doesn't feel like enough." He exhaled, long and slow. "And all those times you or Joe have prayed … I don't know. Sometimes it sticks with me."

Paul raised an eyebrow. "What do you mean?"

Chuck's jaw tightened slightly, as if wrestling with the words. "I'm not … a praying man, Paul. Haven't been for a long time. But lately, I've started wondering if I've got it all wrong. That there's got to be more to … life. It can't be just flying around and trying to hold it together."

Paul didn't respond right away. He let Chuck sit in the moment, giving him the space to keep going.

"I remember when you told me about a 'God-shaped hole.'" Chuck gave a wry chuckle. "I'll be honest, at the time, it sounded like a load of nonsense. But lately, I keep thinking about it. Maybe it makes sense. No matter what I do, it feels like something's missing. And I don't know what to do about it."

Chuck shifted his weight and looked down. "Maybe it's too late for me to change anything."

Paul's expression softened. "You know, it's never too late to start thinking about these things. To ask questions."

Chuck nodded slowly. "I'm not saying I'm ready to start showing up to church or anything, but … I guess I'm just trying to figure things out. That's all." He hesitated. "And maybe ... maybe you were onto something that night."

Paul offered a small smile. "That's a good start, Chuck. And if you ever want to talk about it, I'm here. No judgment. No pressure."

Chuck nodded again, his posture easing slightly. "Thanks, Paul. I appreciate it."

For a long moment they stood there, watching the heat shimmering off the tarmac, feeling the warm breeze, and listening to the faint bustle of the airfield in the distance.

Finally, Chuck glanced toward the barracks. "We should probably catch up with the others. Don't want to give Joe any more reasons to talk."

Paul chuckled. "Good idea. But for the record, Chuck, you're a good leader. Don't sell yourself short."

Chuck didn't reply, but the faintest hint of a smile tugged at the corners of his mouth as they started walking again.

CHAPTER NINE

Hamilton Field - October 1, 1942

The late afternoon sun cast long shadows across Hamilton Field as Alta guided the car through the base entrance. Her hands gripped the steering wheel tightly, her nerves a mix of excitement and anxious anticipation. She hadn't seen Paul in almost two weeks, and though she knew he was safe, a part of her wouldn't fully relax until she had him in her arms again.

She pulled into the small lot near the main building, scanning the area for any sign of him. The airfield was busy. She caught glimpses of airplanes moving about the runways and men moving between hangars. The roar of engines filled the air with arrivals and departures. All this activity amazed her, and she was proud that Paul was a part of it.

Then she saw him.

Paul stepped out of the building, his flight bag hanging from his right hand. He looked tired but well, his uniform slightly rumpled from the long journey. The timing amazed her. She thought she would have to wait an excruciating amount of time to see him. But now, there he was. As their eyes met, his face lit up with that million-dollar smile she knew so well, and Alta felt her heart leap. She parked quickly, not even bothering to shut off the engine before stepping out.

"Paul!" she called, her voice breaking with emotion as she hurried toward him.

"Alta Fae," he said, his voice low and full of warmth. He dropped his bag just in time to catch her as she flung her arms around his neck. For a moment, everything else faded away—the sounds of the base, the distant roar of engines. It was just the two of them.

"You're here," she whispered, holding him tightly. "You're really here."

"I'm here," he said, his hand resting on her back. "And I've missed you, and I've thought about you every day."

She pulled back slightly, looking up at him. "You look tired."

"I am," he admitted with a soft chuckle. "But seeing you? That's better than any rest I could ask for."

They lingered for a moment longer before Paul picked up his bag and followed her to the car. As they pulled away from the base, Alta glanced over at him. The rigid set of his shoulders after the stress of the long journey seemed to soften with each passing mile. She noticed the way his hands rested more loosely on his knees, his gaze shifting from the road ahead to the landscape around them. Alta kept stealing glances at him, as if making sure he was really there.

The forty-five-mile drive from the apartment in San Mateo to Hamilton had been pleasant enough. It was a nice day for a drive, but the anticipation had made her feel anxious. Now she felt relaxed with Paul in the passenger seat. She had wanted him to drive back to the apartment, but he was too tired to drive and wanted to unwind on the way home. She had gladly taken the driver's seat for the trip back to San Mateo.

Alta adjusted her grip on the large, circular steering wheel, the ridges of its smooth surface fitted comfortably under her fingers.

The 1939 Ford Deluxe handled well enough, though it took a bit of muscle to turn the wheel, especially at low speeds. She appreciated the car's reliability, especially now, as they drove away from the base with Paul finally by her side. It wasn't flashy, but it was theirs—a small piece of stability in an otherwise uncertain world. And Paul is a "Ford Man," Alta thought with a smile.

As she shifted gears with the floor-mounted lever, the engine hummed steadily, a sound she had come to associate with stability. The rhythmic thrum was almost soothing, a reminder that the car was dependable, just like Paul. She smiled at the thought as she looked over at him—she couldn't stop looking.

He was exhausted. He kept trying to tell her little details about the trip, but his head kept bobbing forward, his words trailing off into quiet murmurs. Then he would drift off for a couple of seconds before jerking awake again. She wanted to ask him so much—about the trip, how he felt, what the Pacific was like. But there would be time for that later. Right now, she was just glad he was here. Let him sleep.

As she drove, Alta thought about their own journey to this moment. Sometimes, she could look back and see how God had worked in her life, weaving moments of grace and faithfulness into her days. This moment, with Paul beside her, safe at last, was one of them. It wasn't the end of their journey, but he was here, and she was happy. Smiling softly, she tightened her grip on the wheel, silently giving thanks for every mile that had brought them here. God is good. God is faithful. Amen.

***

Hayden, Colorado - October 5, 1942

The tack room was cool, even a little chilly. This time of year, the weather could be wildly different from one day to the next. Yesterday it had been in the upper sixties; today, it was just in the mid-forties. And at 6,500 feet, winter-like weather could come without warning. But the tack room was always pleasant—not necessarily in temperature, but in comfort and peace.

Joe liked hanging out in the barn's tack room. It was a little safe haven, a place to think. And today, his thoughts kept circling back to Luke.

His brother's saddle hung where it had always been. The stirrups were still adjusted the way Luke liked them, the latigo stowed neatly, just like it was cinched up. Nine years had passed, but the saddle had hardly been touched, except to be cleaned. It wasn't a shrine, but it wasn't just a saddle either. It was a tether to a time before loss had reshaped everything.

Joe had always been the wild one of the family; Luke, the steady and responsible one. Their father had depended on Luke, their mother adored him, and Joe had idolized him. Sage was born on the ranch, and Luke had helped Joe with her from the very beginning. From halter training to reining, Luke had been by his side through all of it.

Joe could still picture their last ride together, with him on Sage and Luke on Thunder, the two of them riding a fence line along the edge of the ranch's eight hundred acres. They hadn't talked much, just the occasional exchange, letting the quiet speak louder than words.

Luke had always been the contemplative type, always lost in thought. There were times when they were having a conversation and Luke would just stop talking. He would be a million miles away. On that ride, Luke was just like that—miles away.

"Little brother," Luke had said as they paused at the top of a ridge, "this place is special. Promise me you'll always come back, no matter what happens. And if something happens to me, take care of Thunder."

Joe didn't think much of the comment in the moment. It was just another one of Luke's musings, something to file away.

But the next day, Luke was gone, and Joe's world changed forever.

Joe's chest tightened as he reached out to touch the saddle horn. The leather was cool under his fingers, smooth from years of use.

A horse whinnied in the distance, bringing him back to the present. He was glad to be home for this short break, but he missed Paul.

Paul reminded him of Luke in so many ways. He had the same quiet fortitude, the same knack for leading without trying, the same warm smile that could diffuse tension in an instant. Maybe that's why Joe had taken to him so quickly. Paul didn't just remind him of his brother—Paul had become a brother.

But then there was Chuck. Joe's jaw clenched as the memory of the argument resurfaced. Chuck didn't get it—he didn't understand that there were things more important than flying or being in charge. He didn't understand the importance of relationships with other people. And more importantly, a relationship with God. At least that's how it felt.

Joe exhaled, leaning against the wall of the tack room. Maybe he'd been too harsh. Maybe he'd let old wounds cloud his judgment. But even that realization didn't make it any easier to forgive. And he was called to forgive. After all, he couldn't know everything about Chuck's life, what struggles he faced and what obstacles he had to overcome.

He let out a soft sigh, running a hand along the smooth leather of his saddle. The familiar feel grounded him, pulling him away from the swirling thoughts of the argument with Chuck and the memories of Luke. He had only a couple days of leave left and wanted to spend as much time with Sage as possible. The ranch was his refuge, a place he would always come back to. It was a promise.

Later, he would head into town with his parents for a bite at the diner. Hayden wasn't much to look at, but it was home. The main street was simple—Jefferson Avenue was a dusty stretch lined with wooden buildings that hadn't changed much in decades. There was the general store with its creaking wooden floors, the barber shop with its striped pole out front, and the hardware store that always seemed to have whatever you needed, even if you didn't know you needed it.

The diner was the heart of the town, where ranchers gathered over coffee and pie to swap stories or catch up on the latest news. Joe could already picture the familiar faces he'd see when he walked in. You could always spot a newcomer—they either didn't have boots on or they ordered chicken instead of beef.

Out on the edges of town, fields stretched wide and open, dotted with cattle and the occasional weathered barn. Beyond that were the rolling hills and the shadow of distant mountains, a reminder of just how small the town really was in the grand scheme of things. But to Joe, Hayden was everything. It was where he'd learned to ride, where he'd worked alongside Luke, where the memories of simpler times were etched into every building and blade of grass.

The thought of going into town brought a faint smile to his face. It wasn't the food or the company he looked forward to most, it was the sense of belonging. In Hayden, he wasn't just Joe

Mitchell, the co-pilot. He was Joe, the youngest son of the Mitchell family, the kid who used to race his brother down the main street on horseback. He was the kid who used to get in trouble for putting a snake under the counter at the post office. And he was the kid who helped his dad stack hay bales until his arms ached.

Sage neighed outside the barn, bringing him back to the here and now. She knew what was coming and she was getting anxious. His old friend was always there for him.

"That's enough, time to get moving," Joe muttered to himself as he reached for his saddle. Less thinking, more riding. He stepped out into the paddock, the crisp autumn air filling his lungs. "C'mon Sage," he called to the mare, who stood waiting by the fence. "Let's make the most of it."

He paused and leaned against the door frame of the barn, watching Sage as she shifted in the paddock. He might've been biased, but to him, she was the most beautiful horse he'd ever laid eyes on. Standing a solid fifteen hands high, she was powerfully built yet moved with an easy grace. Her brown and white pinto coat gleamed in the afternoon light, the sharp contrast of colors making her stand out against the faded grasses. A wide blaze ran down her face, softening her strong features.

Her dark brown mane and tail rippled in the breeze as she lazily turned her long neck to glance at him, ears flicking forward with quiet curiosity. Joe chuckled, recognizing that look—she was expecting a treat.

"Alright, girl," he murmured, putting the saddle down and pulling a carrot from his jacket pocket and holding it out. "I came prepared."

Joe stroked the smooth line of Sage's neck as she crunched the carrot, the sound breaking the stillness. He let his gaze drift over the pasture toward the distant mountains, their peaks already dusted with snow. Soon, more would come.

Winter was coming. Before long, he'd be back in California, gearing up for the next mission. The thought weighed on him.

He wrapped his arms around Sage's neck, thinking, I wish I could stay.

***

Newton, Massachusetts - October 6, 1942

The moment Chuck stepped into his childhood home, he felt a weight being lifted off his shoulders, one he hadn't realized he'd been carrying. At first he thought it was the whiskey he'd had in Boston before coming home, but it was really just this place. This house—his home—had a way of grounding him. It didn't hurt that his mother greeted him so warmly, her hug enveloping him in the scent of lavender and something faintly sweet, like cinnamon.

The house itself never seemed to change. The front hall greeted him with its polished hardwood floors, gleaming even in the soft afternoon light. The grand staircase still had the same dark wood banisters, their finish worn smooth from the years of hands sliding down them. Family photos lined the walls, and he couldn't help but notice how crowded they'd become. At this rate, his mother would need to start overlapping frames or move them to another wall.

He had made his way to the kitchen, passing through the dining room with its long oak table and simple but elegant lace tablecloth. The kitchen was the heart of the home, as warm and familiar as ever. The faint smell of coffee lingered in the air, mixing with the scent of something simmering on the stove—stew, maybe, or a roast. The checkered curtains over the windows swayed slightly in the breeze, letting in slivers of sunlight that danced on the enamel countertop.

Chuck had already spent the better part of an hour with his father out in the garage, tinkering with the old Indian motorcycle that had been his father's pride and joy since Chuck was a teenager. They'd gotten along well enough, but his father always found a way to remind him he wasn't quite measuring up. "You're holding that wrench wrong," he'd said with a chuckle, or, "Guess they don't teach you that in flight school, huh?" They were small jabs, said with a grin, but they carried just enough weight to sting.

Now, standing in the kitchen, Chuck felt the lingering traces of those moments with his father. He poured himself a glass of water and leaned against the counter, watching his mother move around the room with practiced ease. She was stirring something on the stove, her apron tied neatly around her waist, and humming a tune he didn't recognize.

"How was the garage?" she asked without turning around.

"Same as always," Chuck replied. "Still smells like grease and sawdust. Dad's still trying to get that thing running smooth. But he's still handy with a wrench."

His mother laughed softly. "That garage his is kingdom. You know, he'll never admit it, but he's always been so proud of you, Chuck."

Chuck huffed. "He has a funny way of showing it."

She turned then, wiping her hands on her apron and giving him a knowing look. "Oh, he's tough on you, but that's just his way. He's proud, even if he doesn't always say it."

Chuck didn't respond right away, letting his gaze drift to the window. Outside, the backyard looked the same as it always had, with neatly trimmed hedges, the small vegetable garden his mother insisted on keeping, and the swing hanging from the big oak tree where he used to push his younger brother and sister.

"At least he doesn't make me call him 'Colonel' like the DiAngelos down the street." A smirk tugged at the corner of his mouth. "How are the twins?"

His mother smiled, her face lighting up. "Oh, you know them. Full of energy, always running off to some school event or the other. They'll be back soon. They'll be thrilled to see you."

Chuck nodded. "It'll be good to see them too." He crossed to the counter where his mother had been working on a salad and casually plucked a carrot from the cutting board.

"Hey!" She swatted his hand away. "Go steal something from the icebox if you're that hungry."

Chuck snickered, chewing. His smile faded as he leaned against the counter. "Do you still go to church?" he asked, the question slipping out before he could stop it.

His mother raised an eyebrow. "Every Sunday, you know that. Why?"

Chuck hesitated, fiddling with the carrot in his hands. "There's this fella on the crew, Paul. He, uh ..." His words trailed off.

Before he could continue, the back door creaked open, and his father stepped into the kitchen, wiping his hands on a rag.

"Did you see the papers last month?" his father said without preamble. "The Eastern Solomons—those Navy pilots flying Wildcats off the *Enterprise* really gave it to the Japs. Took down a whole mess of their planes and saved our carriers. Now that's fighting."

He paused, glancing at Chuck. "Those boys did real damage out there. Brave pilots. Too bad you couldn't be flying one of those Wildcats off the *Enterprise*. I still don't exactly understand what you're doing out there in that bomber."

Chuck's grip tightened around the carrot, snapping it in two. The words hit him hard, slamming into his chest. His father didn't even notice. Suddenly that weight was back on his shoulders.

His mother shot a sharp look at her husband but stayed silent.

Chuck's jaw tightened. "What I'm doing out there is just as dangerous as flying a Wildcat. I could die out there. I almost did several times on our last mission. I can't believe—."

He stopped himself. What's the point? He's never going to see it differently.

His father grunted, already turning back toward the garage. "I'll be out back."

Chuck stared after him for a long second, the tension in his chest tightening before he finally let out a slow breath.

His mother's voice was softer now. "Don't let him get to you, Charlie."

Chuck let out a dry laugh, but there was no humor in it. "Yeah, I know. I just wish he could understand. It's never enough with him. Not graduating at the top of my high school class, not honors from MIT, not my commission, nothing."

His mother touched his arm gently. "It's not you he's disappointed in."

Chuck didn't answer. He wasn't so sure about that.

He stepped back, the tension still simmering. "I'm going out."

His mother's face pinched with worry. "But, Charlie, dinner's almost ready. When will you be back?"

Chuck shook his head. "I don't know. Don't wait for me."

He grabbed his coat from the hook and marched to the door. The latch clicked sharply as he pulled it open, and the cool October air hit him as he stepped out onto the front porch. The door closed harder than he meant it to behind him.

For a moment, Chuck just stood there, staring out at the quiet street. The fading light stretched long shadows across the well-kept lawns. Somewhere down the block, a dog barked.

He shoved his hands deep into his coat pockets and started walking, the chill biting through the fabric. He wasn't sure where he was going. For now, he would just walk.

***

San Rafael, California - October 6, 1942

The bowling alley was smoky and loud but strangely comforting. The steady crash of pins and bursts of laughter blended into a rhythm that made the place feel inviting. Victory Lanes was packed. Servicemen in uniform crowded the lanes, some with dates on their arms, others sharing pitchers of beer and baskets of fries. The air smelled of spilled beer and the faint burn of fried foods.

A hand-painted banner stretched across the wall above the lanes:

Bowling for the Brave
Half-Price Games and Drinks for All Servicemen!
Every Thursday Night - Show Your ID!

Dim lights glinted off the polished wooden lanes, and the jukebox in the corner hummed with Glenn Miller's "In the Mood" barely cutting through the chatter.

Stan weaved through the crowd, balancing two frosty beers, and slid one across the table to Jimmy.

"New game?" Jimmy asked, stretching out his arm lazily.

Stan smirked, settling into his seat. "I guess you don't mind getting beaten again."

Jimmy chuckled, taking a long sip. "I'm just warming up."

Stan leaned back, scanning the lively crowd. "Feels good to be out, around other people, having a good time, huh? No pressure, no engines roaring in your ears. Just ... this."

Jimmy grinned, "Yeah. Beats listening to Chuck and Joe snap at each other."

Stan laughed. "Ain't that the truth. You think they'll kill each other before the war's over?"

"Nah," Jimmy said, setting down his drink. "But I wouldn't be surprised if Paul's gotta play referee again."

Stan shook his head with a grin. "Better him than me."

A cheer erupted from a nearby lane as a sailor nailed a strike and turned to slap hands with his buddies.

Jimmy raised his beer. "To a quiet night off."

Stan clinked his glass against Jimmy's. "I'll drink to that."

They both sat for a moment, letting the comfort of the night settle in.

Stan took another sip of his beer, then glanced at Jimmy, tilting his head slightly. "So what got you into the Air Transport Command?" he asked casually. "No offense, but you don't exactly strike me as the military type. Just sayin'."

Jimmy chuckled softly, swirling the beer in his glass. "Yeah, you're not wrong. A high school geography teacher from small-town Iowa doesn't exactly scream military material." He paused, staring at the condensation on his glass. "I didn't enlist right after Pearl Harbor. Took me a bit. But I wanted to do something. Couldn't join the Army proper—old knee injury from college. But navigation? Maps, charts ... that made sense. ATC felt like the right fit."

Stan leaned back, considering that. "Geography, huh? Guess that makes sense now. You always seem to know where we are, even when we're flying over nothing but water."

Jimmy smirked. "Well, I'd hope so. Otherwise, we'd be in real trouble."

Stan laughed, raising his beer. "Fair enough. To keeping us off the ocean floor."

Jimmy clinked his glass against Stan's. "I'll drink to that. What about you?"

Stan tapped the bottom of his glass lightly on the table. "I come from a long line of mill workers back in Fall River. Spent my summers sweeping floors in the mills, watching my old man and brothers work. Good, honest work, but it wasn't for me. I wanted something different. So, after high school, I skipped the mill and went off to Boston for mechanic school. Got into aviation mechanics after that, did a few apprenticeships."

He paused, his fingers tracing the condensation on his glass. "But I gotta be honest. Sometimes I feel a bit out of my league here with all you smart, college-educated types. I don't have that. I just don't want people to look down on me because of where I came from."

Jimmy leaned forward, resting his elbows on the table. "Let me tell ya something—you've got nothin' to worry about. There's different kinds of education, and I know college folks who wouldn't know a piston from a hammer."

He hesitated for a moment, studying Stan before leaning forward and jabbing a finger at him.

"And as far as anyone looking down on you? I wouldn't trust anyone else with that plane. Heck, you caught that overheating engine over Fiji before it turned into a real mess. You know that bird better than most ground crew."

Stan allowed a small smile. "Yeah, well ... maybe."

Jimmy grinned. "No 'maybe' about it. You're the reason we're still flying."

Stan leaned back, relaxing a little more. "Appreciate that, Jimmy."

Jimmy raised his glass again. "To the man who keeps us in the sky."

Stan chuckled and clinked his glass. "And to the man who keeps us from flying in circles."

They both took long pulls from their pints. Jimmy drained his glass and slammed it down on the table with a satisfied, "Ahhh."

At that moment, the jukebox crackled and shifted to a slower tune: "I Had the Craziest Dream" by Harry James. The rich brass swelled, and Helen Forrest's soft, wistful voice floated through the air. For a second, it felt like the noise of the bowling alley softened, or maybe someone had turned up the volume. Either way, the ballad seemed to drift into every corner of the room, slowing the steady rhythm of crashing pins.

Stan leaned back, his eyes half-closed as he listened. For a few minutes, both fell silent as a woman's clear, silky singing rose above the sounds of woodwinds and brass and floated across the room. "Oh, man. Helen Forrest—what a sweet voice," he said, almost dreamily.

Jimmy smirked. "Didn't peg you for a romantic."

Stan chuckled. "Nah, it's not that. Just ... songs like this make you forget for a second, you know? Almost makes me forget about that flap actuator."

Jimmy's smirk faded slightly.

Stan exhaled, rubbing the back of his neck. "I don't want to sound like a broken record, but I just can't get that out of my mind.

We get up in the air again, and if that thing jams at the wrong time ..."

Jimmy hesitated for a beat, slowly tracing with his finger a ring of condensation left on the table by his empty glass. He didn't say it aloud, but the thought had crossed his mind too. He leaned in, voice lower. "You're doing everything you can. We all know that, and it's holding up. If it weren't, you'd be the first to ground us. Don't let it eat at you."

Stan stared into his glass, then gave a small, resigned nod. "Yeah. Maybe you're right."

The song lingered for a moment longer before the jukebox shuffled on, and the noise of the alley swelled back to life.

"I wonder how the rest of the crew is doing," Jimmy said, tipping his chair back.

Stan leaned back, staring at the ceiling for a moment. "Yeah, I hope Paul's getting some real time with his new bride. Must be hard. Newly married, then flying off for weeks at a time." He swirled his drink slowly. "All that distance—it can wear on a man."

A ball thundered down the lane behind them, scattering pins in every direction. The cheers of excitement filled the space again, but Jimmy and Stan sat quietly, lost in their own thoughts.

Jimmy finally spoke, his voice quieter this time, barely heard above the background noise. "Yeah, that's tough—lots of distance."

Stan didn't answer but nodded slowly, eyes still on the swirling amber in his glass.

***

Golden Gate Park, San Francisco - October 8, 1942

Alta walked with Paul, arm in arm, through the Conservatory of Flowers at Golden Gate Park, one of their favorite places. The late afternoon sun was low on the horizon, casting a warm, golden light through the canopy of trees. Shadows stretched long across the paths, and the crisp scent of autumn leaves mingled with the soft fragrance of flowers.

She gently adjusted the gardenia in her hair—the one Paul had bought her earlier in the day. It had become their little tradition, and now, whenever she saw one, she thought of him. A soft smile touched her lips at the thought, but it faded as the weight of his upcoming departure settled back on her chest.

Two more weeks without him. Two more weeks in the small, quiet apartment. Two more Sundays sitting alone in the pews, answering polite questions about Paul, but feeling the void where he should be. Two more weeks with a hole in her heart.

She tightened her grip on his arm. Say something, she thought. But she didn't want to spoil this perfect moment with the sadness gnawing at her.

The distant roar of aircraft engines pulled her gaze skyward. A pair of military planes crossed the sky, trailing faint white lines behind them. The sound rumbled through the trees and slowly faded.

Before she could stop herself, the words slipped out in a breathless whisper.

"I don't want you to go. Please don't go."

The second she said it, she regretted it, feeling foolish. She knew he had to go. But knowing didn't make it any easier.

Paul's hand instinctively went to his wedding ring, twisting it slowly around his finger. She knew that gesture well.

"Dearest Alta," he said softly, his voice steady but warm, "I wish I could stay. More than anything, I want to stay here with you. But you know why I have to go."

Alta's throat tightened. "I know," she murmured. "I just didn't think it would be this hard."

Paul slowed their steps, turning slightly to face her. His eyes, tired yet loving, searched hers.

"Every time I leave, I carry you with me. You're here," he lifted her hand to his chest, resting it over his heart, "and here," he tapped his temple lightly.

Alta smiled faintly, though her eyes shimmered.

"Please," she said, her voice trembling, "just promise me you'll always come back to me."

Paul leaned in, pressing a tender kiss to her forehead. "Every time I come back, I'll buy you a gardenia. Every. Single. Time."

Her breath caught. She would cling to those words.

They walked in silence for a few moments, the rustle of leaves and distant buzz of the city filling the space between them.

Then Paul tilted his head slightly, his eyes tracing the treetops. "What do you think of Joe?" he asked suddenly.

Alta let out a soft laugh, the sudden shift catching her off guard but easing the weight of the moment. "He's a character, that's for sure. But I don't think you could find a better friend." She squeezed Paul's arm. "We just need to find a wife for him."

Paul chuckled. "Yeah, but he might already be married to his horse."

Alta giggled.

Paul hesitated for a moment, then glanced at her. "Actually, I wanted to ask you something."

Alta raised an eyebrow, teasing. "Oh? Sounds serious. What kind of question?"

Paul smiled. "Well, Joe wanted me to ask if you and I might want to visit his ranch in Colorado after the war. Said he could make a cowboy out of me."

Alta laughed—a bright, genuine laugh. "You? A cowboy? I'd pay good money to see that."

Paul grinned. "Yeah, well, I told him I'd think about it. But it might actually be fun. I'd get to see him in his natural habitat."

Alta squeezed his arm, leaning her head briefly against his shoulder. "I think we should. It sounds ... nice."

Paul nodded, his gaze drifting back to the trees, his fingers tightening gently around Alta's hand as they continued down the winding path. The golden light filtering through the trees was beginning to fade, casting long shadows across the garden beds. The hush of the park settled around them, broken only by the distant rustle of leaves and the soft chatter of couples passing by.

Neither of them spoke for a while. There didn't seem to be much left to say.

As they neared the exit of the conservatory, Paul slowed. "How about we stay out a little longer?"

Alta looked up at him, curiosity softening her eyes.

"There's that little cafe near the water," Paul continued. "We could grab a coffee. Maybe sit for a bit before heading home."

Alta smiled faintly. "One more gardenia for the road?"

Paul chuckled. "Only if they serve them with the coffee."

They made their way toward the cafe, the quiet between them comfortable. Paul ordered two cups of coffee, simple and black, the way they both preferred. They sat on a bench outside, the steaming cups warming their hands against the cooling air.

The distant sound of waves brushing the shore mingled with the quiet hum of the city beyond the park.

Alta watched a small group of children chase each other near the edge of the park, their laughter bright in the dimming light.

Paul followed her gaze. "One day, maybe we'll bring our own kids here."

Alta's breath caught, and she glanced at him, surprised but touched.

"Would you like that?" he asked softly.

She didn't answer right away, but the small, steady smile that spread across her face was answer enough.

The sky deepened to a dusky purple, and the first stars began to peek through.

Paul finally broke the silence. "We should head home soon, I guess."

Alta nodded, but her fingers tightened slightly around his arm, reluctant to move, as she tried her best to lengthen the moment.

When they finally rose to leave, Paul paused for a moment, looking back at the park as if trying to memorize it.

As they started walking, Alta slipped her arm back through his, leaning into him.

Tomorrow would be upon them soon enough. At least they had this moment. Alta would remember it forever.

CHAPTER TEN

Nouméa Airfield, New Caledonia – October 23, 1942

T he outbound trip from Hamilton to Brisbane had been long and grueling. Each leg dragged on endlessly—tension high, tempers thin. The storms from their first mission hadn't followed them this time, but in their place came minor equipment failures and fatigue-driven mistakes. Now, in New Caledonia, the crew finally had a moment to breathe.

Tropical air clung to Lieutenant Joe Mitchell's skin as he leaned against the fuselage of their C-87, arms folded. The steady noise of ground crews working nearby filled the humid afternoon air. Joe squinted at a group of mechanics clustered beneath another C-87 a few planes down. Wing panels were stripped away, exposing flap mechanisms and hydraulic lines, vital systems laid bare.

"That's the second one this week with flap issues," a voice muttered beside him. "Had to come in with a flaps-up landing."

Joe turned to see Lieutenant Frank Harper, a pilot he'd gotten to know in Brisbane. Harper's flight suit bore streaks of oil, his face carved with exhaustion.

"What are they saying?" Joe asked, nodding toward the grounded transport.

Harper sighed, dragging a hand through his damp hair. "Flap actuators again. Same thing your engineer was griping about, right? Parts are scarce out here. Command says replacements are coming, but I've been hearing that same ol' song for days."

Joe's jaw tightened. Stan had been quietly stewing over their own flap issues for days. It wasn't like Stan to voice concerns without reason, and when he did, Joe paid attention.

"What are they doing about it?" Joe pressed.

Harper gave a half-shrug. "Lubing things up, swapping parts between planes when possible—makeshift fixes. Not much else to do when replacements crawl through the pipeline, thousands of miles across the Pacific. It's a mess."

Joe's gaze drifted toward Stan, crouched by their plane's landing gear, hands black with grease, brow furrowed in concentration.

"Any word if these issues have caused ... incidents?" Joe asked quietly.

Harper's eyes darkened. "Nothing official. But rumors? Yeah. Hard landings. Close calls. Command's keeping it quiet. Can't afford to ground these planes, not with cargo piling up."

Joe exhaled slowly, the weight of it all pressing down. "Appreciate the heads-up, Harper. Stay safe."

Harper gave a tired nod and drifted back to his crew.

Joe lingered, the distant drone of engines settling around him. His eyes found Chuck leaning against the other end of the fuselage, arms crossed, staring into the middle distance.

The time at home had cleared Joe's head. Being back at the ranch with Sage had grounded him. He'd been trying to see things from Chuck's side. Joe didn't know much about Chuck's past, but something weighed heavily on him. A conversation with his mother had shifted Joe's perspective.

At dinner in downtown Hayden, Joe had vented to his parents about Chuck—how self-absorbed and distant he seemed. He'd told them about their argument in Brisbane.

His mother had listened patiently, then asked, "Joe, what's Chuck's favorite color?"

Joe blinked. "How should I know?"

"What did he do for fun before the war?"

"I don't know. Argue over the finer points of leaf raking?"

"Does he have siblings?"

Joe's defenses slipped.

She leaned in slightly, tilting her forehead toward him as she said softly, "You don't even know the simplest, most superficial things about him. How can you possibly understand what he's struggling with?"

Then she quoted Scripture: "How can you say to your brother, 'Let me take the speck out of your eye,' when you yourself fail to see the plank in your own eye?"

Joe dropped his head, closing his eyes. She was right.

"Get to know him, Joe. Then be the man I know you are."

Her words echoed in his mind as he slowly walked toward Chuck.

"Chuck. Got a minute?"

Chuck glanced over, guarded. "What's on your mind, Cowboy?"

Joe rubbed the back of his neck. "Talked to Harper. They're seeing the same flap issues. Stan's on edge. Might be worth pushing this up the chain."

Chuck's jaw tightened, then loosened with a slow nod. "We've logged it. Maintenance says it's within tolerances, but yeah. We need to escalate if it's not getting fixed."

Joe hesitated, then stepped closer. "Thanks, Chuck. And ... about Brisbane. I was out of line. You're the pilot, and I respect that. I'm here to support you. I'm praying for you. Just wanted you to know that."

Chuck blinked, caught off guard. His posture stiffened briefly before he let out a quiet breath.

"Thanks, Joe. I owe you an apology too. And ... I probably need those prayers."

Joe gave a small nod. "Anytime. I'm going to grab a bite to eat before we have to depart for Fiji. Want to come along?"

Chuck hesitated, then glanced up at Joe. "No thanks. I'll grab something later. But thanks for asking."

Joe offered a brief nod and turned toward the mess hall. His mother had been right, as usual. He'd do his best to know Chuck better. Even though Chuck was a tough nut to crack, Joe sensed he'd just seen a different side of him—something quieter, more open. And that comment about needing prayer? Joe hadn't expected that.

As Joe walked away, he sensed the wall between them beginning to crumble. Grudges were a strange thing. You tell yourself they make you stronger, help you stand firm in your convictions.

But really, they're just stones in your pockets—an unnoticed burden at first, but over time, they drag you down. Forgiveness—that's where real strength lives.

And maybe today, he'd finally taken a step toward it.

Maybe today, he could move on.

***

Kiritimati (Christmas Island) - October 27, 1942

Kiritimati, also known as Christmas Island, is little more than a speck in the vast Pacific—a remote refueling and maintenance stop between Canton Island and Hawaii. Normally, the crew would've flown straight to Hickam Field, but orders had them divert here to pick up personnel heading home. Isolated and sweltering, the island sits about 1,300 miles south of Hawaii and 1,100 miles northeast of Canton. Hot, humid, and bare boned, it wasn't a place anyone lingered by choice.

Despite its small size, the airfield buzzed with activity. Ground crews moved briskly among the transport planes, trucks rumbled over coral-packed paths, and distant voices echoed from the scattered buildings. But there was something else in the air—a quiet tension that clung heavier than the heat.

Paul wandered along the edge of the tarmac, boots crunching on coral dust. His eyes followed a group of mechanics clustered around a grounded plane, their movements subdued. He noticed several low buildings in the distance and began walking toward them, seeking some shade or maybe a quiet corner to rest.

"Paul!"

The sharp call made him turn. Jimmy sprinted toward him flushed and breathless.

"Where are the other fellas?" Jimmy panted, barely slowing.

Paul frowned. "Scattered. What's going on?"

Jimmy stopped up close, voice lowered. "I just overheard a radio operator. The Navy's in bad shape. Battle of the Santa Cruz Islands—real bad. The *Hornet's* gone."

Paul blinked, stunned. "Gone?"

Jimmy nodded grimly. "Sunk. The *Enterprise* took hits too. She's all that's left out here."

Paul stared past Jimmy, the airfield quieter now it seemed. The USS *Hornet*—gone. The star of the Doolittle raid and one of the last fleet carriers holding the line in the Pacific.

"That leaves the *Enterprise*," Paul muttered, as if saying it out loud might make sense of it.

Jimmy's voice dropped lower. "And she's limping. *Saratoga's* still in drydock, and *Wasp*—gone last month. We've got nothing else."

Paul exhaled slowly. The Pacific had always felt vast. Now it felt empty—exposed.

"This changes things." His voice was quieter now.

Jimmy nodded. "Yeah. No carriers means no cover. Supply runs like ours are wide open."

Paul's jaw tightened. The roar of engines around them came back into focus, but still seemed distant, like echoes off a distant mountain range. The war felt closer now, heavier. The fragile thread holding their operations together had frayed even more.

"We need to find Chuck. He should hear this."

Jimmy wiped sweat from his brow. "Yeah. Feels like the war just got a whole lot bigger."

Paul glanced toward the horizon, where the endless blue ocean and sky seemed to stretch on forever. Somewhere out there, the *Enterprise* was fighting to stay afloat. And here they were, one more vulnerable cargo plane over a very unforgiving ocean.

"Let's move."

Paul led Jimmy toward the small cluster of buildings he'd spotted earlier, hoping to gather the rest of the crew. As they rounded the corner into the shade, Paul nearly collided with Joe.

"Hey, easy there, fella." Joe took a step back, raising his hands, outstretched. "Who put a burr under your saddle?"

Paul sidestepped around Joe but didn't slow down, saying, "Jimmy's got news everyone needs to hear. You seen Chuck and Stan?"

Catching up with Paul and Jimmy, Joe sensed something amiss. "Yeah," he replied, "just a minute ago. They should be close."

The three cut around the side of the building, spotting Chuck and Stan emerging from a doorway, each holding a bottle of Coca-Cola, the glass sweating in the humid air.

Stan raised his bottle with a faint grin. "Luke-warm Cokes inside if you're thirsty. Better than nothing."

Paul motioned them over, his expression serious. Once they were gathered, he quickly relayed what Jimmy had overheard about the *Hornet* at Santa Cruz. His words hung in the thick air as the group fell silent.

Chuck's eyes darkened. He stared at the ground for a long moment, jaw tight, then slowly nodded. When he spoke, his voice was quieter than Paul expected.

"That's ... hard to swallow." Chuck looked up, scanning the faces around him. "I'm thinking about the men we lost. Fathers, sons, husbands. Families who'll never see them again." His gaze drifted for a moment before he caught himself. He straightened slightly, the weight of command settling back on his shoulders.

"But we still have a job to do. It was dangerous before—now it's worse. For us, the only thing that's changed is how sharp we need to be. Focused in our thoughts. Deliberate in our actions. No mistakes."

Chuck's tone shifted, steady and deliberate. "Before we leave, I want full mechanical checks, debriefs with the ground crew, and a run-though of every checklist we've got. This is no time for slip-ups."

Paul felt a quiet pride stir in his chest. *This* was the Chuck they needed.

"Get something to eat and get some rest. Tomorrow, we've got work to do. After breakfast, we'll start the mechanical checks and talk with the ground crew. That's all."

The crew dispersed without hesitation, their steps purposeful. Yet Paul lingered. Something in Chuck's expression made him pause. He wasn't sure what he planned to say, only that Chuck needed some encouragement.

Paul stepped closer. "The men responded well to that. You turned bad news into something solid. Gave us direction instead of letting us stew in the negative."

Chuck's gaze softened for a moment. "Yeah. We all need that."

He hesitated before continuing, his voice quieter. "I'm glad you stuck around. I've got something to ask you."

Paul raised a brow. "Sure. What's on your mind?"

Chuck's eyes didn't meet his at first. "I don't get it. Surely there were godly men on the *Hornet*. Good men. Gone in an instant. Why?"

Paul was quiet for a beat, weighing his words. "The honest answer? I don't know. Maybe it was their time. Maybe it's something we can't understand. God doesn't promise us safety, Chuck—just that He's with us through it all. If we could understand everything He does, well … He wouldn't really be God, would He?"

Chuck seemed to mull that over, his brow tightening slightly. The tension in his shoulders didn't ease, but something in his eyes shifted—an acknowledgment, maybe.

"I suppose that's true," Chuck murmured, almost to himself.

Without another word, he turned toward the mess hall. Paul fell in a step beside him, giving him space to think.

Sometimes, Paul thought, you don't need all the answers, just the right question to start looking for them.

***

250 Miles Northeast of New Caledonia - October 28, 1942

Lieutenant Frank Harper rubbed the back of his neck, trying to ease the dull ache that had been with him since sunrise. He hadn't slept well—hours of tossing and turning, mentally flying every leg of their return trip. By the time sleep finally claimed him, it was nearly morning, and he woke with a pounding headache and a stiff back.

Now, hours into the flight, the C-87 droned steadily over the endless stretch of Pacific. Below them, nothing but blue. Above them, more blue. Behind them, New Caledonia—three frustrating days of repairs finally behind them. Ahead, Fiji. Beyond that, Hawaii.

But Hawaii felt very far away.

Frank thumbed the intercom. "Skip, how's everything looking back there? Anything I need to worry about? I'm still thinking about those flaps."

The flight engineer's voice crackled in his ears.

"So far so good. But honestly, sir, we won't know for sure until we drop them."

Frank gave a quiet grunt. "Fair enough. Keep me posted."

He released the mic and leaned back in his seat, but the tension in his shoulders wouldn't ease. Maybe it was the extra cups of bitter coffee that morning, but something else gnawed at him. The news of the *Hornet*—sunk just hours ago at Santa Cruz—was still fresh. A fleet carrier gone.

They were flying over waters that felt thinner, less defended—closer to the fighting than Frank liked to admit.

He glanced at his co-pilot, Dan Cromwell, quietly scanning the instruments. Maybe he'd hand over the controls later, let Dan log some hours while he cleared his head. But not yet. Something felt off. This wasn't time to relax.

He shifted in his seat and keyed the intercom again. "Sparky, picking up anything unusual on the radio?"

"Nothing on standard frequencies, boss. But I'm only scanning the frequencies in the mission profile. Want me to poke around a bit?"

Frank hesitated. It was probably nothing, but that feeling in his gut hadn't let up. "Yeah. Scan the other bands. Let me know if anything jumps out."

"Roger."

Frank leaned back, eyes fixed on the horizon. Back on New Caledonia, just before he'd climbed into the cockpit, a wave of nausea had hit him. He seemed to have a knack for sensing trouble—something in his gut warned him when things were about to go sideways. Sometimes it was a flicker in the back of his mind, other times it was like a stone in his stomach. He'd initially blamed the nausea on breakfast—God knew the food on New Caledonia could turn a man's stomach—but the feeling was still there, coiled like a snake ready to strike.

His mind drifted to a memory from years ago. He and his younger brother had been swimming in the river near their home. Frank was stretched out on the bank, half-asleep, when a sudden wave of nausea jolted him upright. That's when he saw his brother being swept downstream, thrashing in the current. Frank hadn't hesitated. He'd sprinted along the bank and pulled him out just in time. He never forgot that feeling—that internal warning bell.

And now, that same warning was clanging louder by the second. A bead of sweat slid down his temple and he shook his head trying to free it.

Frank keyed the intercom. "Sparky, anything?"

There was a tense pause, then Will's voice crackled through. "Sir, I'm picking up some broken chatter. Something about Zeroes …"

Frank sat up straighter. "Say again?"

Before Sparky could answer, Dan snapped his head around, eyes wide. "What was that?"

Frank's pulse hammered. "Son of a gun! We've got company."

Almost on cue, two small fighters burst from the sun, diving hard—sleek silhouettes of menace. Frank barely had time to think. Instinct kicked in.

He shoved the yoke forward and banked as hard as he dared to the left. The lumbering C-87 groaned under the strain, but the sudden drop sent a stream of gunfire slicing harmlessly through the air where they'd just been.

"Sparky! Get a distress call out—NOW!"

"I'm on it!" Will barked, already flipping switches.

Dan strained against his harness, scanning frantically.

"Where'd they go? I can't see 'em!"

"They're circling for another pass," Frank growled. "We can't outrun 'em, and we sure as hell can't outfly 'em."

The engines roared as Frank started a shallow weave, banking just enough to throw off the Zeroes' aim. It wasn't much, but it was all the C-87 could handle.

The sharp *tat-tat-tat* of machine guns tore through the air. Holes punched through the fuselage, jagged light cutting across the cabin.

"Will! That call—how are we looking?"

"Signal's out! Trying to raise Efate now!" Sparky's voice was thin with strain. "They should be close enough to hear us."

More rounds ripped through the tail section, the plane shuddering under the assault.

Frank's mind raced. "Hang on! Diving for speed!"

He shoved the yoke forward again, and the engines screamed in protest. The C-87 nosed down hard, clawing for more airspeed.

"Careful, Frank!" Skip's voice crackled through the intercom, forced calm edging toward panic. "You push her too hard, she'll come apart before they finish the job!"

Frank ignored him, eyes locked on the altimeter as they dropped—9,000 feet ... 8,500 ...

The plane screamed in the wind, groaning under the strain.

Then—a violent jolt.

BOOM.

The left wing shuddered violently, smoke and flame belching from engine number one.

"Engine one's hit! FIRE!" Skip shouted.

Warning lights flared. The plane lurched, yawing hard to the left.

Frank wrestled the yoke, gritting his teeth.

"Shut it down! Feather the prop!"

Skip was already on it. "Feathering one!"

Dan's knuckles were white on the throttle.

"They're coming around again!"

Frank's mind sharpened. No time to think—just survive.

"We're not done yet. Brace yourselves! Dan, throttle up remaining engines." Frank ordered, as he pulled back on the yoke and banked hard to the right.

"Frank, is it time to ditch?"

"Negative. We still have a chance. We'll make it to Fiji, even if we have to glide there."

Will's voice broke through on the intercom. "Frank, cavalry is on the way. Except in the form of P-39s instead of flying horses."

"Let's hope they get here soon!" Skip snapped. "Engines two through four are redlining—they can't take much more!" His usual humor was gone, replaced by pure strain.

Frank's grip tightened on the yoke.

"Here they come again!" Dan shouted, eyes locked on the canopy.

A deafening boom rocked the plane. The right wing pitched violently downward as engine four erupted in a flash of smoke and fire.

"Engine four's gone! Shutting it down—feathering the prop!" Skip's voice was thin, taught. "We're in bad shape, Frank. I'm not sure we can stay up."

Frank fought the controls, but the plane bucked hard, nose dipping toward the ocean. "Dan! On the yoke! Now!"

Dan lunged, gripping the co-pilot's controls. Together, they wrestled the shuddering beast, the airframe groaning under the strain. Instruments blurred from the violent shaking.

"Come on ... come on ..." Frank growled, muscles burning.

The plane leveled, barely, but the drag from the missing engines and gaping holes in the fuselage were fighting them every inch.

Frank's mind raced: Ditch or fly?

They could try to hold out, hope the fighters arrived, and limp to Fiji. Or ditch now. Neither option promised survival. Ditching in the Pacific was a roll of the dice—if the impact didn't kill them, the ocean might. Then there were the possible strafing runs by the Japanese pilots. But staying airborne on two strained engines, dragging half a wing, wasn't much better.

His pulse hammered in his ears.

Then, out of nowhere—salvation.

Four dark shapes streaked in from above, cutting through the sky like knives. The distinct snub-nosed profile of P-39 Airacobras dove in, machine guns blazing. Tracer rounds lit the air as they tore into the pursuing Zeroes.

Dan's breath caught. "They're here!"

Frank barely exhaled. "Thank God."

The P-39s split off, chasing the Zeroes in a vicious dogfight. The sky exploded with twisting metal and gunfire.

"Sparky!" Frank barked, "can you raise those fighters?"

"I'm trying, sir!" Will's fingers flew over the radio, desperate to reach their saviors.

Skip's strained voice filled the cabin. "Frank, engines two and three are still running hot. We've got maybe minutes if we don't ease off."

Frank's jaw tightened. The P-39s had bought them breathing room, but they were still hanging on by a thread.

"Hold her steady, Dan. Sparky, get me those fighters. Skip, keep those engines alive. We are not dying out here today."

Frank leaned into the yoke, forcing the crippled bird onward.

The fight wasn't over. But for Harper and his crew, it was far from clear who would win.

***

Hickam Field, Hawaii – October 30, 1942

If felt good to be back at Hickam Field—really good.

Even with the occasional moments of rest during layovers, every mission over the Pacific carried a weight of tension that never fully let up. But here, in the relative safety of Hawaii, Chuck felt an unexpected sense of peace, almost surreal, like waking from a long, restless dream.

He guided the C-87 into its designated parking spot, hands steady on the controls, and worked through the shutdown and post-flight checklists with Joe. The familiar clicks of switches and murmured confirmations grounded him in routine.

As the engines whined down and the plane settled, the crew began disembarking. Chuck noticed it immediately—shoulders dropping, faces easing. Stan stretched his arms overhead, groaning like an old man. Jimmy cracked some offhand joke—something about the difference between a pilot and a peacock—but Chuck missed the punchline. Paul laughed anyway, giving Jimmy a playful shove that nearly knocked him off balance.

Chuck watched them with a quiet pride. They'd gotten through it. The trip had been rough—full of tension, conflict, mechanical problems—but they'd held together. No, they'd *grown* together. Piece by piece, flight by flight, they were becoming a real team.

His eyes drifted past them, scanning the sprawl of the airfield. The distant thrum of other aircraft, the organized chaos of ground crews moving with practiced purpose. Civilization.

Chuck took a slow breath, letting it fill his chest. The ground felt firmer here. The air smelled cleaner. And the war—the war felt just a little further away.

The mission had been a personal milestone. It had challenged him more than any flight, any training session, any long hour spent in the cockpit. But something had shifted in him back on New Caledonia. When the crew heard about the *Hornet*, and he stepped up—without thinking, without hesitation—it had just ... clicked.

It reminded him of solving a stubborn engineering problem. You grind away at it, turning it over and over, and then—suddenly—the answer reveals itself, as if it had been there all along. That's how leadership felt to Chuck in that moment. Natural. Clear.

And now, standing on solid ground, he understood something he hadn't before. Leadership wasn't about barking orders or holding rank. It was listening. It was holding steady when everything inside was unraveling. It was being the anchor, the steady hand, the quiet strength that held the crew together when the world threatened to come apart. He couldn't help but wonder if he'd unconsciously learned some of that from Paul.

Chuck was brought back from his thought by Stan, his Massachusetts accent thicker than usual.

"I gotta get a real showah."

"Yeah, you do!" Joe shot back.

"Well, you're no bundle of flowahs yourself, yah know."

Jimmy chimed in, grinning. "You fellas suit yourselves. I'm gonna find something more refreshing to drink than warm Coke."

Chuck smirked faintly. They'd forgotten about the post-flight briefing—but that was alright. Let them enjoy this moment. He'd handle the briefing himself and catch up with them later.

As he made his way toward the operations building, Chuck passed two officers deep in conversation. He caught bits and pieces of their exchange.

"Transport shot up ... somewhere near Fiji..."

"Rumor it was a C-87 from New Caledonia ..."

"... think it was Harper's ..."

Chuck froze. His mind immediately jumped to Frank Harper, recalling his grumbling about flap issues. Harper's crew had been delayed, a couple of days behind them. Could it be?

Then the doubt crept in. Their own flap problems surfaced in his thoughts. Should he have pushed harder for a more thorough inspection? What if they were next?

No. He wouldn't go there. Panic and second-guessing wouldn't solve anything. Focus. Preparation. Discipline. That's what he told the crew. That's what he needed to remember himself. Stirring them up with rumors wouldn't help anyone. Still, the thought gnawed at the back of his mind.

Chuck lifted his gaze to the soft blue Hawaiian sky. A warm breeze brushed his face. He closed his eyes and quietly murmured.

"If you're listening, keep them safe."

He wasn't sure why he said it—or who he was even talking to. Part of him felt foolish. But another part of him knew it was necessary.

The debriefing lasted less than thirty minutes, a relief to Chuck, who was eager to unwind. Leaving the operations center, he headed toward the transport office, where he found the crew lounging in the shade, talking in low, relaxed tones.

As he approached, Joe looked up, his face curious. "Chuck, you look a little tense. Everything good?"

Chuck nodded, his expression steady. "We'll debrief after we clean up and eat. I do have something to share with the team, but it can wait for a bit."

Though his tone was composed, he could see the flicker of unease in their eyes. He didn't blame them. They had been around each other enough to know when something was bothering another crew member. But now wasn't the time to stir up concerns over something that might only be a rumor.

They made their way to the barracks together, the late afternoon sun casting long shadows on the ground. The warm light felt good on Chuck's face, and the breeze carried the scent of the ocean. Overhead, palm fronds swayed with the wind, their soft rustling a reminder of simpler, more peaceful places.

Chuck lingered in the shower longer than usual, letting the warm water cascade over him. It wasn't just about washing off the grime of the mission, it was about resetting. He let the tension flow away with each drop, clearing his mind. By the time he put on a fresh uniform and stepped outside, he felt refreshed—lighter and steadier.

The crew gathered again for the short walk to the open-air mess hall, where the smell of roasted meat and fresh-baked bread greeted them. As they sat down, the sun dipped low on the horizon, painting the western sky in streaks of red and orange that seemed almost too beautiful for a world at war. Chuck paused, taking it in. What had he done to deserve being here, now, with these men?

The meal was the best they'd had in weeks—hot, hearty, and enough to fill every belly. Laughter and light conversation passed easily between them, the camaraderie palpable. It felt good to just be, to exist in the moment without the weight of a mission pressing on them.

As they lingered at the table, Paul finally voiced the question that had hovered unspoken. "Chuck, you said earlier you had something to share with us. Is now the right time?"

Chuck glanced out at the darkening sky and took a steadying breath before turning back to his crew. "Yeah, I think now's the right time."

He recounted what he had overheard on his way to the operations center—the tone of the two officers, their obvious concern as they spoke in hushed voices.

"Now, fellas, this might just be a rumor. But I suspect there's some truth to it. That area northwest of New Caledonia was heating up as we were leaving. The Japanese could've very well shot down a transport."

Jimmy's voice cut through the silence, his concern plain. "Do you think it was Harper?"

Chuck hesitated, weighing his words. "I really don't know. But one thing I do know—we can't let it affect how we do our jobs. Keep that crew in your prayers, sure. But worrying ourselves sick over it won't do a lick of good. We've got seven days off before our next mission. Use that time to rest, unwind, and clear your heads. We've got more work ahead."

The men nodded, their solemn agreement unspoken but understood. They rose from the table and filed out together, their conversation fading into the night as they made their way back to the barracks.

Chuck lingered behind, shuffling along at his own pace, savoring the coolness of the evening air. He looked up at the sky, now sprinkled with stars that seemed impossibly far away. The vastness of it all pressed gently against him, making the war—and his place in it—feel both monumental and insignificant.

Let's hope he made it; the thought was half-prayer, half-plea. He finally turned toward the barracks to join his crew.

CHAPTER ELEVEN

San Mateo, California - December 1942

They had fallen into a rhythm. It was never easy when Paul had to leave on a mission, but Alta had found ways to fill the long stretches of quiet. Sundays were for church, followed by lunch with the friends she'd made there. During the week, she volunteered in the church office, tackling light administrative work that kept her busy. Wednesdays were for women's Bible study, and once a week, she joined a neighborhood bridge game. It wasn't the same as having Paul at home, but it gave her days some structure, a way to pass the time while she waited for his return.

When Paul was home, they slipped into a routine of their own—a routine that, despite the uncertainty of war, felt wonderfully familiar. On warm evenings, they'd pull lawn chairs outside and sit together in front of their modest apartment building. Sometimes they'd talk about the future, dreaming of what life might look like when the war was over. Other times, they'd reminisce about the past, weaving old memories into stories they never tired of telling. And some evenings, they wouldn't talk at all, content just to be near each other, the silence between them as comfortable as an old quilt.

Tonight, as the stars began to sprinkle the December sky, their conversation turned to Joe. Alta had come to admire Joe in the short time she'd known him. He was different from Paul—more outgoing, quick to laugh or make a joke, and always full of energy—but she could see why the two had become close friends. What puzzled her, though, was why he was still single.

"He's such a good man," Alta said, leaning back in her chair. "Kind, loyal, loves the Lord. I don't understand why he hasn't found someone."

Paul smiled, the corner of his mouth twitching slightly. "Well, you know Joe. He's not the type to go looking for a wife. He's trusting God to handle that for him."

Alta nodded thoughtfully. "I know, and I respect that. But sometimes I wonder if God might use someone to help move that process along."

Paul chuckled. "Are you suggesting we play matchmaker?"

"Not just suggesting," she said with a mischievous smile. "I might already have someone in mind."

"Oh really?" Paul leaned back in his chair, his smile widening as he gave a slow, knowing nod. "And who might his future Mrs. Mitchell be?"

"I've told you before about Lucy, haven't I? From my Bible study?"

"Yes," Paul said thoughtfully. "Sounds like the two of you really hit it off. You've mentioned her a few times—getting to be good friends, right?"

"We are," Alta said, her tone softening as she thought of Lucy. "She's smart, caring, attractive—and most importantly, she loves Jesus as much as Joe does. Honestly, I think they'd make a great match."

Paul raised an eyebrow. "You've been giving this a lot of thought."

"Of course I have!" Alta said, grinning. "You know me—I can't help myself."

She thought back to some of the conversations she'd had with Lucy during their weekly Bible study. Lucy came from an upper-middle-class family that had been rooted in the Bay Area for generations. Growing up in Burlingame, she'd always felt the weight of her family's expectations—a subtle but steady pressure to follow in their carefully laid footsteps. Although she loved her parents dearly, and she knew they wanted the best for her, she always felt that she wanted to make her own way.

At twenty-two, Lucy was at a crossroads. While many of her peers had settled into predictable roles—working for their families, marrying into similar social circles, or quietly waiting for the war to end—Lucy was different. She had taken a job as a secretary at a local bank, a position her parents had initially regarded as temporary. But Lucy was proud of the work and found satisfaction in the independence it gave her.

Still, she often spoke of wanting something more. She wasn't entirely sure what that "more" was—whether it was furthering her education, starting a business, or simply carving out a path that felt distinctly hers. Alta admired her for that. For all her self-doubt and uncertainty, Lucy possessed a quiet determination to create a meaningful life, even if it meant veering off the course her family had mapped out.

It wasn't just her ambition that Alta appreciated. Lucy's faith was woven into everything she did. Whether it was offering heartfelt prayers at Bible study or volunteering to help coordinate church events, her conviction was as steady as her character. She was smart, caring, and approachable, with a down-to-earth quality that made her easy to like. And yet, Alta had noticed a certain wistfulness in Lucy's voice when they talked about relationships, as if she, too, was waiting for God to reveal the next step.

Paul leaned forward, resting his elbows on his knees. "So, what's the plan?"

"Well ..." Alta hesitated, a hint of playfulness in her voice. "I was thinking we could invite them both to do something casual—like some tennis. Lucy doesn't play much, but she's willing to try. And Joe, well, he's so outgoing, I'm sure he'd make her feel comfortable."

"Tennis, huh?" Paul said, rubbing his chin. "So this isn't just matchmaking—it's matchmaking on the court."

"Exactly!" Alta said, laughing. "And besides, even though tennis isn't really my thing, it'll be fun. What do you think?"

Paul considered it for a moment, then nodded. "Well, you know how much I like tennis, alright. Let's set it up. Worst-case scenario, Joe and Lucy end up with a funny story to tell about a disastrous tennis game."

"And best case?" Alta asked, a hopeful smile playing at her lips.

"Best case?" Paul smiled back. "We might get to dance at their wedding."

"Great! So, you talk to Joe, and I'll talk to Lucy. How about we set it up for Friday afternoon?"

"Friday afternoon?" Paul raised an eyebrow. "You don't waste any time, do you?"

"Why waste time when love is on the line?" Alta shot back, flashing a big smile.

Paul laughed, the sound warm and genuine. "Alright, Friday it is. And hey, we can also work on your tennis game while we're at it. Believe me, it needs a lot of work."

"Hey!" Alta exclaimed, giving him a playful swat on the arm. "I'm pretty good ... for someone who doesn't have much of an aptitude for tennis."

"And I love you anyway," Paul said, grinning.

Alta smiled and reached over, slipping her hand into his. The size and warmth of his hand were a comfort, an anchor she clung to in the ever-shifting uncertainty of their lives. She didn't want this moment to end. She was happy.

Soon, he'd have to fly off again to places she could only imagine—places she hoped, one day, he might show her. She pictured him pointing out distant landscapes and sharing stories of the skies he'd flown, things he'd experienced. But for now, she was content. Content to sit here, her hand in his, feeling the stillness and knowing he was by her side.

***

Joe adjusted the brim of his hat as he strolled into the small tennis court just down the street from Paul and Alta's apartment building. He'd been roped into a lot of things over the years, but a tennis double date? And a blind date at that? That was a first.

Paul had sold it well enough. "Just a friendly game. Good way to relax. Oh, and Alta's bringing a friend." Joe had raised an eyebrow at that, catching the no-so-subtle hint. A setup. Wonderful.

The sun was bright and the temperature was in the mid-sixties, although the air was crisp for December. The court looked decent enough. Joe wasn't much of a tennis player, but he figured he could fake it well enough to make it through the afternoon. He thought that he was there early enough to be first, but then he spotted Paul setting up a net on one side, a casual grin on his face. Joe shook his head. That grin was trouble.

Then he saw her.

Lucy Hathaway walked up with Alta, both women laughing about something Joe couldn't catch. She was tall and poised, with a confident stride that didn't quite match the modest way she glanced around. Her blonde hair caught the sunlight, and Joe noticed her smile first—warm, open, and completely disarming.

"Joe, this is Lucy," Alta said as they approached. "Lucy, this is Joe."

Lucy extended her hand. "Nice to meet you. I hear you're the tennis pro of the group."

Joe blinked, caught off guard by the playful jab. For a brief second, uncharacteristically, he was at a loss for words. Then he laughed, shaking her hand. "Not quite. I'm just here to keep Paul humble."

"Good luck with that," Lucy quipped, her eyes twinkling.

Joe's legs suddenly felt like rubber. He had never expected someone to have this affect on him. This woman, Lucy, had somehow completely enchanted him in less than a minute.

"What about you, Miss Hathaway? I'd be willing to bet you can hold your own on the court," Joe said, his confidence returning.

Lucy tilted her head slightly, a teasing smirk tugging at her lips. "I'm mostly just a spectator, but I'll give it my best shot." Her voice had a warmth that caught him off guard again.

He glanced briefly at Paul and Alta, who both wore matching grins, their attention glued to the exchange. Not exactly subtle.

"Well, whaddya say we pair up and start playing?" Paul said, clearly enjoying himself. "Alta and me against Joe and Lucy."

"Sounds good to me," Alta chimed in, picking up her racket.

Lucy adjusted the strap on her racket bag and turned to Joe. "Guess that makes us teammates," she said with a soft laugh. "Try to go easy on me."

Joe grinned. "Oh, I'm sure you can handle things. I'll try to keep up."

She laughed, and the sound seemed to linger in the air, light and effortless.

Joe had hit the ball a few times with Paul—he was good. But as Paul served, Joe noticed he was clearly holding back, keeping the game light and fun. The serve sailed directly to Lucy, who pivoted slightly and returned the ball with an effortless backhand.

The ball floated toward Alta, who swung with all her might—missing it completely.

Paul stifled a laugh and stepped up behind her, placing his hands over hers on the racket. "That was a powerful swing, sweetheart. Your form's getting better. Just keep your eyes on the ball, follow through, and look it right into the racket."

Joe raised an eyebrow at Lucy, smirking. "I thought you were just a spectator. That return looked pretty smooth. What gives?"

Lucy shrugged, her eyes sparkling. "Oh, I may have hit a ball or two before. But mostly beginner's luck."

"Yeah, right," Joe said, shaking his head as he glanced back at Paul and Alta. Paul stood behind Alta, their heads close as he guided her grip. Joe wasn't sure how much actual tennis advice was being shared, but it didn't seem to matter.

"Hey, lovebirds!" Joe called, holding up the ball. "I think it's our serve."

Paul grinned at Joe without moving. "Give us a minute. Alta's got a mean forehand coming your way."

"Oh, I'm shaking in my boots," Joe shot back, earning a soft laugh from Lucy beside him.

As Paul stepped away, Joe leaned toward Lucy. "Looks like I've got the better teammate anyway."

Lucy smirked, twirling the racket lightly in her hand. "Don't get too confident, Mitchell. Let's see if you can keep up."

They played for a short time with Paul and Alta squaring off against Joe and Lucy. The volleys were generally short—Lucy was surprisingly good, Joe and Alta ... not so much. Alta's swings were enthusiastic, but frequently off the mark, and Joe, distracted by Lucy's quick reflexes and effortless grace, missed more that he hit.

After a particularly chaotic rally that ended with the ball bouncing far out of bounds, Lucy called out, "Why don't we switch it up? Boys against girls."

"Oh, now you're in for it, Hathaway," Joe said, his grin widening. "Now who's too confident?"

"Sounds like fun," Alta replied, already walking toward the opposite side of the court. "Let's see what you fellas have got."

Paul chuckled as Joe joined him. "This should be interesting." He smirked. "Don't let me down, Cowboy."

Joe picked up the ball and turned to Lucy. "Better brace yourself, Hathaway. We're bringing the heat."

Lucy adjusted her grip on the racket, her eyes narrowing playfully. "We'll see about that. Alta and I have strategy on our side."

Joe raised an eyebrow. "Strategy, huh? This I've gotta see."

"Yep." Lucy tapped her racket lightly against her palm. "Don't underestimate us, boys."

The banter continued as the match kicked in, the energy light and infectious. Alta managed to return a few serves with surprising accuracy, eliciting cheers from Lucy and teasing groans from the men. Lucy, on the other hand, was a force—her precise returns and quick footwork kept Joe and Paul scrambling to keep up.

Joe leaned toward Paul during a pause in the action, his voice low. "She's good. Too good. You sure this wasn't a setup?"

Paul grinned. "Don't look at me, pal. You're the one who's supposed to be keeping up."

"Keeping up?" Joe muttered. "I'm just trying not to look bad."

Lucy caught their exchange and called out with a knowing smile. "Talking strategy over there, boys? Won't help."

The next rally was the best yet, lasting the longest of the game. Paul and Lucy exchanged quick returns, the ball zipping back and forth with growing intensity. Lucy's next swing sent the ball toward Joe, who deftly returned it to Alta.

Joe watched as Alta focused, her eyes locked on the ball as it arced toward her. She swung her racket with determination, her form surprisingly precise—just as Paul had coached. The ball connected solidly, sailing cleanly back toward Paul.

Caught off guard, Paul scrambled to return it, swinging with a rushed backhand. His shot veered sharply out of bounds.

Alta let out a joyful squeal, dropping her racket and bounding over to Lucy. The two embraced, jumping up and down in celebration.

Joe turned to Paul with a smirk. "Nice one, buddy."

Paul shrugged, grinning. "What can I say? I'm a good coach."

"Yeah, right." Joe chuckled, glancing back at the girls who were still celebrating like they'd won a championship. "Oh well, it's worth it. Look how much fun they're having."

The two men stood watching for a moment, smiling as Alta and Lucy reveled in their hard-fought victory. The sun dipped lower in the sky, casting a warm glow over the court, the laughter and lightheartedness of the moment lingering in the air.

Paul called out as he started walking toward the other side of the court. "Should we head back to the apartment for something to eat?"

Alta looked over, her wide grin still lighting up her face. "Yes, that sounds like a good idea."

Paul reached for Alta's hand as they walked off the court together to gather their things. Joe lingered behind, slowly making his way toward Lucy, hands tucked into his pockets.

"That was pretty impressive, especially for a beginner," Joe said, the corner of his mouth curling into a sly smile.

Lucy's eyes sparkled as she glanced at him. "Well, I have a confession to make. My family belongs to a tennis club. I played almost every weekend through high school."

Joe let out a low laugh. "Ah, a ringer. You had me fooled." His grin widened. "Well, you got me." In more ways than one, he thought.

Lucy's expression softened, a playful edge still in her voice. "You're not so bad yourself, Cowboy. And I'm not just talking about your tennis skills either."

For a moment, Joe was at a loss for words for a second time that afternoon. He felt the warmth rising to his cheeks, wondering if he might actually be blushing. He looked at Lucy, her confidence and charm balanced with an unmistakable kindness.

And right there, in the fading golden light of the evening, Joe Mitchell knew that Lucy Hathaway was someone special.

***

The apartment was quiet and relaxing. Lucy had left a little earlier, and Joe had gone home just a couple of minutes ago. It had been a fun afternoon playing tennis, and the light dinner shared among the four friends had been the perfect end to the day. Paul was in the kitchen making coffee, while Alta relaxed on the small sofa.

The radio played softly in the background, tuned to *Command Performance*, the variety show created specifically for the Armed Forces. Tonight's episode would feature Bing Crosby, the Andrews Sisters, and Bob Hope.

"That went well. I think those two really liked each other," Alta said, glancing up as Paul walked into the living room carrying two steaming cups of coffee.

Paul handed her a cup and settled onto the sofa beside her, his smile warm and relaxed. "You do have a knack for matchmaking," he admitted, blowing lightly on his coffee. "But don't let it go to your head."

"Oh, it's already gone to my head," Alta teased, taking a sip. "I think Joe and Lucy complement each other well. She's grounded and steady, and he's so full of life. They balance each other."

Paul chuckled. "That's one way to put it. I thought Joe was going to trip over his own feet with all that gawking at her on the court."

Alta laughed, the sound blending with Bob Hope's lively chatter coming from the radio. "It was pretty obvious, wasn't it? And Lucy seemed to enjoy his humor. Did you see how she kept smirking at his jokes?"

Paul leaned back, crossing his legs. "Yeah, I noticed. But it's not just that. Joe's been through a lot. If anyone could bring him a sense of calm and keep him grounded, it's someone like Lucy."

Alta's expression softened. "And she could use someone like Joe—someone who'll remind her to laugh and take risks. It's not easy to find your own path when you've spent your life living under other people's expectations."

Paul looked thoughtful. "You've really gotten close to her, haven't you?"

Alta nodded, her gaze distant for a moment. "She's a good friend. I hope this works out for both of them."

"And let's face it," Paul added with a grin. "They're a great-looking couple."

"They are at that," Alta agreed.

The melody of Bing Crosby's "White Christmas" drifted from the radio, filling the small apartment with a warm, nostalgic glow. Paul smiled at the sound, then turned his attention back to Alta. "This will be our first Christmas together. I'm glad I'll be home for it. One more mission before Christmas, and then we'll have it together."

Alta leaned over, resting her head on his shoulder. "That will be nice."

"What about us?" Paul asked quietly. "Have you ever wondered what our lives will look like when the war is over?"

Alta nuzzled further into his shoulder and took a deep, relaxing breath. "All the time," she said softly. "I dream about it, actually. A house with a little garden. A place we can really call our own, where we can put down roots. Where we don't have to say goodbye every few weeks."

Paul's voice was low. "I think about that too. A lot. This war … it's hard not knowing what's ahead. But these little stretches keep me going."

Alta lifted her head and took his hand. "And you keep me going. Every time you walk out that door, I pray. I pray for you to come back safely. And when you do, it makes it all worth it."

The music swelled in the background, and for a moment, neither of them spoke. They just enjoyed each other's presence.   ·

Alta broke the silence, smiling softly. "Do you think Joe and Lucy could have something like this?"

Paul squeezed her hand gently. "I hope so. Joe wants it, and they deserve it."

Alta leaned back into the sofa, her fingers still intertwined with Paul's. "Well, if they end up together, I expect full credit."

Paul laughed softly. "Deal."

They sat in comfortable silence as the radio transitioned to the Andrews Sisters singing "Boogie Woogie Bugle Boy." The lively tune filled the room, a cheerful counterpoint to the weighty thoughts lingering in their minds.

"Care to dance?" Paul asked.

"Do we have room in here?" Alta giggled.

"We'll make room if we need to."

Paul took Alta's hand, and they danced together as the Andrews Sisters' lively tune filled the small apartment. They twirled and laughed, their movements weaving around the limited space. When the song ended, Bing Crosby's voice returned, shifting the mood with the slower, romantic strains of "Moonlight Becomes You."

Paul pulled Alta closer, the gentle rhythm guiding their steps. He thought about spending Christmas—and every moment beyond it—with her.

"What about children?" he asked softly, his voice almost a whisper. "We've talked a little about it, but what do you think?"

"Children? Yes, I would like that," Alta replied, leaning into him. "I think it would be nice to have a little family. Of course, we'd need a bigger place. Maybe a house."

"Would you want to stay here in California after I finish my service with the ATC? Or would you want to move somewhere else?"

"I wouldn't mind moving back to Ohio," Alta said thoughtfully.

"Or maybe Nebraska," Paul added, with a slight grin.

"Yes, or maybe Nebraska. Wherever you want to go, darling," she replied warmly.

As the music faded, the radio show concluded with the familiar melody of "The Star-Spangled Banner."

Paul held Alta close, feeling a pleasant peace settle over him. Next week, duty would call again, taking him back into the vastness of the Pacific. But for now, he was home, and his thoughts lingered on Christmas—just weeks away—and the promise of coming back to her again.

CHAPTER TWELVE

Half Moon Bay State Beach, California – January 30, 1943

The air was bright and crisp, with a sharpness that hinted at winter's lingering presence, though the midday sun offered enough warmth to make it pleasant. The beach stretched wide and inviting, the golden sand speckled with small clusters of driftwood and scattered seashells. Waves rolled in steadily from the Pacific, their white crests dissolving into frothy foam as they met the shore. A gentle breeze carried the faint scent of salt and seaweed, mingling with the occasional cry of a distant gull.

Joe and Lucy had chosen a spot just beyond the reach of the tide, where the sand was soft but firm enough for their picnic blanket. Nearby, a weathered piece of driftwood stood like a natural marker, offering a bit of rustic charm to their impromptu setup. A wicker basket sat open on the blanket, revealing an assortment of simple fare: Sandwiches wrapped in wax paper, a thermos of coffee, and a few apples adding some color.

The beach wasn't deserted, but it was far from crowded. A few families and couples strolled along the shore, their laughter and conversation blending softly with the rhythm of the waves. Children darted after retreating water, leaving small footprints in the damp sand before scampering back to safety.

Lucy had slipped off her shoes, tucking her feet beneath her on the blanket, the hem of her wool skirt fluttering lightly in the breeze. Her blond curls were pinned back, though a few strands had escaped, framing her face in soft, windswept waves. She looked out toward the horizon, her expression serene, yet with a hint of something reflective in her eyes.

Joe inhaled sharply as he caught a glimpse of her. She had that effect on him. He would catch her in random moments—just a glance—and she would take his breath away. They had known each other for less than two months, but in that time, they had formed a deep bond.

Joe, sitting cross-legged beside her, reached for the thermos, pouring them each a steaming cup of coffee. He handed one to Lucy, his hands brushing hers for just a moment.

"It's a perfect day for this," Joe said, his voice warm and soft, barely audible over the waves.

Lucy smiled and nodded, wrapping her hands around the cup to keep them warm. "It really is. I'm glad we came here instead of going to the cafe. It feels so ... peaceful." She glanced at Joe, her gaze softening. "Thank you for suggesting it."

Joe leaned back on his hands, letting the sun touch his face as he looked out over the water. "I thought we could use a little escape," he said, his tone light. He glanced over at Lucy and grinned. "And I figured I owe you a good picnic after being hopeless on the tennis court."

Lucy laughed, the sound a bright note against the steady rhythm of the waves. "Our first date. I'll admit, I was impressed with your ability to miss every ball. It's a skill in its own way."

Joe chuckled, shaking his head. "Hey, I was distracted by my teammate. Hard to focus on the game with someone on the court that looks like you."

Lucy's cheeks flushed faintly, and she turned her gaze back to the ocean. "Well, you weren't so bad yourself. I guess we were quite the pair that day."

Joe shifted his gaze to the horizon, the crisp breeze fresh on his face. That first date on the tennis court was still vivid in his mind. At first, he'd been annoyed with Paul for dragging him into what he thought would be an awkward setup. But it hadn't been awkward at all. From the very start, being with Lucy felt ... right. Comfortable in a way that surprised him. Now, he couldn't imagine things any other way. He owed Paul and Alta in a big way.

His eyes flicked to Lucy's hand and the delicate ring on her finger. Some might think they were moving too fast, but he didn't care. It felt right. Since that afternoon on the tennis court, they'd spent every spare moment they could together—even if it was just for a quick cup of coffee. And with each meeting, their connection deepened, their bond growing stronger. His trips made it a little more difficult, but nothing they couldn't handle.

Last week, without hesitation, he'd walked into a small jewelry store near the base and picked out the ring. When he'd slipped it onto her finger, her expression wasn't one of surprise but of quiet certainty. They'd both known where this was headed from the very beginning. And Paul and Alta? They seemed even happier about the engagement than Joe and Lucy were.

"Should we try to pick a date?" Joe asked, his voice casual, though his grin betrayed the excitement bubbling beneath the surface. "You know, for the day we get hitched?"

Lucy raised a playful brow. "Wow, Cowboy. How romantic."

"What can I say?" he replied with a wide grin. "I really know how to charm the ladies."

Lucy tilted her head thoughtfully, her smile softening. "How about May? Spring. Life in bloom. All that jazz."

Joe nodded, the thought of a spring wedding bringing warmth to his chest. "That sounds good to me. The sooner the better."

Lucy's gaze flicked to him, her eyes bright. "Do you think your folks will be able to make it out here?"

"Oh, I've told them all about you," Joe said, his grin widening. "They wouldn't miss it for the world."

Joe stood, brushing the sand from his pants, then extended a hand to Lucy. "Come on," he said, pulling her gently to her feet. "Let's stretch our legs a bit."

Hand in hand, they wandered down the shoreline, their footsteps sinking softly into the cool, damp sand.

"Where are we going to go for our honeymoon?" Lucy asked, glancing up at Joe, her eyes glinting with playful curiosity.

"How about Colorado?" Joe suggested. "The Mitchell Quarter Horse Ranch has a guest cabin we can stay in. You'll get to see the ranch and meet Sage."

Lucy's lips curved into a smile. "That sounds perfect."

Joe gave her hand a gentle squeeze, his grin widening. "It'll be great. My two best girls in the same place—doesn't get much better than that."

Lucy laughed, leaning her head against his shoulder as they walked. The rhythmic sound of waves lapping at the shore mixed with the occasional cry of a distant gull, creating a serene backdrop to their conversation.

Joe glanced at the horizon, the sun hanging low and casting the ocean in hues of gold and amber. He couldn't believe how much his life had changed in just two months. Here he was, walking with the woman he loved, planning a wedding, dreaming of a future he'd long prayed for. His heart swelled with gratitude.

This is what he'd always wanted.

God is good.

***

San Rafael, California - February 2, 1943

Chuck walked slowly through the rows of bookcases in the downtown San Rafael bookstore. The store was small and slightly cluttered, its mismatched chairs scattered in corners like quiet invitations to linger. Most were unoccupied, but a few patrons browsed in hushed solitude, their movements as unhurried as the tick of the old clock near the entrance.

The faint smell of aged paper mingled with cedar, the kind of scent that reminded him of the comfort of a warm study on a cold night. Chuck let it settle around him as he strolled, his boots creaking against the uneven floorboards. Even the sounds added to the ambiance of the store—this was a place he could relax.

He paused in front of the Religion and Faith section, his eyes trailing over the titles. They were a mix of slim devotionals, hefty theological tomes, and everything in between. He wasn't sure what he was looking for, but something told him to stop here. Maybe it was the same voice that had started to whisper more insistently since his last mission—the one he couldn't quite place but couldn't seem to ignore either.

The trip back to Newton had left a mark on him. Shortly after returning from his last mission, he'd received a letter from his father. That alone had been enough to unsettle him. His father had never been much for writing letters—his words had always been reserved for the rare moments when they were face to face, and even then, they were usually few.

The letter was brief, almost awkward in its tone, but the message was clear: I'd like to see you if you have the time.

Chuck hadn't known whether to feel worried or curious—or both. He sent a telegram back saying he'd get there as soon as he could. The visit had been ... unexpected. And now, here he was, miles away from Newton but still carrying pieces of that trip with him.

Just then, Chuck heard the creaking of footfalls on the floor behind him. He turned around slowly, and there was Paul.

"Didn't take you for a bookworm, Chuck," Paul teased, a crooked grin curling on his face.

"I'm just looking," Chuck replied with a faint smile. "Needed to get off base for a while, and I ended up here."

"Anything in particular you're looking for? I might be able to help—I stop by here occasionally."

Chuck glanced back at the rows of books, his hand hovering near the spine of a well-worn volume. "Just looking for something worth reading. Not sure why I stopped in front of this section."

Paul nodded, his gaze briefly skimming the titles. "I see. Well, I'll be around for a little while."

As Paul turned to walk away, Chuck felt a push—a subtle but insistent nudge within him. Before he could overthink it, he called out, louder than he intended, "Paul. Actually, there is something ..."

Paul turned back, his expression shifting to quiet curiosity. "Sure, Chuck. What's up?"

Chuck hesitated, his fingers brushing the edge of a book he wasn't really seeing. "I just got back from a visit home. A very short visit, but interesting." His tone changed, softening slightly. "Paul, we get along well, right? I mean, I'm your commanding officer, but we have something outside that, don't we?"

Paul stepped closer, his posture easy but attentive. "Of course, Chuck. I think we do."

"I've told you a little about my father. The way he needles me, puts pressure on me. The way he sometimes makes me feel ... insignificant. Right?"

"Yeah," Paul said gently. "You've mentioned it. Is everything alright?"

Chuck exhaled slowly, as if blowing out the weight of the words. "Actually, everything is alright. More so than I ever expected." He looked at Paul, his shoulders relaxed. "I went home, and my dad and I went out for a beer the first night. It was his idea. He told me he'd read about the Air Transport Command and our mission. He said he'd heard about the dangers of flying over the Pacific."

Paul remained silent, giving Chuck the space to continue.

Chuck's voice grew quieter, but more steady. "He told me he was proud of me. And then ... he apologized. For disregarding me. For the way he's treated me." He paused, the memory still raw. "I wasn't expecting that. Not from him. Not ever."

Paul nodded, his gaze steady. "That's something, Chuck. That's big."

"It is." Chuck exhaled slowly, his hand brushing against the spines of the books. "When I got back here, I couldn't stop thinking about it. How did that happen? Why now? I started realizing I don't have all the answers. My old man has always said, 'There's no shame in not knowing—just in not trying to find out.' And now, I think I'm trying to find out. But I don't know where to start."

Paul's face softened, his voice carrying a quiet assurance. "I think you're already starting. You went home for a reason, Chuck. That conversation with your dad—that happened for a reason. Even this moment right here, it's not an accident." He placed a hand on Chuck's shoulder, a steadying gesture. "That's where faith comes in."

Chuck looked at him thoughtfully. "But what is faith, Paul? Really?"

Paul glanced down the row of books and paused. His fingers settled on a title, pulling it gently from the shelf. "*What Is Faith* by J. Gresham Machen," he said, holding the book out to Chuck. "It's a good place to start."

Chuck took the book, turning it over in his hands as though searching for answers with that simple touch. His skepticism lingered, but so did a flicker of curiosity.

"Just give it a try," Paul said, his tone calm but insistent. "Take it one step at a time. And if you have questions—about anything—you know where to find me."

Chuck stared at the cover for a moment longer, then nodded. "Alright. I'll give it a shot."

"I also suggest a couple Bible verses. I'll write them down for you. And if you don't have a Bible, you can buy one here, they're right over there."

Paul pointed to the next bookcase, on the top row. Then he took a notepad and pencil out of his pocket and jotted down some Scripture references: "Romans 3:23, Romans 3:10–18, Romans 6:23, Romans 5:8, Romans 10:9, Romans 10:13, Romans 5:1, Romans 8:1, Romans 8:38–39."

"Read them in that order—look in the index to help you find the book of Romans. The first number is the chapter and the second number after the colon is the verse. Read those tonight, then let's talk about it tomorrow."

Paul tore out the sheet of paper and handed it to Chuck.

"Thanks, Paul. I'll read those tonight. I can't say I'll understand, or agree with it, but I'll read it."

"That's why we're going to talk about it tomorrow," Paul said, with a slight grin.

As Paul turned to leave, he hesitated, glancing back with a thoughtful expression. His voice softened, almost reverent. "Chuck, your father's apology? That wasn't just coincidence. God's in it. Jesus is with you, even if you're only starting to sense it. This is a new beginning, and when you see your father again, it'll feel different—because now you'll know there's a purpose behind it all. He's with you."

For a moment, Chuck didn't reply. He just stood there, holding the book, the weight of the moment settling over him. Then he gave a small nod, his voice barely above a whisper. "Maybe He is."

***

Hamilton Field - February 4, 1943

Stan supposed it might be a character flaw, always feeling like he was missing something. Was he obsessive? He didn't think so. But here he was, late in the evening, still inspecting the C-87. As flight engineer, it was his responsibility; if he missed something, it could spell disaster.

He moved around the aircraft like a mad scientist, flashlight in hand, muttering under his breath to no one in particular. Occasionally, a laugh or muttered expletive escaped him, but there was no one around to notice. Anyone with half a brain was enjoying some downtime or catching up on sleep.

The problem was, once he got into this mode, he couldn't shut his brain off. He'd be lying awake, replaying the evening in his mind, worrying over what he might have missed. It was something he'd wrestled with for as long as he could remember. Back in school, he'd lie awake fretting over test answers he might've gotten wrong. Some habits never die.

He swept his flashlight across the wheel well, scanning for anything out of place. The faintest glint caught his eye. Squinting, he leaned in closer. There it was—a loose safety wire on a hydraulic line. It wasn't catastrophic, not yet, but if that fitting worked itself free during flight, it could lead to a hydraulic leak. Landing gear or flaps—both could be affected. A chill ran through him at the thought.

"Ha! There you are, you little bugger." Stan crouched lower, his flashlight beam steady on the fitting. A thin sheen of hydraulic fluid had already formed, faint but unmistakable. He ran his gloved finger across it, holding it up to the light. The glistening film confirmed his suspicions.

"Landing gear hydraulics," he muttered. "Could've been worse, but this also could've gotten ugly real quick."

He set to work, pulling a wrench and a spool of safety wire from his tool bag. The fitting wasn't torqued properly, and the wire was barely holding. With practiced precision, he snugged the fitting to spec and looped a fresh length of wire through the bolt, twisting it tight. He wiped the area clean, ensuring no stray fluid remained to collect dirt or grime during the mission.

"Alright, let's see how you look now." Stan leaned back, inspecting his handiwork. The fitting was solid, the new safety wire gleaming under his flashlight. He let out a satisfied chuckle, some tension easing.

"There's always something, isn't there?" Stan muttered, giving the fitting one last nudge to test its security. "But you're not getting one past me."

He stood and pulled off his gloves, the faint scent of hydraulic fluid still lingering in the air. This was why he was out here—to catch the little things before they became big things. Every issue he found and fixed felt like releasing a knot in a tightly twisted rope. Slowly, he was unwinding the tension. Maybe tonight, he'd actually get some sleep.

His family still didn't understand why he'd leave the steady work of the mills for this. But in the mills, there were no problems to solve, just the mindless repetition of the machines. Here, every moment mattered. Every decision had weight. And every bolt tightened was one step closer to ensuring the crew's safety.

He resumed his inspection of the plane, using his flashlight to reveal the little spaces that most people would bypass. As he worked his way around the aircraft, he felt the tension continue to ease.

Finally, done, he turned off his flashlight and leaned against the landing gear for a moment, letting the subtle vibrations of the airfield settle over him. Out here, under the vast expanse of the sky, he felt more alive than he ever had back home.

***

Hamilton Field - February 4, 1943

Seth would love this, Jimmy thought, as he jotted more notes into his journal. The notebook was nearly full now, with measurements, observations, and rough-drawn maps. One map in particular, scrawled with care, depicted the vast Pacific. California lay in the east, with Australia thousands of miles to the southwest. A thin line traced the islands scattered along the way—those tiny stopping points that broke the endless blue expanse.

It was a map he couldn't wait to show his class back in Iowa, especially Seth. That boy could be a handful, but he had a knack for geography. Jimmy could picture him now, leaning forward in his desk, eyes wide with curiosity, as Jimmy explained the isolation of

Canton or the importance of Christmas Island. Seth always had a million questions—good questions, the kind that made teaching worth it.

Jimmy leaned back, tapping his pencil against the edge of the table. After his divorce, teaching had become his lifeline. He poured everything into it, determined to make his classroom a place of discovery and wonder. Geography wasn't just a subject for him; it was a gateway to understanding the world. His enthusiasm was contagious, and it wasn't long before his classroom became a favorite among the students. Watching them connect with the material, seeing their eyes light up with curiosity—it gave him purpose.

But so did this. Navigating these missions felt like a continuation of the same thread. In the classroom, he'd taught about the world. Now he was experiencing it firsthand, charting courses over the same waters he once described to his students. The work was dangerous, no question about that. But there was something deeply satisfying about applying his knowledge in a way that was practical. A way that mattered, contributing to the war effort.

Jimmy laughed out loud. "Of course, teaching high schoolers has its own dangers," he bellowed.

The sound of his own laughter echoed in the empty briefing room, and for a moment he felt the weight of the quiet settle over him. Late at night, the space was his alone. Maps spread out before him, their edges curling slightly, illuminated by the soft glow of a desk lamp. He traced a finger over the Pacific, his mind following the path of their next mission. He knew the risks. He'd seen enough near misses to understand just how precarious it could be. But tonight, something felt ... different. A faint unease lingered at the edge of his thoughts, unshakable despite his efforts to brush it aside.

He shook his head, forcing himself to focus. Worrying about what-ifs wouldn't change anything. The best he could do was prepare, planning every leg of the route meticulously, leaving no detail unchecked. That was his job, and he took it seriously. He'd do his part to ensure they all came back in one piece.

Jimmy leaned over the map again, making a few final notations. The worry still lingered, indistinct but still present. But so did the thought of his students, and the stories he'd tell them one day. Maybe, he thought, that's what kept him grounded—the knowledge that what he was doing now might inspire those kids to dream bigger, to see the world differently.

He hoped he would make it back in time to teach that same group of kids before they graduated. He hoped he would be able to accurately relay the beauty and danger of the Pacific. He hoped he would have a good story to tell them.

"Alright, Seth," he muttered softly to himself, "I'll make sure this story's a good one."

He closed the notebook and folded the maps. He was ready. He would bring the notebook with him, adding details to each page.

He couldn't wait to see his kids again when he was finished with this adventure.

***

San Mateo, California - February 5, 1943

Paul folded the last shirt into his flight bag, his movements slow and deliberate. From the kitchen, the soft scrape of the coffee pot broke the morning stillness, followed by the faint, familiar hum of Alta's voice. She wasn't just humming, she was singing, and as the melody reached him, Paul recognized the hymn.

BE THOU MY WISDOM, AND THOU MY TRUE WORD;

I EVER WITH THEE AND THOU WITH ME, LORD;

THOU MY GREAT FATHER AND I, THY TRUE SON;

THOU IN ME DWELLING, AND I WITH THEE ONE.

As the melody faded, Paul's gaze lingered on her. The sunlight filtered through the curtains, catching the faint curl of her hair as she moved gracefully between the stove and the counter, her apron fluttering slightly. Paul paused, his hand resting on the flight bag zipper. He wanted to remember her exactly like this: a picture of quiet strength, even in the face of a difficult goodbye.

"Breakfast is ready," Alta called gently, her voice carrying the warmth of home. She turned to him with a muted smile, holding a plate of eggs, bacon, and toast.

Paul zipped the bag and joined her at the small kitchen table, where the scent of breakfast—bacon, toast, and the rich aroma of coffee—greeted him. It felt like home, yet the weight of the up-coming mission pressed heavily on his chest. He sat down and let out a slow, deliberate exhale. He looked down at his plate. This was usually his favorite breakfast, but he didn't have much of an appetite this morning.

"How's the weather looking?" Alta asked, trying to keep the mood light.

"Clear skies. Should be a smooth flight," Paul replied, reaching for the toast.

She looked up at him and lingered on his face. She remembered the first time she saw him at the Cleveland airport. His big smile and friendly manner.

Alta poured coffee into his cup and slid it across the table before sitting down across from him. She was trying to be strong, but Paul noticed her hands trembled slightly as she buttered her toast. She fidgeted with her napkin, folding and unfolding it with meticulous care, her appetite nonexistent.

"Is something on your mind?" Paul asked softly, setting his fork down and meeting her gaze.

Alta hesitated, dropping her eyes to the table and tightening her fingers around the napkin. She opened her mouth, then closed it again, her lips pressing into a thin line. Finally, she looked up, her eyes glistening.

"Paul, there's ... something I need to tell you," she began, her voice barely above a whisper. "I was going to wait until you got back, but I feel like I should tell you now."

His brow furrowed, and he reached across the table, taking her hand in his. "What is it, sweetheart?"

"I'm ... we're going to have a baby."

The words hung in the air, their weight palpable. Paul's expression shifted from surprise to joy, then to something deeper—a mixture of love, wonder, and understanding. He stood, his chair scraping softly against the floor, and knelt beside her, taking both of her hands in his.

"A baby," he repeated, his voice tinged with awe. "Alta, that's ... that's the best news I could have heard."

Tears welled and spilled down Alta's cheeks as she leaned into him, her voice muffled against his shoulder. "I'm scared, Paul. You're leaving again, and I ..."

Paul gently framed her face with his hands, his thumbs brushing away her tears. "I'll come back," he said, his voice steady, full of conviction. "I promise you, Alta—I'll come back to you. And when I do, I'll be the husband you deserve. The father our child needs. Whatever it takes, I'll make it back to you both."

They sat there, holding each other, the quiet ticking of the kitchen clock marking the passing moments. Finally, Paul broke the silence. "I hate this, but I should probably get going."

Alta nodded reluctantly as Paul stood, pulling her gently to her feet. He wrapped her in one last embrace before stepping back to grab his flight bag.

At the door, he paused, turning to her one more time. "I love you," he said, his voice steady, but thick with emotion.

"I love you too," she replied, her voice trembling. "Come back to us, Paul."

"I will. I'll be back in two weeks," he said, the promise anchoring him as he turned to leave.

Outside, the taxi waited, its engine idling softly. Paul walked down the gravel path, his boots crunching with each step. When he reached the curb, he turned back. Alta stood in the doorway, her arms wrapped around herself, one hand raised in a small wave.

The sight seared itself into Paul's memory, every detail vivid—the soft morning light catching her hair, the strength in her posture despite the tears threatening to spill, and the small but hopeful wave. He carried that image with him as he climbed into the car, the weight of the promise heavy in his chest but steadying his resolve.

Alta stayed in the doorway long after the car disappeared from view, her hand resting protectively over her stomach. She closed her eyes, whispering softly, "Lord, please bring him back to us."

CHAPTER THIRTEEN

Hamilton Field - February 5, 1943

S tan didn't really need to be there this early, but he couldn't help himself. He could never sleep the night before a mission, and last night had been no different. The lingering flap issues gnawed at the back of his mind, despite their best efforts to keep the actuator well-lubricated. There had been no replacement parts, no real solution, just maintenance workarounds and hope.

The hydraulic issue had been minor, and he was confident in his repairs. But confidence wasn't certainty.

Hamilton Field was quiet at this hour, the kind of silence that only existed in the brief window before dawn. A few mechanics moved in the distance, their voices low, the occasional clang of tools breaking the stillness. In just a couple of hours, the base would be alive with activity, but for now, it was just him, the plane, and the ever-present sweeping of the Pacific winds across the air-field.

Stan moved through his standard preflight inspection, running his hands along the aircraft's underbelly, checking every fitting and joint with a methodical patience that had become second nature. Everything else looked clean, and the maintenance report showed nothing major. He crouched by the landing gear, running his flash-light along the hydraulic lines. Dry. Good sign.

He exhaled and straightened, rolling the stiffness out of his shoulders. The aircraft loomed in front of him, a mechanical beast that was both a miracle of engineering and an unpredictable brute.

He turned his gaze toward the east. The first streaks of twilight stretched across the horizon, the dark giving way to the soft glow of impending dawn. For a moment, he just stood there, hands on his hips, listening.

He thought of a conversation he'd had yesterday; Chuck said he'd handle the altimeter calibration—Stan made a mental note to remind him.

Not much else he could do now. He rubbed his hands together, the chill of the morning air biting at his fingers. Maybe he'd head over to the briefing hangar, get off his feet for a bit before the others started rolling in.

He took one last look at the plane before turning toward the hangar. No matter how many times he checked, no matter how many missions he flew, there was always that feeling in his gut—the one that never quite went away.

Not fear. Not exactly.

Just a whisper of something else—something unsettling.

Stan sank into a chair in the hangar, stretching his legs out in front of him. His mind drifted. It had been a while since he'd seen his family. Some of the other guys had taken trips home, but he hadn't gotten around to it. Not that he didn't want to—he just didn't feel like dealing with all the inevitable questions: Don't you miss Fall River? Why couldn't you just get a good job here? Why don't you go down the street to visit Joan? She's been asking about you.

He sighed, rubbing the bridge of his nose. Maybe after this trip, he'd just suck it up and deal with it.

Footsteps echoed across the hangar floor, pulling him back to the present. He turned as Chuck strode in, his usual sharp gait carrying him with purpose.

"Mornin', Stan. You got the maintenance logs handy?" Chuck asked, all business.

Stan raised an eyebrow. "Good morning to you too, Chuck." He reached for the clipboard beside him. "Yeah, I've got them here. Anything in particular you're looking for?"

Chuck took the log, flipping through it with quick precision. "Just want to make sure we're not missing anything."

Stan leaned back slightly, watching him scan the pages. Chuck looked tired, but there was something else in his expression—something tight, like he had more on his mind than just routine checks.

Didn't hurt to have a second set of eyes on the report, though.

"You're going to do the altimeter calibration this time, right?" Stan asked casually.

Chuck gave a distracted, "Uh-huh," without looking up from the clipboard. "I'm going to go have a look."

"Suit yourself," Stan said, stretching out again. Then, after a pause, "You're going to do the altimeter calibration at each stop this trip, correct?"

Chuck barely looked up. "I said yes." The sharpness in his tone caught Stan off guard.

Then, just as quickly, Chuck turned on his heel and strode off.

Geez, just askin', Stan thought, shaking his head. Then he leaned back, enjoying the last bit of quiet as the first streaks of sunrise painted the horizon.

He must have drifted off because the next thing he knew, someone kicked his chair. He sat bolt upright with a start.

Paul stood over him, grinning. "You look comfortable. Getting some last-minute beauty sleep?"

Stan blinked, rubbing his eyes. "Hey, I was here before anyone else this morning. Already finished my inspection, so cut me some slack, would ya?"

Paul smirked. "I'd expect nothing less. You probably checked that bird a hundred times already."

Stan exhaled, shaking off the haze of sleep. "Yeah, well. It only takes one thing going wrong."

Paul's grin softened slightly. "I know."

For a second, there was a pause, a flicker of understanding passing between them. Then Paul clapped him on the shoulder. "Come on, want some coffee? We still have several hours before the briefing."

"Yeah, I'd love some."

As they approached the mess hall, the unmistakable sound of Joe's voice carried through the open doorway.

"... and I said, 'What do you mean you don't have any? I just dumped a truckload of it in your lobby this morning!'"

A burst of laughter followed, loud and unrestrained.

Paul chuckled. "I think Cowboy's here."

Stan smirked. "Sounds about right."

They stepped inside to find Jimmy slapping Joe on the back while half a dozen other guys sat around the table, most in various stages of convulsive laughter. Joe leaned back in his chair, grinning like a man who had not a care in the world.

"Hey, Joe," Paul said as they approached. "Sounds like you're wide awake already. What's the scoop?"

"Just filling these fellas in on the time I tried to get a bank loan." Joe tipped his chair back, shaking his head with exaggerated exasperation. "You know, back when I thought all you had to do was walk in with a smile and a firm handshake."

More laughter erupted.

Paul grinned. "Guess that didn't go how you planned."

"You could say that." Joe shot him a wink. Then, noticing both with coffee in hand, he added, "We all here?"

"Yep. Chuck's with the bird," Stan said, taking a sip. "You and Jimmy make five."

Joe nodded, looking around as if taking stock. "Good. The gang's all here."

The energy in the room was light, almost like any other morning before a mission. But under it, just beneath the surface, there was that same quiet understanding they all carried. The weight of where they were going, what they were doing. For now, though, this small moment was what they needed, and they would take it.

Stan took a long sip of his coffee, letting the warmth settle into him. "At least the coffee's hot."

Joe smirked. "Enjoy it while you can. Not much of that coming up at 10,000 feet."

After a few more minutes, the crew left the mess hall to check their stations aboard the C-87. Stan settled into his position behind the cockpit, running through his final checks before the briefing. The engines, hydraulics, electrical—everything looked as good as it was going to.

At five minutes before 1000, he grabbed his notepad and headed back to the hangar, taking a seat. Chuck was already there, flipping through some paperwork.

Stan crossed his legs and leaned back slightly. "Chuck, I don't want to be a bother, but you seemed a little distracted earlier when I mentioned the altimeter calibration."

Chuck didn't look up from his clipboard. "Yep, I've got it taken care of." His tone was terse and abrupt.

Stan studied him for a second but let it go. He had to trust that Chuck would handle it.

A moment later, the rest of the crew filed in, taking their seats. Chuck straightened, flipping to the first page of his notes.

"Weather's looking solid—clear skies, slight tailwind. Should be a smooth flight. Since we're not departing until 1130, we'll be landing at Hickam after dark, so everyone needs to be sharp."

Joe exhaled, shaking his head. "Great. I'm not too keen on flying into Hickam at night."

"Yeah, me too," Chuck admitted, glancing up from his notes. "But we'll handle it."

He flipped a page. "We're light on cargo this trip, but we'll be carrying sixteen passengers. Mostly colonels and majors catching a ride, so let's be on our best behavior." He glanced pointedly at Joe.

Joe raised his hands in mock innocence. "Why are you looking at me? Jimmy cracks just as many jokes as I do."

Jimmy smirked. "Yeah, but mine are actually funny."

A few chuckles rolled through the room before Chuck brought them back. "Last but not least—flap actuator's still a known issue. They've been keeping it lubed, and it's been working fine for the last few months, so we should be good." His eyes flicked toward Stan, who gave a subtle nod. "We're flying a good bird."

Chuck scanned the room. "Questions?"

The crew exchanged glances, but no one spoke up.

"Alright. Grab a snack, relax a little, and hit the head before boarding. Everyone in place by 1100. Engines fire up at 1115, wheels up at 1130. Dismissed."

The crew filed out, each man lost in his own thoughts. Stan lingered a moment, letting out a breath as he ran through the long hours ahead in his mind. Each trip seemed to stretch longer than the last. That visit back home after this one was sounding better and better.

He grabbed a banana and some crackers from the mess hall before heading down the path toward the barracks. Finding a quiet spot beneath a tree, he sat and watched the airfield stir with movement—ground crews loading cargo, mechanics making final checks, the steady drone of aircraft engines preparing for departure.

As 1100 approached, he got up, stretched, and made his way toward the tarmac.

Preflight checks went smoothly. Engines fired up without a hitch. Before he knew it, they were taxiing down the runway, the familiar vibrations of takeoff rumbling through the aircraft.

As they climbed, Stan glanced out the small window, watching the shoreline of California shrink beneath them. He always felt a pang leaving, even after all these flights. But now, his focus shifted. Time to do the job.

He exhaled, rolling his shoulders, and turned his attention back to the instruments. He wondered what this trip had in store.

***

Airborne, Flight out of Hamilton

The C-87 climbed steadily, banking gently as it left the coastline behind. Jimmy settled in at his station, adjusting the strap on his navigation kit—a compact canvas pouch packed with folded maps, a plotter, and his well-worn flight log. He slipped out a chart and began tracing their course. He ran a quick mental checklist of course settings, wind adjustments, magnetic variation, all second nature by now.

For him, this was the best part of the flight. Looking at the lines and figures drawn on the maps at the start of a mission was like seeing the future unfold in ink. A course plotted with precision, confirmed in real time by calculations. No guesswork, no maybes—just certainty. It gave him a sense of peace. If he had a bowl of rocky road right now, life would be just about perfect. The thought made him chuckle softly to himself.

The aircraft hummed around him, a steady vibration that he had long since learned to tune out. The crew had settled into their usual rhythm: initial banter, then silence as they focused on their tasks. Later, as the hours stretched on, conversation would pick up again.

The passengers sat toward the front of the plane, just around the wings. They were mostly quiet, their faces unreadable. Officers, some non-commissioned, mostly Army, catching a lift out to the Pacific. No small talk, no idle chatter. Jimmy had seen it before—some men talked to distract themselves, others got quiet. The quiet ones were usually the ones who had seen too much.

He glanced up from his charts and looked toward the front of the aircraft and around the bulkhead as best as he could. Chuck was steady at the controls, Joe beside him. Paul was already tuned into the radio, occasionally flipping between frequencies. Stan looked like he was running through another round of checks.

He checked their heading again, frowning slightly as he reworked the numbers. Nothing was wrong exactly, but they were just a fraction of a degree off from his initial mark. He adjusted, making a quick notation, but the feeling of something being slightly off lingered. Maybe it was nothing. Maybe it was just the fact that another long mission stretched out before them.

One more check—everything looked good. He exhaled, stretching his fingers before picking up his pencil again. His mind drifted, as it often did during these long flights, back to his students. He could picture them now—especially Seth—leaning forward in their desks, peppering him with questions about atolls, prevailing winds, and how far you could fly before running out of ocean. This is what I'll tell them, Jimmy thought, making a mental note. Between his first-hand experiences, his maps, and his knack for storytelling, he could make one heck of a lesson.

His thoughts then shifted to a more personal memory. A memory that still hurt him deeply.

The divorce had left him feeling hollow. Alone. Confused. Angry, even. He didn't talk about it much—not because it didn't matter, but because he didn't know how to. Not in a way that made sense. The finality of it had hit him like a punch in the gut, and if it weren't for his job—mostly his students—he probably would have made a mess of things.

The war had become his escape. It gave him purpose, adventure; and, for a time, it dulled the ache that had settled deep in his chest. But what about after? When the flights were done, the maps were put away, and there was nowhere left to run?

He needed to talk to someone.

Jimmy thumbed the intercom. It didn't matter about what—he just needed something to break the silence.

"Hey, Paul, how are things looking over there? I don't suppose you've picked up the beacon from Hickam yet?"

It took a couple of seconds before Paul's voice crackled through. "Not yet. A little too far out. But I'll let you know when I do."

"Appreciate it." Jimmy leaned back, tapping his pencil against his knee. "You hungry? I could go for some rocky road about now. You got any stashed away over there?"

Before Paul could answer, Joe's voice cut in. "Can I get in on that?"

A pause. Then Paul came back, feigned seriousness. "Sorry, fellas. I did pack extra, but I dropped it while boarding."

Jimmy scoffed. "Some friend you are."

Joe chimed in again. "Alright, that does it, Paul. No more best man for you."

Laughter crackled over the intercom, and just like that, Jimmy's mood lightened. He could always count on these guys to do that. Even when tensions ran high, someone—usually Joe—would crack a joke, throwing a wrench in the stress before it could take hold.

Then without warning, the plane dropped.

Jimmy's stomach shot into his throat. His harness snapped tight against his shoulders, the metal frame of the aircraft groaning with the sudden shift. Loose items rattled, and for a moment, everything seemed to hover in the air before settling back into place.

"What was that?" Paul's voice came over the intercom.

"Thermal turbulence, most likely," Joe responded. He sounded calm, but Jimmy knew him well enough to hear a subtle edge. "We're bound to get some of that this time of day. Stan, let's keep an eye on things."

"Roger," Stan replied.

Jimmy took a breath, forcing his pulse to slow. He would have thought by now that he'd be used to turbulence, but it always unsettled him, especially when it seemed to come out of nowhere.

The hours ticked by. Miles slipped beneath them.

At this point in the flight, they were roughly 1,300 miles from Hamilton, a little more than halfway to Hickam. The sun had dipped below the horizon, leaving behind a fiery glow that faded into deep blues. Darkness was settling in fast, swallowing the ocean below.

Inside the aircraft, the lighting had dimmed. The cockpit was illuminated only by the soft green glow of the instrument panel, casting faint shadows over Chuck and Joe. In the navigator's station, Jimmy had a small adjustable lamp casting just enough light over his maps. Paul's radio station had a similar low-intensity work light, just enough to keep his frequencies visible without ruining night vision.

The passenger compartment was almost entirely dark, save for a few overhead dome lights, which were kept low to avoid disrupting night adaptation. The occasional flicker of a flashlight beam could be seen as one of the passengers adjusted in their seat.

Jimmy shifted slightly, glancing up from his maps. Outside the small window, the stars had begun to appear, sharp and brilliant in the inky sky. The vast Pacific stretched endlessly below, unseen but always present.

Long, dark hours lay ahead.

***

Hickam Field, February 6, 1943

Paul was exhausted. Not just physically, but mentally. Night flights had a way of draining a man, even when everything went smoothly. The vast blackness outside the plane, the lack of any visible horizon, the instruments glowing softly in the cockpit—it all made for an eerie, almost dreamlike experience. He knew that approach and landings were the hardest on Chuck and Joe, and tonight had been no exception. Every descent in the dark carried its own brand of tension. But if there were two men Paul trusted to get him safely on the ground, it was them. They were competent, sharp, and steady, and he wouldn't trade them for any other flight crew.

They had touched down just after midnight. Headwinds and a weather reroute over the Pacific had slowed them more than expected, and by the time post-flight checks were completed and the aircraft secured, it was well past 0130. The usual barracks at Hickam had been full, so instead of a half-decent Army bed in a proper bunkhouse, they had been given space in an older building with rickety frames and mattresses that felt as soft as a sheet of plywood.

It seemed to Paul that he had barely shut his eyes before the early morning stirrings of the airfield had begun creeping through the thin walls. The dull roar of engines spooling up, voices carrying outside, the shuffle of boots over pavement. Sleep was fleeting on these layovers, but at least they had a full day ahead of them before takeoff.

Despite the rough accommodations, the passengers seemed to have gotten along alright during the flight. Even a colonel had taken time to personally thank Paul after they landed.

"Smooth flight, son," the officer had said, clapping him on the shoulder. "We appreciate the lift."

Paul had waved a hand. "I'm just the radio operator. The guys you really want to thank were up front."

The colonel had frowned. "That's a bunch of malarkey. Every man up there plays an important role. Doesn't matter if you're flying the plane, tuning a dial, or keeping track of fuel—you don't make it across the Pacific without each other. So thank you. For your service and your sacrifice."

Caught off guard, Paul had managed only a quiet, "Thank you, sir."

Now, as he stretched out on the uncomfortable cot, staring up at the ceiling, he found himself replaying the exchange. It wasn't often that someone outside the crew acknowledged what they did—not just the pilots, but all of them. He thought about Alta, about home. About the child growing inside her. The word "sacrifice" stuck with him.

He just hoped the sacrifice was worth it.

After breakfast the crew had a short briefing with the base personnel to review the next leg of the trip. They were to leave the next day around 1130 with more cargo and the same passengers, making their way further into the Pacific.

A rumor had been circulating that there were cold Cokes in the mess hall, so Paul and the rest of the crew headed over to investigate. Sure enough, frosty bottles of Coca-Cola sat nestled in buckets of ice, condensation dripping down the glass of each bottle.

Joe's eyes widened. "Do you think we can take more than one?"

Paul smirked. "How about we start with one each, make sure everyone gets a shot?"

"Yeah, yeah, fine," Joe muttered, already popping the cap off his bottle.

They carried their Cokes outside and found a table under the shade of a palm tree, the breeze off the ocean making the moment feel almost like a vacation—if you ignored the uniforms, the looming mission, and the fact that a war was still raging across the Pacific.

"Now this is the life," Jimmy sighed, stretching out as he took a sip. "Sun, breeze, ice-cold Coke. Even if I do have to share it with the likes of you fellas."

Joe leaned in, deadpan. "Yeah, well, you're no Rita Hayworth yourself, Jimmy."

Jimmy shot him a look, and Paul chuckled, taking a long sip of his Coke as Joe continued. "In fact, you remind me of this donkey I once met. One day, this ass starts talking and says ..."

"Well, what do we have here?" A voice interrupted from behind them. "Didn't think I'd be running into you fellas so soon."

Paul turned, blinking in disbelief.

There stood Frank Harper, walking toward them with a moderate limp, his uniform crisp, but his movements still a little tentative. His face was leaner than Paul remembered, though there was no visible sign of injury other than the limp. But there was something in his eyes—maybe a weariness that hadn't been there before.

Joe shot to his feet. "Lieutenant Frank Harper! Back from the dead. I can't believe my eyes."

Harper smirked. "Yeah, well, guess it wasn't my time yet."

Paul stood, eyeing Harper carefully. "We heard about a C-87 out of New Caledonia that was attacked by the Japanese. Rumor was it went down. At the time it sounded like it could've been your plane."

Frank's gaze drifted toward the horizon, his expression darkening. "Yeah. We ran into a couple of Zeroes. They weren't just passing through, either—they were hunting." His voice was calm, but the weight behind it was unmistakable. "We did what we could to evade, but I just couldn't maneuver fast enough. Before I know it, we were taking hits. A couple of P-39s finally showed up, gave 'em something else to shoot at, but by then ..." He exhaled, shaking his head slightly.

The crew listened in silence.

"We lost engine one almost immediately. Engine four got hit soon after, and they weren't in a hurry to let us go." He forced a tight chuckle. "Took some serious flying just to keep her in the air."

Chuck, arms crossed, spoke up. "How'd you make it to Fiji?"

Frank let out a slow breath. "We didn't." His voice was quieter now, the memory weighing on him. "I thought we could, gave it everything I had, but the wings were chewed up. After a while, I knew we weren't gonna make it. Had to put her down in the drink—hundred miles out."

No one spoke.

Frank's jaw tensed before he continued. "It was rough. Two of my boys didn't make it." His gaze lowered. "The rest of us floated for a day before a PBY spotted us."

The weight of his words settled over them. Paul swallowed hard.

"What about Sparky?" he asked, his voice quieter.

Frank just stared at the ground, shaking his head.

Paul felt the hit deep in his chest. Will "Sparky" Spencer had been a good guy. They had spent hours talking in the mess halls, swapping stories, comparing notes on radio equipment. Gone.

"You look like you're recovering well, though," Paul said finally, trying to shift the conversation.

Frank huffed out something close to a laugh. "You should've seen me four months ago. Leg and arms busted up. Face a mess. Took me a while to get back on my feet." He hesitated. "They'll probably send me home soon. But, uh ... some things, you don't really recover from."

Paul nodded, understanding more than he could put into words. "I'm sorry, Frank."

Harper forced a small smile. "Yeah. Me too." He looked around at them, as if memorizing the faces of men still flying missions, still rolling the dice every time they took off. Then he straightened up. "But hey, I'm here, right? And now that I know you're here, I'll be drinking up all the Cokes before you get a chance at more."

The mood lightened slightly.

Joe shook his head. "That's what I was afraid of."

Harper perked up slightly. "Alright, boys. Just wanted to let you know I'm still breathing. Hope I'll see you all again. Look me up when this thing's over." He hesitated for just a second. "You take care of yourselves out there."

Paul watched as Frank turned and walked away, disappearing into the flow of men moving across the base.

The crew sat in thoughtful silence, the Coke in their bottles slowly losing its chill in the Hawaiian heat. Paul stared after Frank, his thoughts staying with him. Would he ever see him again? He hoped Frank would fully heal, that he would find his way forward.

Then his thoughts shifted. He hoped this mission would go by quickly. He hoped, more than anything, that he'd be home soon—with Alta and his new baby.

***

Hickam Field, February 7, 1943

The cot was stiff, the air warm, and Chuck woke early, staring at the ceiling. He hadn't really slept—not in any meaningful way. Maybe he had drifted off for a couple hours, but it hadn't been restful. His body ached with exhaustion, but his mind refused to quiet.

He had been dreaming. Or at least, he thought he had. It was the kind of dream where you aren't fully asleep and not entirely awake but caught somewhere in between. He was in the cockpit, hands gripping the yoke. Something was wrong—he couldn't tell what, but the aircraft wasn't responding the way it should. He made slight adjustments, but none of them seemed to work. No matter what he tried, he couldn't correct it. The controls felt sluggish, just out of sync. Strange.

Then, a shift. The dream changed. The elusive problem remained, but now the co-pilot's seat was empty. He was alone.

Chuck exhaled and rubbed his hands over his face. It was just a dream. A stupid, meaningless dream. But still, something about it unsettled him. He had flown this leg of the mission before, plenty of times. There was nothing unusual about it. Nothing different.

So why did it feel different?

Maybe it was just the nerves. The standard pre-flight tension, the weight of command. That had to be it.

He sat up, ran a hand through his hair, and decided there was no use trying to sleep anymore. He'd feel better once they were in the air.

After a quick shower and shave, he leaned against the sink and stared at his reflection in the small mirror. He looked awful. His eyes were distant, ragged—just like he felt. He needed a break. After this trip, he'd take a few days off, maybe even head home again. He promised himself that. But for now, there was coffee.

Stepping outside, the air was cool with the lingering remnants of night, and the eastern sky was just beginning to lighten. He took a slow breath. He used to marvel at this place, the ocean breeze, the palm trees swaying in the morning wind. His first time here with the crew had been filled with adventure—trying to surf, the luau. It felt like a lifetime ago.

Now, it was all routine. Long miles ahead, the same stretch of ocean, the same long hours in the cockpit. It wasn't about adventure anymore, it was about endurance. He didn't dwell on it. He just needed to get through this trip, and then he'd be home.

He stepped into the mess hall, grabbed a cup, and poured himself some coffee. Breakfast wasn't quite ready yet, but that was fine. His stomach felt too knotted to eat anyway. He took a sip, letting the warmth settle in his chest, when he heard footsteps behind him.

"Mornin', Chuck. Glad they have the coffee ready at least."

Chuck turned to see Joe reaching for a cup. "Morning, Joe. How'd you sleep?"

Joe shrugged as he poured himself some coffee. "Not great. I can never seem to get much sleep before a flight."

"Yeah, me too," Chuck admitted, leaning back against the counter.

Joe took a slow sip. "How's Lucy handling this? Must be new for her—having you gone for his long."

"She's doing alright," Joe said, his gaze distant for a moment. "As good as can be expected, I guess." Then he looked up. "You doing OK, Chuck? Other than being tired?"

Chuck hesitated, then gave a small nod. "Yeah, I'm fine."

Joe studied him for a second, then spoke. "You know, Chuck. I know we've had our differences, but I respect you. I think we've put all that other stuff behind us."

Chuck glanced at him, then exhaled, nodding slightly. "Yeah. We have."

Joe leaned on the counter next to him, turning his coffee cup in his hands. "If something's on your mind, you can talk to me. You're not carrying all this weight alone."

Chuck stared down at his coffee for a long moment, the steam curling up in thin wisps. Finally, he spoke. "I suppose there is something. I feel ... anxious. Uneasy. Like I'm forgetting something. Like there's something I should be remembering to do."

Joe didn't interrupt. He just listened.

Chuck shook his head, running a hand over his face. "And then there's this other thing. I've been talking with Paul ... about God, about faith. I've actually been reading some of the Bible." He exhaled sharply, shaking his head. "I don't know, Joe. It's like I know it's true, but I can't quite get it to click in my head." He let out a dry chuckle. "But that's different from the other stuff I'm feeling. Heck, Joe, I don't even know what I'm talking about."

Chuck glanced over at Joe, watching as his friend processed his words. Joe didn't say anything right away, just nodded slightly, as if turning something over in his head. Chuck wasn't sure why, but that small pause—Joe's quiet consideration—meant something. It made him feel less ridiculous for saying any of this out loud.

"Thanks for listening, Joe. I probably made absolutely no sense, though."

"You made perfect sense." Joe looked down at his coffee cup, turning it slightly in his hands. "We're friends now, I think. Right?"

Chuck smirked. "Yeah, I'd say we're friends—when I'm not your commanding officer."

"Well, that goes without saying." Joe hesitated for half a second before continuing. "Uh, you know Lucy and I are getting married. April seventeenth. I'd like it if you could be there. The rest of the crew will be. Paul's going to be my best man." He glanced up. "Whaddya say, Chuck?"

Chuck looked at Joe, surprised. Of all the things he expected this morning, an invitation to Joe Mitchell's wedding wasn't one of them.

"I'd be honored, Joe. Thanks for asking." He clapped Joe on the shoulder, then stood, stretching. "Well, I'm heading over to check on the bird. We've got several more hours, so get something to eat and relax a bit."

"Aren't you going to get any breakfast?"

"I'll grab something later. Want to chat with mechanical first." Chuck turned and stepped out into the early morning light. The air was cool, the sky shifting from deep blue to the warm glow of sunrise. The conversation with Joe lingered in his mind, unexpectedly lifting the weight off his chest. He still felt that nagging sense of unease, but for the first time all morning it wasn't quite as heavy.

Maybe things were going to be alright.

***

Aboard ATC-903, February 7, 1943

Joe had to concentrate. The preflight checks had become so automatic that sometimes, by the time they were airborne, he barely remembered running through them. His hands moved by habit, adjusting the dials, flicking switches, verifying readings—a dance of precision burned into muscle memory.

Across from him, Chuck worked methodically through the checklist, his voice steady.

"Hydraulics feel good. Brakes holding pressure," Joe reported, pressing the rudder pedals lightly.

Chuck nodded, eyes flicking to the fuel gauge. "Alright, we're topped off on mains. Crossfeed valve?"

Joe reached up and flipped the switch. "Off."

Chuck scanned the instrument panel, then reached for the altimeter knob, tapping it absently. "Altimeter ... should be 29.92 ... wait." Chuck's fingers paused over the knob. "We're at Hickam. Local pressure'll be different."

Joe glanced up. "Is that going to change much from Hamilton?"

"Not by much," Chuck said, adjusting it a click or two. "I'll double-check with the tower before descent."

"Just remember—we're headed to Canton."

Chuck smirked. "Yeah. They're not exactly chatty with local conditions."

Joe let it go. The checklist moved on—engine readings, control surfaces, nav settings. Everything clicked into place. He was ready to get in the air, finish the leg, and get home.

They were set. Joe glanced over at Chuck as they taxied down the runway. He was focused, but something about him seemed just a little off—too rigid, too intense. But there was no time to dwell on that now. The engines roared as they lined up, and the runway stretched out ahead.

"V1 committed," Joe called out as they thundered down the runway.

The C-87 picked up speed, the rumble of the wheels against the concrete vibrating through the airframe.

"Rotate."

Chuck pulled back on the yoke, and the nose lifted smoothly into the sky.

"V2 positive rate." Joe glanced at the altimeter, confirming the climb. "Gear up."

Chuck flipped the lever, and with a dull thud the landing gear locked into place inside the fuselage. The familiar sound faded into the background as they cleared the airfield, the Pacific opening up beneath them in an endless expanse of blue.

"That was one smooth ride. You fellas are top-notch." Jimmy's voice came through the intercom.

"Yeah," Paul chimed in. "Didn't even feel it. My feet didn't slip off the table."

"That's nothin'," Stan's voice crackled in. "Didn't even spill my drink."

Joe smirked. "Hey, you fellas settle down back there. Chuck and I have important work to do up here. And besides, no one wants to hear your opinions anyway. Isn't that right, Chuck?"

He turned his head, expecting a quick quip in return—but Chuck didn't say anything. He just stared ahead, his expression unreadable.

Joe frowned. "You alright, Chuck?" he called out over the hum of the engines, this time without the intercom.

Chuck nodded, but the gesture felt mechanical. Forced.

Joe held his gaze for a second longer before turning back to the controls. Whatever was on Chuck's mind, he wasn't talking about it now.

The flight continued on, the vast ocean stretching endlessly before them, familiar yet always humbling. The steady drone of the engines settled into a rhythm, and Joe started thinking about home.

About Lucy.

He pictured them together on the ranch—her laughter as they rode through the open fields, the way she clung to him when he first showed her how to sit in the saddle. Earlier, Lucy had talked about how she had been searching for her place in life, and when Joe told her about the ranch, she had lit up.

She'd never been on a ranch before, never even ridden a horse. But she was ready. Ready to start a new life—with him.

They were about four hours into the flight, just around the halfway point—around 950 miles from Hickam. Joe heard Chuck exhale slowly and looked over at him. Chuck rolled his shoulders, adjusted his grip on the yoke, and returned Joe's glance.

"Hey, Cowboy. Take over for a bit?"

Joe shifted slightly in his seat and nodded. "Yeah, I got it," he replied as he placed his hands on the yoke, getting a feel for the aircraft. "You alright?"

"Yeah, just need to stretch a little." Chuck rubbed his temple, blinking away the exhaustion creeping in behind his eyes. "Didn't sleep much last night."

Joe smirked. "No kidding. You look like youve been breaking horses all night instead of catching shut-eye."

Chuck gave a dry chuckle, shaking his head. "Something like that."

Joe still couldn't get over the change in Chuck the last few weeks. A couple of months ago, he never would have been able to have an exchange like that with him. Joe scanned the gauges, cross-checking their altitude and airspeed. "Alright, I've got the controls."

"You've got the controls," Chuck confirmed, lifting his hands from the yoke.

Joe felt the slight shift as he took full command of the aircraft. The C-87 was steady in the air, responding smoothly to his touch. "Go on, get up and stretch a little. Take a lap around the cockpit or go talk to the passengers a little. "

Chuck leaned back with a quiet sigh, rolling out the tension in his shoulders. He could already feel the stiffness settling in from hours in the seat.

Joe glanced quickly at him. "You gonna catch a few winks, or just sit there looking pretty?"

Chuck snorted. "Maybe I'll just sit here and make sure you don't screw it up."

Joe smirked. "Fair enough."

Chuck shifted in his seat, stretching as best he could, while Joe settled into the rhythm of flying. The sky stretched endlessly ahead, the ocean a dark blue canvas below. The droning hum of the engines filled the cockpit, steady, unwavering.

As time and miles slipped by, the sun dipped lower over the Pacific. The cockpit glowed with deepening shades of orange and gold, eventually giving way to twilight. Joe reached forward, flipping the panel lighting to red—less strain on the eyes now that darkness had taken hold. The transition always felt like a shift into a different world, where time blurred and only the soft glow of instruments connected them to reality.

"You guys still awake up there?" Paul's voice cracked over the intercom. "It's awfully quiet."

Joe shook his head, smirking. "Geez, Paul, now you've gone and woke us up. Thanks a lot."

"Just doing my part," Paul shot back. "I was thinking—this is almost relaxing. Smoothest flight we've had on this leg."

Joe groaned. "Now you've gone and done it. We'll probably fly into some major turbulence now."

The minutes passed, the plane slicing cleanly though the night sky. Joe stole a quick glance at Chuck. His shoulders had tensed again, his easy posture from just a few minutes ago replaced by something tighter, more rigid.

Chuck finally spoke, voice quieter than before. "That's enough fellas. I'll take control back now."

Joe hesitated for just a beat before responding. "You've got control."

He lifted his hands from the yoke, feeling the shift—not just in the controls, but in the air around them. The cockpit seemed smaller somehow, pressing in just a little.

Something had changed. Joe felt it.

***

ATC-903, 60 Miles from Canton Island, February 7, 1943

Joe adjusted his headset and shifted slightly in his seat. Something felt off. He felt it just before he turned the controls over to Chuck. It wasn't dramatic, not yet, but there was definitely a faint shift in the way the aircraft moved. A subtle tug, a slight resistance against the yoke.

Maybe it was nothing, but something had felt different about this flight ever since they'd taken off. He glanced at Chuck, who was focused ahead. Joe scanned the instruments—everything looked alright. The drone of the engines remained steady, the altimeter reading was stable—at least, it seemed to be.

Joe's eyes flicked to the attitude indicator. Was it just his imagination, or was the aircraft rolling ever so slightly to the left? He frowned, watching for a few more seconds. He glanced at the suction gauge—that looked alright.

"Hey Chuck, you feeling that?" Joe asked, keeping his tone even.

Chuck gave a small nod, his fingers tightening slightly on the yoke. "Yeah—could just be wind. We're getting closer to the island. Might be some shifting currents."

Joe wasn't convinced. The air had been smooth for most of the flight. And even if there were shifting winds, the plane shouldn't feel like this—like it was dragging its feet on one side.

He flicked the trim wheel slightly, trying to correct it. The roll persisted. A slow, steady pull to the left.

Joe checked the altimeter—800 feet.

His stomach clenched. Something felt wrong.

They were lower than they should be. His pulse quickened as he flicked his gaze to the artificial horizon. Level. No abrupt dive, no sudden drop. He tapped the altimeter, willing the needle to jump. It didn't.

Chuck's jaw tightened. He had noticed it too. "That doesn't make sense."

Joe swallowed hard. "No, it doesn't."

Chuck exhaled sharply, his voice losing its steadiness. "Give me half flaps."

Joe's fingers hovered over the lever. Half flaps? Here? It didn't make sense. They were still miles out. But Chuck had been flying longer than he had. He had to comply.

Joe reached over and eased the lever down.

Then it hit.

A dragging sensation from the left side, slight at first—almost imperceptible—then growing. Chuck shifted in his seat, compensating with an instinctive nudge on the yoke.

Joe's pulse pounded in his ears. This wasn't right.

Then, suddenly—a jolt.

The roll sharpened. The nose pitched down.

Joe's breath caught. He instinctively grabbed the yoke. Something was wrong. The resistance felt off, sluggish. He knew that feeling. Uneven drag. A flap issue. One wing grabbing more lift and drag, the other on the verge of stalling. And at this altitude, there was no room to recover.

His throat tightened. It had caught up with them.

He turned sharply toward Chuck, voice edged with urgency, not bothering to use the intercom. "Flaps—check the flaps!"

Chuck fought the yoke, jaw clenched, his hands tense around the controls. Joe reached for anything that would stabilize them.

Then, for a split second, he happened to glance back—just for a moment—and met Paul's eyes.

Uncertainty. Worry. The beginnings of fear.

Joe's chest tightened. He forced himself to turn back to the controls, hands sweating. His voice was tight when he spoke again, intercom forgotten.

"Chuck! Something's wrong!"

Chuck's grip on the yoke tightened even more. His voice was sharp, almost too quick. "Maybe if we fully deploy flaps, things will even out."

Joe's gut twisted. That didn't seem like the right thing to do. If half flaps cause this much drag, full flaps could make it worse.

Then, over the intercom—Chuck's voice, firm. "Full flaps."

Joe's hands hovered over the controls, hesitating. This wasn't standard procedure. Everything in him screamed, "Don't do it!"

He stole a quick glance back at Paul. Paul's eyes met his—uncertainty. A silent question.

Joe turned forward again and moved the lever.

The roll sharpened.

Joe's breath caught. The left wing dragged harder, pulling them into a deeper bank. They were tipping. He yanked the flap lever back, trying to retract, but nothing happened.

Panic surged through him. "Flaps aren't responding!"

He flicked his gaze to the altimeter. It read 700 feet.

His stomach dropped. That can't be right.

He punched the intercom, voice tight. "That can't be right." Unless the local pressure's way off ...

Then the nose dipped. The engines whined.

A sharp burst of static, then Paul's voice through the headset. "Joe, are we losing altitude?"

Joe barely heard him. His mind was racing. No training had covered this.

This wasn't normal.

This wasn't supposed to happen.

His hand clenched around the yoke, knuckles white. He forced himself to respond, his voice clipped, strained.

"Working on it. Stand by."

His heart pounded as he yanked at the flap level one more time. Still nothing. His mind raced. They were losing altitude—fast.

Joe turned to Chuck, his voice rising, nearly a shout. "Chuck! Should we try reducing power on three and four, increasing one and two?" His hands were already moving toward the throttle.

Chuck didn't respond.

"Chuck!" Joe shouted, waving a hand to get his attention. "We have to do something—should we try asymmetric power?"

Chuck blinked, snapping back to focus, but his hesitation was clear. His face was pale, drawn tight with concentration—and something else. Fear.

"I ... I'm not sure." Chuck swallowed. His voice was hoarse. "Yeah. Yeah, let's do it. I'll put in right rudder. Maybe that'll counteract it. We do it together—on three."

Joe's pulse thundered in his ears as he placed his hands on the throttles.

"Three ... two ... one."

As Joe adjusted power, Chuck stomped the rudder.

The plan jerked violently left.

The cockpit lurched—a sickening roll.

Joe slammed against the airframe, the harness biting into his shoulders as the C-87 pitched down sharply.

The engines screamed as the aircraft plunged.

"Chuck! Straighten out! Pull up!" Joe's voice cracked with urgency, but it was too late.

The altimeter spun downward. The horizon tilted.

Over the roar, Paul's voice cracked through, calling a desperate Mayday.

Then, in an instant, everything slowed.

The sound faded into a low hum, like the world had suddenly pressed pause. The chaos, the panic—it dissolved. The weight of it all lifted.

Joe turned.

Chuck was looking at him.

For the first time, really looking.

Joe reached out, his hand steady. He rested it on Chuck's shoulder.

"Chuck, you know the truth." His voice was calm, unwavering. "Now is the time."

Chuck's chest rose and fell sharply. His lips parted, but no words came. His eyes burned with something raw, something breaking open inside him.

Then he nodded—slowly, deliberately.

Joe sat back.

He thought of Lucy—her laugh, the way she squeezed his hand when they talked about the future. He thought of Paul and Alta. Of their baby.

And Sage.

She'd wait for him by the fence. He could almost hear her nicker, feel the brush of her coat against his hand.

Joe let out a slow breath.

He closed his eyes.

He was not afraid.

Impact.

CHAPTER FOURTEEN

Aftermath

STATEMENT OF: 2nd Lt. Joseph D. Mitchell, Army Transport Corps, US Army

Recorded at Canton Island - February 8, 1943

"As I remember, we were approaching Canton, about sixty miles out. The aircraft started pulling slightly to the left. At that point, we hadn't sighted the runway lights yet, and we hadn't started our final approach.

"The tower called us, said everything looked normal. The captain called for half flaps, which I set.

"Immediately, the roll to the left became more pronounced. I checked the altimeter—it read 700 or 800 feet. The reading didn't seem right. I tapped the instrument, but the reading held steady. Something felt wrong.

"The radio operator called the tower, but I don't know if he got a response.

"The captain then called for full flaps. I hesitated but complied. As soon as I deployed them, the plane rolled sharply left. At the same time, the nose pitched down.

"We tried to correct—reduced power on the right engines, increased on the left, applied right rudder. But that only made things worse. The roll increased, the nose pitched down further.

"At that point, I don't remember what I said, maybe something about altitude, but before I could react further, we hit the water.

"I think one of the main landing gears struck first because we had two or three distinct jolts. My head hit something, probably the wheel. Then next thing I knew I was thrown from my seat.

"By the time I got free, the plane had already split apart. I saw the navigator and engineer ahead of me, struggling toward the break in the fuselage.

"I don't know what happened to the radio operator.

"The captain's windshield had torn loose. I crawled toward it and managed to squeeze through. When I finally got free, I'd say there were fifteen to twenty feet of water between me and the surface.

"The water was murky. I was disoriented. Couldn't see much. But I just swam up.

"When I broke the surface, I saw the rudders still above the water. The plane floated for a minute or two, then I watched as the tail slipped beneath the surface.

"I spotted a suitcase nearby, one of these affairs that splits in the middle. The top half had been torn off. I grabbed it, thinking I could use it to float, but it just got in the way. I let it go.

"I saw a raft overturned in the water. I tried to swim for it, but I couldn't make much headway.

"I stripped off my shirt and pants, but left my stockings on. Don't know why—maybe I was too exhausted to take them off. I kept trying to reach the raft but couldn't turn it over.

"After a few minutes, I decided to just float and wait. About fifteen or twenty minutes later, a PB2Y flew overhead and switched on its searchlights.

"As I floated there, I could hear several voices calling out for help. The cries were weak, men in pain. I don't know how many, but it wasn't many."

***

Q&A Interrogation - February 9, 1943

Q: What type of aircraft was it?
A: C-87 Consolidated

Q: How many personnel were on board?
A: Twenty-one total. Five crew members, sixteen passengers.

Q: Were you wearing life jackets?
A: No. The passengers were supposed to be wearing them. Some were, but I don't know if they all had them on when we hit.

Q: Do you know if the passengers were strapped in at impact?
A: No, I couldn't see them at that moment.

Q: The pilot was 1st Lt. Charles Carter?
A: Yes.

Q: Do you believe the plane sustained severe structural damage on impact?
A: Yes. It split almost immediately.

Q: How long before the aircraft sank?
A: Less than two minutes.

Q: How long did it take you to get out?
A: Ten to fifteen seconds, but it felt longer. I fumbled with the hatch before deciding to go out the windshield break.

Q: Did you see anyone else escape?
A: I saw two or three crew members trying to get out. But I didn't see that they were successful.

Q: How do you account for the low altitude?
A: The altimeter was off. We had no accurate reading from the tower. It had been calibrated back in Hamilton, but local settings weren't updated. When we hit, it was reading 200 to 300 feet.

Q: How do you account for the sharp roll to the left?
A: The flaps malfunctioned. The flap actuator had been unreliable for months—we'd been keeping it lubricated, but there were no replacement parts available. When full flaps deployed, we lost control. Too much drag on the left. The aircraft rolled, and we couldn't correct it.

Q: How many hours had you been flying before the crash?
A: We left Hickam at 1145 local time. We had about a twenty-four-hour rest before takeoff, but the captain didn't sleep much. He said something about bad dreams, not feeling rested.

Q: What is your assessment of landing at Canton after dark?
A: Extremely dangerous. There's no reliable altimeter reading from the tower. Crews need a confirmed setting before descent.

Q: What's your recommendation for future flights?
A: Arrivals should be scheduled before sundown. Ideally, at least one hour before dark. I'm not too keen on night landings at Hickam either. I wouldn't recommend it.

Q: Did you ever see 1st Lt. Carter again?
A: No.

/s/ 2nd Lt. Joseph D. Mitchell
Army Transport Corps
US Army

                            ***

War Department
Washington, D.C.
March 03, 1943

Mrs. P. F. Carlson
San Mateo, California

Dear Mrs. Carlson,

On the night of February 7, 1943, while on
an authorized flight, the aircraft on which
Mr. Carlson was assigned, a C-87 Consolidated
transport, crashed into the Pacific Ocean approximately one mile east of Canton Island at
approximately 2100 hours (Canton time). There
were sixteen passengers and five crew members
on board. Three individuals survived—two were
rescued by a naval vessel, and one swam
ashore. An immediate search was conducted by

air and sea for several days following the accident, but I regret to inform you that no further survivors were found.

The cause of the crash remains undetermined, though a full investigation was conducted. We understand the difficulty of receiving news under such circumstances, and I want to extend my deepest sympathies to you during this time of grief.

Mr. Carlson served honorably and with distinction. His dedication to duty and his service to his country reflect the highest traditions of the United States Army Air Forces. His sacrifice will not be forgotten.

Please accept my heartfelt condolences on behalf of the War Department, the United States Army and Air Transport Command. If there is anything we can do to assist you during this difficult time, please do not hesitate to reach out.

With deepest sympathy,

/s/ J. A. ULIO
Major General,
The Adjutant General

***

Boonville, Missouri - March 23, 1943

Frank limped down to the river by his house, his footsteps uneven on the soft, damp earth. The doctors said the limp would never go away. It didn't really bother him, or at least that's what he told himself. He would learn to live with it.

The war was over for him. That part of his life was over—not just the war, but the flying. He would never fly again. He was grounded now, in every sense of the word.

The warm March air carried the scent of fresh earth and new grass, the promise of spring hanging in the air. The little tributary ran high and fast, swollen with snowmelt from upriver, its current a restless, murmuring voice in the quiet afternoon.

The news had hit him hard.

Chuck's plane—gone. Just like that. He still couldn't wrap his head around it. He remembered standing with them at Hickam not long ago, swapping stories, trading jabs, sharing the easy camaraderie of men who had been through it together. Now, most of them were gone. That had been their last full day. It didn't seem real.

Frank felt a tear slip down his cheek before he even realized it was there. He let it go, let it fall. What was one more? The war had taken so much already.

Joe Mitchell had survived. That was something. Frank had written him a letter, but no response had come yet. He figured Joe had his own demons to wrestle. Maybe they both did.

He stared out over the rushing water, watching it tumble over the rocks and swirl in eddies, never stopping, never looking back. Maybe that's how he needed to be. Maybe that was the only way forward. But right now, he wasn't sure how to let go.

He reached down, picked up a small, smooth stone, and turned it over in his hand. Then, without thinking, he flung it into the river. It hit the water with a hollow plunk, disappearing beneath the surface.

Frank exhaled slowly.

Maybe one day, he and Joe could talk it through. Maybe it would help. Maybe it wouldn't.

But at least they were still here.

He was here.

He was home.

***

Hayden, Colorado - June 1943

Joe sat astride Sage in the north pasture, staring toward the horizon. The tall grass danced in the early summer breeze, swaying like waves rolling across the field. Off in the distance, the horses grazed, their tails flicking lazily. The scene was almost perfect.

Almost.

For the second time in his life, Joe's heart was completely broken. Sage was here for him again, solid beneath him, steady, grounding him when the weight of it all threatened to pull him under. If it weren't for the ranch—if it weren't for Sage—he didn't know if he could continue. But that wasn't entirely true. His faith pulled him through. Joe had named Jesus his Lord years ago, and when he did that, it defined his entire life. So yes, he would go on.

Still, the guilt was relentless. It clung to him, gnawed at him from the inside in the quiet moments, making it hard to breathe when he least expected it. Why him? Why had he survived when Paul—when Stan, when Jimmy, when Chuck—had not? He thought of Alta, of the child she was carrying. Paul's child. That baby would grow up never knowing his father. Paul would have made a great father. It would have made more sense for Paul to be the one who made it. But then again, none of this made any sense.

And then there was the anger.

It was a quiet, simmering thing, not easily defined, not easily directed. Maybe he was angry at Chuck for not pushing harder for those replacement parts. Maybe he was angry at himself for not insisting on getting the altimeter setting from the tower. Maybe he was angry that he hadn't trusted his gut and overridden Chuck's order for full flaps. Maybe—though he hated to admit it—he was even angry at God. Not for what happened, but because he couldn't understand why.

He'd written to Alta, though he had no idea what to say. What could he have said? Nothing could make up for what she had lost. She'd sent a short reply, saying she had moved back to Ohio, that she had received many letters from people she didn't even know. Joe's heart ached for her. Paul had talked so much about their plans, about where they would live, what they could do after the war. Paul had mentioned briefly that he was already thinking about baby names.

And Chuck. Chuck had been on the cusp of something—of making peace with his father, of letting go of his bitterness. He had been wrestling with faith, trying to find his footing in something that had always felt so far away to him. Joe hoped—prayed—that Chuck had grasped it in those final moments. He recalled those final moments. Chuck had seemed at peace. Not just calm—but the kind of peace Joe had only ever seen in people who believed and trusted in Jesus as their Lord and Savior.

As his thoughts lingered there, Frank Harper came to mind. Frank had made it home, but he hadn't come back whole. He was walking and breathing, but the weight of what he'd been through clung to him. Joe had received a letter from Frank but hadn't found the words to reply. Maybe he was being selfish, still trying to heal in his own way. Or maybe it was just that they'd never known each other that well. Still, one day soon, Joe would try to write back.

The early evening light stretched long across the pasture. The mountains in the distance glowed deep red and gold as the sun dipped toward the horizon. Joe let his mind drift back to the accident, to the cold darkness of the ocean, to the endless waves. Now, months later, it felt like a dream—a nightmare he couldn't shake.

He could still hear the engines screaming, still feel the sudden weightlessness of the final descent, the sharp jolt as the plane hit the water. He remembered the cold pressing in, the way the salt burned his eyes. He had been in shock, he supposed, floating there, waiting for rescue. He had kept thinking—absurdly—that it wasn't a very nice night for a swim. That he would have to jab Chuck for making him go swimming that night. Why would he have thought that?

He remembered the planes circling overhead, the flare light flickering on the water. He remembered the exhaustion, the ache in his limbs, the moment when he had considered just letting go. Then the tugboat, the rough hands hauling him aboard. The blurred faces. Someone had wrapped him in a blanket, and he had wondered, numbly, what he was supposed to do next.

Joe sighed, looking out across the pasture. His gaze drifted to the silhouette of a lone rider in the distance, moving at an easy lope. A tall sorrel, its mane catching the breeze. Thunder.

The rider sat straight in the saddle, looking comfortable there—then stopped and turned toward him, lifted a hand, and waved.

Joe exhaled slowly, nudged Sage forward, and galloped out to meet her.

Epilogue

Chatham, Ohio - August 1949

"Paul, get in here this instant, or we'll be late!"

Sometimes living on a farm was difficult. Well, really, it was almost always difficult. What she meant was that sometimes living on a farm with a young boy was difficult. Especially when that young boy had a pony. Paul had gotten Flower several years ago, and between the pony, the dog, and the endless rows of corn, it was often a battle to rein things in.

Alta shook her head, thinking back to just a few days ago. Paul, convinced he could make the tractor go faster, had been tinkering under the hood, his small hands smudged with grease. His grandfather had come out, offering to help.

"No, I can do it myself. I'm pretty sure I know what to do," Paul had said, his voice steady, sure.

That quiet confidence. That curiosity. He got that from his father.

Alta saw him in Paul every single day—in the way he narrowed his eyes when he was focused, in the stubborn set of his jaw when he was determined. Some days, the resemblance made her heart ache.

Other days, it made her feel like he was still here, just out of reach.

She often caught herself doing things Paul had taught her. Just the other night at supper, she'd started tapping Morse code absent-mindedly under the table. She hadn't even realized it until someone at the table wondered aloud about the odd rhythm. She'd had to stifle a laugh.

Paul's presence was everywhere. In her thoughts. In her heart. In their son.

The first year had been the hardest. After wrapping up affairs in California, she had moved back to Ohio, and then eventually to the new family farm in Chatham. The support she received had been almost overwhelming—letters from people she didn't know, neighbors who showed up unannounced with meals, friends she had nearly forgotten offering help without asking anything in return.

And somehow, through it all, she had kept going. Not because it was easy, but because she had to. Because Paul would have wanted her to. Because there was a little boy who needed her to.

"Paul!" she called again, stepping out onto the porch, shielding her eyes from the morning sun.

A moment later, Paul Jr. came running up the path, hair tousled, a smudge of dirt on his cheek.

"Coming, Mama!"

Alta sighed, shaking her head with a smile.

"Well, I think we'll be late now. Your church clothes are dirty, and you'll have to change. We'll end up sitting in the back."

"Yes, Mama. Sorry. I thought it would be alright."

She crouched slightly, smoothing out his shirt with gentle hands. "It's alright."

Paul smiled up at her—wide, bright, and full of life.

A million-dollar smile.

Author's Note

Million-Dollar Smile is a work of historical fiction inspired by real events and the true story of my grandparents during World War II. At its heart, this novel is based on the life of my grandfather, Paul Carlson, who served as a radio operator on C-87 transport aircraft for the Air Transport Command (ATC) during World War II. The story is deeply personal, shaped by historical records, family recollections, letters, and my family's research into the Pacific air routes used during the war.

One notable use of artistic license was depicting the crew of ATC-903 as a mix of military and civilian personnel. In reality, this specific Air Transport Command flight was operated entirely by civilian pilots and crew under contract with the US Army. I chose to structure the crew differently to allow for richer character development and internal conflict. This decision also created space to explore themes of leadership, duty, and faith in a high-stakes wartime environment.

While this novel is based on real events, most of the characters are fictional, with four notable exceptions:

- Paul Carlson (my grandfather);

- Paul Carlson Jr. (my father), who makes a brief appearance in the epilogue;

- Alta Carlson (my grandmother); and

- Chester Nimitz (who appears briefly in historical context)

All other names, characters, and select events have been fictionalized for storytelling purposes. However, I have worked diligently to remain historically accurate in depicting the aircraft, flight procedures, locations, and challenges faced by Air Transport Command crews during the war.

In the spirit of honoring the real people behind this story, I have included a tribute section listing the actual crew and passengers of the ill-fated C-87 flight that crashed off Canton Island on February 7, 1943. Though *Million-Dollar Smile* tells a fictionalized version of events, this book is dedicated to their memory.

I hope this novel serves as both an engaging story and a tribute to the men and women who served in ways that history often overlooks.

—Paul F. Carlson

In Memory of the Crew and Passengers

The following is a tribute to the crew and passengers of ATC-903, the C-87 Liberator Express that crashed off Canton Island on February 7, 1943.

Thank you for your service. Your sacrifice is not forgotten.

CREW:

Pilot — Christopher V. Pickup
Co-Pilot — Roger H. Moninger
Navigator — Grant L. Judd
Flight Engineer — Edward J. Adams
Flight Radio Operator — Paul F. Carlson

PASSENGERS:

Colonel Ralph F. Love
Colonel John Dibble
Lieutenant Colonel Powhatan M. Morton
Lieutenant Colonel John R. Pitman Jr.
Lieutenant Colonel William H. Bache
Major James J. Gleason
Major Clark W. Mayne
2nd Lieutenant Gerald H. Levine
Chief Warrant Officer Alexander Z. Dale
Warrant Officer Junior Grade Charles J. Hickman
Master Sergeant Kendall M. Taylor
Technical Sergeant Felix M. Padkosky
Staff Sergeant Charles W. Cotton
Sergeant Percy J. Archdale
Sergeant Robert Lambie
Sergeant Alfred B. Collandar

This story is told in their honor.

Acknowledgements

Writing Million Dollar Smile has been an incredible, interesting and satisfying journey. I never thought I could write a book like this—especially one so personal. I could not have done it without the support, encouragement, and expertise of so many people.

First, I would like to thank my father (you guessed it), Paul Carlson. He was the one who originally conceived of this story. He did all the initial research into our family history and the details of the actual accident. He found all the documentation and scanned the letters that became the foundation of this story.

Next, I want to thank my wife, Lisa, for putting up with all the late-night writing sessions and the distant, far-off looks as I tried to think of what to write next. She would often ask, "Are you okay?" And my response was usually, "Yes, I'm just thinking." Thank you for understanding. I love you very much.

To my daughter, Brooke—my biggest cheerleader. Thank you for being a constant source of joy and encouragement. You carry on the million dollar smile.

A heartfelt thank-you to my beta readers: Michael Bay, Paul Carlson, and Skip Englebrecht. Your thoughtful feedback helped shape this manuscript into something far stronger than I could have achieved alone.

I am deeply grateful to my copy editor, Courtney Oppel, for her keen eye, insightful edits, and commitment to making this book the best it can be. Your expertise and attention to detail were invaluable in refining this story.

Most importantly, I thank my Lord and Savior, Jesus Christ. Without Him, none of this would be possible.

Finally, to you—the reader—thank you for taking this journey with me. This story was written to honor unsung heroes, and I hope it resonates with you as deeply as it has with me.

With gratitude,
Paul F. Carlson

For Book Club Discussion Questions, visit:
www.milliondollarsmilebook.com/discussion

*Paul and Alta Fae Carlson -
Carlson Family Collection*

*Ready to Leave on a Trip - Carl-
son Family Collection*

www.ingramcontent.com/pod-product-compliance
Lightning Source LLC
Chambersburg PA
CBHW020124120726
47903CB00007B/2094